To Ziter

# The Other Side of
# Black Rock

# the GREAT PROVINCE

Pine Plateau

Great Basin

crest
ridge

black
rock

Two Rivers

~ 1 Day Travel

Olos Island

# THE FORBIDDEN

# SCROLLS

*by* John W Fort

## BOOK ONE

## The Shadow of Black Rock

## BOOK TWO

## The Other Side of Black Rock

## BOOK THREE

## Under the Burning Sun

# The Forbidden Scrolls

—·◇·—

# John W Fort

## Book Two

—·◇·—

# The Other Side of Black Rock

*Illustration & cover design by Sydney Six*

Pacific Publishing

ISBN-10: 1727002873
ISBN-13: 978-1727002874

Printed in the U.S.A.

To My Wife, Anna
My rock of stability

# PROLOGUE

Erif thrust his sword in the stand, leaving it standing nearly as tall as he. *I believed I was used to its weight,* he thought to himself, rubbing his bicep. *That sword may be perfect for dealing with dragons, but otherwise it is too heavy to do any good. I only hope I grow strong enough before I'm expected to use it.* He sat on a log by his fire pit.

The Warrior removed a skewer of roasted goat and gazed out to sea as he ate. Erif tried to imagine he could see the distant shore where his wife and younglings were. I hope they are not suffering. Tama's last letter said they were nearly out of food.

"Zul, where are you!?" Erif shouted to the cloudless sky. "How am I expected to train when all I can think of is my family? They need me!"

His only answer was the warm breeze. He ate quickly and released his stallion from the tree it was tied to. With a leap he mounted the steed and headed toward the beach. It was time for another vision. The stallion trotted for a tide pool bounded by barnacle covered rocks. Erif knew what visions awaited him, reflecting from the water.

"I do not want to watch Raef again," Erif said inot the wind, "it is too painful."

"You were chosen for this," came an ancient voice in reply.

Erif turned to see Zul himself, the Great Spirit, appearing out of thin air. Erif slowed the horse and the spirit walked by the Warrior's side. They came to the tide pool where Erif dismounted. He removed the harness from the stallion to let it run free a bit. Zul moved his hand above the water and an image appeared within. Eric bent lower to see.

Enormous black claws encircled the torso of a greenling, who appeard to be scarcely more than a youngling. It was Raef. He was high in the air, suspended by the black talons as he passed over the ridge of Black Rock mountain. Raef looked frozen in terror. He wore a long blue robe and hair down to his waste, signifying he was not only an Intercessor by birth, but an Apprentice Keeper, set aside to lead his village in spiritual matters. The image descended and the beast that held Raef came into view—a great dragon, covered in oily, black scales with a mane that ran from its head down to the tip of its tail. It was Rail, the dark spirit and enemy of Zul.

Erif recalled the first time Raef had encountered the beast, chased through a grassy meadow when he had only six seasons. The youngling had run home to tell his mother and father, but his father did not believe him. The dragon had not been sighted in a lifetime. Raef's father, Folor, was a respected Keeper, and had been certain his status would protect his son from such evil.

It had been only a few moon cycles later when Raef was introduced to the dragon again by an older greenling, DeAlsím. Erif remembered how afraid Raef had been to stand next to such a hideous beast, but Rail surprised the youngling and befriended him. Even as a youngling, Raef knew it was prohibited to speak the dragon's name, much less be found with it, yet he felt drawn to it. He returned to the dragon, again and again, in a secret clearing deep in the forest.

Erif understood, to an extent, why Raef continued to visit the dragon in secret. The youngling's earliest friends were sons of Warriors, who did not respect the Intercessor cast. Chaz, the son of the Prime Warrior, had acted as friend, but often turned on Raef, taunting him rather mercilessly. The dragon, sadly for young Raef, was kind to him. As the seasons past Raef eventually dared to introduce an Intercessor friend, Domik, and a younger neighbor, Nilo, to Rail, but otherwise kept it secret from everyone.

When Raef had reached his tenth season he saw a faint vision of the Great Spirit, Zul during meditation. The Keepers appointed him to be an Apprentice Keeper as a result. Erif did not know what to think of that development. It was unheard of for a youngling to act as any apprentice, must less an Apprentice Keeper. Yet Raef had been given a blue robe and new status in the village at only ten seasons. What youngling could bear that responsibility?

Rae's secret grew harder to keep while surrounded by Keepers and greenling apprentices. Raef managed to sneak away to visit Rail, even with his new duties, though he was frequently reprimanded for arriving to his obligations afterward. In spite of the trouble it brought him, Raef seemed compelled to be in the dragon's presence.

Raef left his home to live with the other apprentices in the dormery when he reached his thirteenth season, as all new greenlings did. He appeared to enjoy the freedom from his parents but had little freedom to sneak away to the forest under the increased scrutiny of his new master.

Then it had happened—while in the village square. Raef had frozen, as if in shock, to see the dragon reveal itself to the village, circling overhead. Raef remained stiff as Rail dove down on him, snatched him in its talons, and flew off with him. Raef yelled in vain to be released as he was carried toward Black Rock mountain, the dragon's lair. Erif shook his head in disgust at the vision.

Raef wrapped his arms over the top talon that gripped him, watching the dark mountain loom closer. Scarcely able to breathe from fear, his stomach was like ice. What would this forbidden place hold? How long would the dragon keep him here? Would the all-seeing dragon allow him to leave at all? Raef felt his insides twist up in knots. He looked down to see his dangling feet pass over the jagged peaks of Black Rock.

# PART ONE

## BLACK ROCK

# 1

Erif sat, hunched over a small tide pool, and watched the dragon carry the greenling over the tips of the dark mountain. A gust of salt air brought Erif back to himself. He shook his head. The wind rippled the tide pool, and the vision was gone. He looked up at the sky. It had turned dark and brooding, unusual for the island. He stood and smelled the air. Rain was coming. He loved the smell of the air just before a rain. He turned slowly in a circle, expecting to see his spirit mentor standing nearby. Zul was gone. Erif shrugged. The old spirit was unpredictable.

Erif stretched from his long spell crouching over the tide pool. He knew the beach faced more or less to the north. He squinted but could not see land beyond the sea, but he knew it was there. The beaches of Salt Marsh were directly in front of him on the other side of the sea. The villages Two Rivers and Crest Ridge were east of Salt Marsh. Raef's home village, Fir Hollow, was further north. East of Fir

Hollow lay vast uninhabited forests and then Black Rock, jutting straight up out of the forest. Erif felt a chill down his spine. Black Rock was a forbidden place; no one dared speak of it in the villages.

He called for his stallion and watched as it pranced to him. He grinned at the powerful animal, amazed he had managed to tame it. The stallion paused and Erif leapt onto its back. Turning slowly away from the ocean Erif headed back to his camp. It was getting cold.

———·◇·———

As the dragon carried Raef over the ridge of Black Rock Mountain Raef saw a world that looked completely foreign. From Fir Hollow Black Rock had looked like a long ridge of sharp rock sticking into the sky. But from the sky he saw what lay on the other side of that jagged ridge. Below him was a vast basin sunk down into the rock. The crater below was entirely dark with no green anywhere. The basin floor looked flat and the color of slate, just like the rest of the mountain. Rail began to circle over the basin, giving Raef a clear view of its entirety.

The sides of the basin were very steep, dropping abruptly to the flattened floor. Raef thought he could see trails here and there on the inside leading from the floor to the top of the rim. The circular rim itself appeared sharp and jagged in most places. There was one conspicuous spot on the south rim where a large flat rock protruded inward from the rim, making a perch of sorts that overlooked the entire basin. Other than that, the only other flattened area of the rim was along the north side, where an expansive plateau overlooked the basin.

The plateau extended away from the basin to the north, where it was covered in a sparse pine forest. A river ran across the plateau toward the basin, where it dropped off a vertical cliff and cascaded to the basin floor. The resulting waterfall fell into a pool on the north floor of the basin, which in turn drained into a river inside the basin. From this pool a dark river flowed through a crack that zigzagged across the basin floor. The crack, and the river within it, ran to the middle of the basin then turned sharply west, running to the western wall where it disappeared under the mountain. Raef craned his neck back to glance over the rim and saw that the river reappeared on the other side of the mountain in the forest and headed towards the villages. Raef wondered which river it might be and if it was one he knew.

The view of the forest vanished behind the crater wall as Rail slowly spiraled down to the basin floor. Raef realized there were villagers in the basin. Many, many villagers, spread out in groups across the basin floor. Raef guessed there were enough to fill two or three villages here, several hundred at least.

Rail landed gently on the basin floor and released Raef. Villagers began to gather around them. Rail stretched its head skyward and let out a loud, guttural roar. Raef jumped and looked up at the beast. In all the seasons Raef had known the dragon he had never heard it make this sound before. A large crowd continued to gather, forming a circle around them. They were mostly men and greenling, though Raef did see several women and a few greenlia. A few, much to his surprise, were youngling, some quite small. A strong rank smell hit his nostrils and made him wince. He held his hand over his nose and looked for the source of the odor. He realized that the odor was coming from the villagers themselves. Raef had never seen anyone as filthy as those who surrounded them. Their clothing, the little they wore, was torn and ragged and covered in oily grime. He could not tell what color any of the clothing had once been. Most of the clothing seemed to have been very crudely sewn together, only vaguely resembling trousers and dresses. Only one or two males wore shirts and those who did had only shreds of cloth covering their chests. None of them wore shoes. Their skin was also darkened with dirt and sweat. Muddied streaks of dried liquid ran down the necks and chests of most of them. It did not appear that any of them had ever combed their hair.

The eyes of the shabby crowd had expressions of mild curiosity and they wore slight grins. A greenlia, with perhaps one or two more seasons than Raef, pulled her long hair out of her eyes. Raef smiled at her but she simply looked blankly at him in return. She seemed mostly curious about his bright blue robe.

Raef shifted uncomfortably only to feel his feet slip beneath him. He looked down to see a damp film covering the dark rock of the basin floor. It was then he noticed the humidity condensing onto his face. He tried to wipe it away with the sleave of his robe but moments later his skin became clamy again.

Raef felt the dragon come up behind him and

stand nearly over him. Then Rail spoke in a deep, resonating voice that vibrated the very ground.

"We have a new brother. A new Dragon Child has joined us."

There was a weak cheer from the circle around Raef and Rail, then they began to clap. The clapping slowly unified into a steady beat. Raef slinked backwards until he touched the dragon's belly. Then he felt something hot and slimy go down the back of his neck and Raef jumped forward. He turned, wiping the back of his neck, to see the dragon's long tongue uncoiled directly over him. Raef had become accustomed to Rail's smell, but the sickly sweet dragon stench from its mouth was still something Raef disliked. The dragon flicked its tongue down and licked up Raef's side and onto his cheek.

"Stop, Rail, that is disgusting!" Raef said, stepping back and wiping his face with his sleeve.

But his voice was lost as the clapping of the dirty Dragon Children became louder and louder. Before Raef could escape the great dragon licked his other side and cheek, then lifted its head and blew clouds of thick smoke into the air. Raef had never seen this, either. The crowd began dancing in a circle around Raef and Rail. Raef clasped his arms across his chest and shivered. The crowd continued to circle him, their heads bobbing slowly back and forth as they danced. There faces remained locked in mused expressions.

The crowd pulled Raef into their crazed circle dance. They linked arms with Raef, not seeming to mind the dragon drool on his robe. Raef smelled the musty scent of Rail wafting off the people on either side of him. None of these people, these Dragon Children, smelled of mankind. It made Raef's stomach feel a little sick. The Dragon Children grinned peacefully at Raef as they danced.

"Raef!" called a familiar voice.

Raef pulled himself from the churning circle and turned to see a young man pushing his way through the spinning crowd.

"Raef, you are finally here!"

Raef could not identify the man, though he did look vaguely familiar. The young man took Raef's wet hand and shook it, ignoring the drool on it. He smiled, and Raef finally recognized him.

"DeAlsím?" said Raef, "are you DeAlsím?"

The young man nodded and grinned. Raef was momentarily glad to see a familiar face. The spinning crowd jostled Raef and DeAlsím as they tried to stand between spinning circles of Dragon Children. DeAlsím was as filthy as everyone else. He was much taller than before and would have twenty seasons by now. DeAlsím clasped both hands on Raef's shoulders. Raef rememberd being much shorter than DeAlsím but noticed they were now nearly the same height. Raef had grown but so had DeAlsím. The last time Raef had seen DeAlsím they were both younglings, but now there was no longer any trace of youngling to DeAlsím's face. His youngling friend was now a young man.

"You are grown now," said Raef.

"Of course," said DeAlsím, "did you think that I stopped growing when I left Fir Hollow?"

"Why are you here? Everyone said you ran away to

Moss Rock."

"Well, I did go to Moss Rock, but not to run away. Rail asked me to visit Moss Rock, and I did. Then Rail brought me here!"

"I...I never heard. Why did the word never come to Fir Hollow that you had disappeared?"

"I did not disappear at all. Several villagers saw Rail fly away with me."

"They saw it take you! But certainly they would have sent word to the other villages about that. We heard nothing at all."

"Moss Rock knows better than to tell other villages when Rail flies off with its children."

"This has happened before?"

"Frequently."

"And no one tries to stop it?"

"Stop Rail? What in all the Province for?"

"But you said everyone saw it."

"Not everyone, just the ones who know Rail. We all visited it out in the forest. There is a big space where we would gather to meet it."

Raef's mind swirled.

"You would gather to meet...Rail? How many villagers? How could the rest of the village not know?"

"A lot of us did, men, women, greenlings, greenlias and younglings too. And I think many of the other villagers did know about it. Except the Keepers, of course."

"And no one cared?"

"Of course we cared. Rail was taking care of us. That's why we were happy when it took one home with it. I was glad when it was my turn."

Before Raef could ask any more questions, the crowd snagged he and DeAlsím and spun them in different directions. Raef could scarcely keep to his feet as the crowd pulled him faster and faster around the circle. Then everyone stopped and jumped, giving one last yell and it was over. Rail opened its wings and lifted to the sky in a great wind. A few Dragon Children clapped, but most just turned and began wandering off in one direction or another. Raef watched as they ambled off, no one seeming to have any place in particular they were going. Raef spied DeAlsím again through the crowd and ran toward him.

"Ho, Raef!" DeAlsím said. "Is it not grand here?"

Raef started to speak but DeAlsím looked behind him and waved at someone else. Raef turned to see a young woman wave gently at DeAlsím, then wander off.

"Who is that?" he asked DeAlsím.

"Narra. You do not remember her?"

Raef could not recall the name, and she did not look familiar.

"She was Serip's daughter, back in Fir Hollow," said DeAlsím. "Perhaps you were too small to remember. She disappeared, and everyone thought the dragon had eaten her."

Raef could vaguely recall the story from when he was small.

"Of course, you and I know that is not what happened," said DeAlsím with a sloppy grin.

"Does anyone know she is here?" Raef asked.

"You know, from the villages?"

DeAlsím grew a puzzled look, "What does it matter?"

DeAlsím took him by the arm and pulled Raef toward the south wall.

"I will show you where I sleep," DeAlsím said.

Raef allowed himself to be drug along by his old friend. It was hard to get used to DeAlsím being only slightly taller than he. As they walked, Raef looked at the Dragon Children around him. He realized how he stood out in his clean, bright clothing, but the Dragon Children no longer seemed to notice he was even there at all. They were sauntering lazily or sitting on the hard ground and a few sat under filthy, tattered tents scattered haphazardly around the basin floor. Only the smallest moved quickly at all, scampering about playing some sort of game, oblivious to the depravity around them.

They approached the south wall, which rose steeply from the basin floor. It was made of the same dark basalt that made up the rest of the basin. The damp walls were spotted here and there with dingy patches of moss, the only sign of life other than the Dragon Children.

"There," said DeAlsím, pointing to a cave several spans up the rock wall, "that is my cave."

The rock wall was dotted with caves, starting near the ground all the way up to the top of the cliff. Raef saw the narrow trails that zigzagged up the wall, connecting the caves. A young man waved down at them from the cave opening DeAlsím was pointing to, halfway up the wall.

"I have some friends who live up there with me."

Raef's eyes continued up. There were more caves far up the steep rock walls. Everything in sight was drab. Even the sky above looked dull and gray, though no clouds were in the sky. Raef blinked and looked down again. He wished the dragon had not taken him wearing this robe. His robe did not belong here.

"Wanna meet my friends?" DeAlsím asked.

Raef looked up at the cave again, and the young man waving.

"I think I will walk around and see more of…of Black Rock."

DeAlsím shrugged, "As you like, see you at mid sun meal."

DeAlsím paced slowly up a steep, narrow path. Mid sun meal, Raef thought to himself. It was not yet mid sun. It felt like he had been gone a full sun's journey already.

Raef turned back and began to walk towards the center of the basin. There were fewer Dragon Children there. As he walked it grew slightly quieter, and the smell was not as bad. When he had gone far enough that he felt alone he sat on the rock floor. He began to think of home, but then shook his head to chase away the thoughts. It was strange here, even frightening, but he could not go back, not now. The entire village had seen the dragon take him. He was not certain he could believe DeAlsím's stories about Moss Rock, but Fir Hollow would definitely care that Raef had been taken by the dragon. The villagers in Fir Hollow would know he was a dragon lover. He could never face his village if they knew that. He stood and turned around, walking quickly back to the place DeAlsím had been. An image of his mother flashed in his mind and he began to run.

He reached the rock wall and slowed to a stop. He did not see DeAlsím and could not remember which cave he had pointed to. There were many dotting the rock face. Raef turned and sat with his back to the wall. The smell was strong here so Raef covered his nose with his robe. It did not seem to help much. A young man and woman came up and sat next to him, acknowledging him only with a nod. They sat, not speaking, looking out into the basin. The excitement brought on by his arrival was gone now. No one was laughing. No one was even smiling. Raef saw Dragon Children sprawled out across the basin floor, sleeping. A few waded in the dark stream in the distance. Some climbed narrow paths on the rock walls up to the caves. No one was in a hurry. Everyone's eyes had a dulled, vacant gaze. Raef put his head in his hands to cry, but no tears came.

At mid sun Rail came into sight, circling the basin several times. All the Dragon Children stopped what they were doing and began to walk to the center of the basin. Raef felt a hand on his shoulder, and he looked up to see DeAlsím.

"Ho, Raef!" DeAlsím said, "it is time to eat. Come, I will show you."

Raef slowly lifted himself off the ground and followed DeAlsím. Rail landed just as they reached the stream at the center of the basin. The dragon's cheeks protruded, and its long neck bulged like an over stuffed stocking. Raef was about to ask DeAlsím why when the dragon stood tall on its legs and arched its neck downward, regurgitating a huge pile of multicolored goop. Raef nearly vomited at the sight.

"Look!" said DeAlsím, "Rail found some melons this time!"

"Melons?" said Raef, "what melons?"

"The orange part, those are melons!"

Raef looked at the half digested pile of orange, green and yellow, trying to discern anything that resembled a melon, or any other kind of food. DeAlsím ran ahead to the pile and shoved his arm into it. Rail flew off, and Raef watched it depositing more piles of slop around the floor of the basin. Dragon Children across the basin crowded the pile nearest them. Raef turned back to DeAlsím and watched him pull a dripping orange chunk from the slimy mass. DeAlsím ate it, and Raef nearly vomited again.

"Come, Raef!" DeAlsím said.

Something orange, which Raef hoped was melon juice, ran down DeAlsím's chin. Raef turned away from DeAlsím. But, everywhere he looked, people were eating. They ate ravenously, and with no manners at all. There were no spoons or trenchers; people used only their hands. Some walked right into the piles of gooey food up to their knees to reach a piece they wanted. Soon all the Dragon Children had frightening things dripping off their faces, hands, and even arms. It got in their hair and on what little clothes they wore. Raef's curiosity temporarily overcame his repulsion, and he turned back to the nearest pile and took a step closer. That is when he smelled the dragon drool that covered the food.

Raef turned and ran. He ran all the way back to the southern rock wall. He climbed up the nearest trail to get as far away from the gruesome sight as he could. He found a cave and crawled in it. The cave turned out to be of little help. It was small, humid, and smelled strongly of sweat. Raef left the cave and stood outside it. Raef noticed Rail watching him from the floor below. The great dragon lifted its head skyward and let out a puff of inky smoke, then turned to face Raef again. It was hard to tell from this distance, but Raef thought it smiled at him.

Raef followed the nearest trail upwards. He passed many caves and grew tired as the rock wall was very tall. The sun had reached nearly three quarters sky when he finally reached the top. Raef looked over the edge to see there were no trails on the other side and the rock was too steep to climb down. He could not leave the basin this way. To his left, some distance away was the flat spot on the southern rim he had seen from the sky. Raef did not want to try to walk that far, but he wished he had a flat place like it upon which to sit. He turned and sat on the rough rim, looking over the basin. He was too high to make out faces from here. He could see the piles of slime Rail had deposited across the basin floor. A few Dragon Children were at them, eating Raef supposed. He could no longer see Rail in the basin. It had left again. It was likely out visiting younglings and greenlings in the villages. He felt more alone than he had ever felt in all his seasons.

When the sun grew close to the horizon Raef

descended the trail until he came to a flat place, wide enough to lie down. He lay down and tested the space to make sure if he rolled over he would not roll off and tumble down the wall. It seemed safe enough, so he wrapped his robe around him and lay still. Raef was surprised it was not colder. It was winter, and it would have been too cold to sleep outside back in Fir Hollow. There was even a little snow already in Fir Hollow. There was none here at all, even though Black Rock was at a higher elevation.

As darkness slowly fell Raef saw the dragon return over the western rim and circle the basin once. It did not land in the basin, but flew to the flat spot on the rim above him. The dragon let out a roar, making Raef's spine tingle, and reclined on its elbows. It looked as if it was holding court over the Dragon Children in the basin. Then it became too dark for Raef to see, and he tried to sleep. It was difficult on the hard rock.

# 2

Raef woke with the dawn. He was surprised to find himself sleeping on the ground outside. Then he remembered where he was. He glanced over his shoulder, but Rail was already gone. He sat up and looked at his gray surroundings. He wondered how any of this could be real. He finally stood and began the long walk down the wall to the basin floor. His stomach was tight and rumbled loudly. He walked quickly and was able to reach the floor before just as the sun became fully visible in the sky. He paused and looked around, expecting to see the others awake and moving about. Not a single Dragon Child appeared to be awake. The caves and tents were silent, and those who had slept in the open still lay sprawled on the ground, snoring. Raef realized there were no washbasins here, so he walked to the center of the basin to the stream. The ritual washings were not for public display, but there was no one awake to see him, even out here in the open. Raef removed his robe and knelt at the stream's edge and did the New Leaf washing. He then sat cross-legged to do a sunrise meditation, which is necessary when a Keeper cannot attend sunrise homage. It was difficult, as he was distracted by the newness of everything around him. He thought he saw Zul, but he wasn't sure. His mind was too full of noise.

When he had sat still for what felt like long enough, he got up, put on his robe and returned to the south wall. Upon his return Raef found the Dragon Children finally awake. Some were eating food left over from the previous sun. Raef realized he was very hungry, having eaten nothing at all since first meal a full sunrise past. Raef felt a bit panicked, realizing he knew of only one source of food.

Raef hesitantly approached a pile of food. It still looked disagreeable. He gingerly reached out and picked out the most solid looking piece he could find. It was green, with a bit of darker rind on one side, and covered in clear slime. His stomach was doing flips. He pulled his robe open and tried to wipe the slime off on his trousers. Raef closed his eyes and shoved the green thing in his mouth. The thought of what was on it made him gag and almost vomit. Then he realized it did not taste particularly bad. A bit like squash. He quickly chewed and swallowed it. His eyes watered and he wiped them dry. In the village they boiled almost all their food. This was raw, but tasted like a kind of squash Raef had eaten raw before. The orange hunks, as DeAlsím had suggested, did appear to be melon. He reached for an orange piece then closed his eyes once it was in his hand. He managed to eat by not looking at what he was eating. It wasn't too bad as long as he didn't have to see what it looked like. It did smell like dragon, but everything did here. He ate a few more bites and his stomach lurched. He decided to stop and not to push his luck.

He walked away from the pile to get away from the smell of dragon drool only to be met with the strong smell of an unwashed Dragon Child as DeAlsím ran up to meet him.

"Ho, Raef!"

DeAlsím was an adult, and adults did not address anyone in this manner. This was a youngling or greenling greeting. Raef wondered how to address the young man back.

"Pleasant Sunrise, DeAlsím."

"Pleasant what?" said DeAlsím. "What kind of talk is that?"

"You are not a greenling any longer. I should show respect."

"We are all Dragon Children here. We are all the same."

"Alright, then, 'Ho, DeAlsím.'"

DeAlsím grinned.

"I see you have finally eaten something," said DeAlsím.

"Well, a little. My stomach could not handle very much. Is there not anything to eat besides the stuff Rail pukes up?"

"Rail does not puke it up," laughed DeAlsím.

"Well, it looks like it."

"The dragon has a pouch in its neck to hold all our food. It does not go into its stomach."

"What is the difference? It still has dragon drool all over it."

DeAlsím laughed, "You will get used to it. We all do."

"Not any sun soon."

"You should be glad you don't have to find your own food, like the villagers do," said DeAlsím. "We do no work at all here."

"I would not mind finding my own food," Raef said, "I am…well, I was an apprentice. I am used to working."

"No food grows in the basin," DeAlsím said, "It would take too long to walk out every sunrise for food. The dragon has to gather food for us."

Raef curled his nose. DeAlsím laughed again. Raef suddenly recalled a question he had long wondered about.

"Ho, DeAlsím, what does Rail eat? The villagers in Fir Hollow say it eats people, but Rail told me it does not."

"Not live people, at least," DeAlsím said. "When Dragon Children get old and die, Rail takes them up to that ledge on the south rim and eats them. That way the bodies don't stink the place up. We could not bury anyone in this solid rock."

Raef's mouth dropped open. He looked back at the ledge where Rail had perched the previous night and tried to imagine it up there, eating a dead Dragon Child. He tried to imagine watching such a gruesome sight, even at a distance. He closed his eyes, and his stomach turned.

"It eats dead Dragon Children, right in front of everyone?" Raef asked.

"It must, what else would become of the bodies?"

"What kind of madness is this place?"

"You must be a bit wild to be a Dragon Child, Raef."

"You must be disgusting to be a Dragon Child, if you ask me," said Raef. "What happens if I do not like it here?"

"Oh, everyone likes it eventually. No one has ever left."

Raef wondered how that could possibly be true. Why would so many former villagers choose to stay here? DeAlsím gave him a knowing look.

"Rail knows who will like it here," said DeAlsím, "It only takes true Dragon Children to Black Rock."

"Well, maybe it was wrong about me," said Raef, "you did not know, but I am a Keeper in Fir Hollow."

DeAlsím put a hand on Raef's shoulder.

"Your robe is blue, you were only an apprentice. Besides, Raef, I have seen you with Rail. Believe me, you are a Dragon Child. You are no Keeper."

Raef looked at his feet, feeling shame well up inisde.

"Come, Raef, do not think of the past. There is something I wish to show you."

Raef followed DeAlsím farther north, along the river. After a lengthy walk, they reached the pool at the base of the waterfall Raef had seen from the air. The water fell from a protruding ledge far above them as a broad, sparkling sheet down into a large circular pool. The rocks around the pool's edge were broken into large black cubes, tilted this way and that. Raef walked up and stood on a rock near the pool and felt the mist from the water brush his face. He could see that the waterfall stood a fair distance in front of the rock wall behind it, leaving enough room for a Dragon Child to stand behind the falling water. Raef thought it might be nice to stand behind a falling sheet of water.

"This is a special place," said DeAlsím.

"The waterfall?"

"No, Black Rock. It is a place for the brave ones. For those who are not afraid."

DeAlsím looked over at Raef.

"It is for people like you, Raef. You belong here."

They lingered at the waterfall until nearly sunset. They tossed rocks in the water, took a drink now and then from the cool water, and cooled their feet in the pool. The tensions of Fir Hollow and Raef's apprentice life were drifting away. His father would not scold him here. He would not need to hide his visits with Rail. No one would tease him here. The sun began to set, and they walked back to the south end of the basin where DeAlsím's cave was. Raef paused at a pile of food on the way and got another bite to eat. His stomach fluttered a bit, but it was not quite as foul as before. Raef slept at the base of the south wall, not brave enough to sleep in a stinky cave.

# 3

Raef woke again as the sun was rising. His stomach hurt in a way he had never experienced. Reluctantly he got up and walked slowly to the nearest pile of food. The food was two sunsets old now and only a small bit remained. What was left was mere mush and had turned a gray color. Raef stood over the remnant of food. It smelled faintly of melons. He closed his eyes and plunged his hand into the mush and forced it into his mouth. He was surprised at how his body swallowed automatically. He didn't even notice a bad taste. He ate more, keeping his eyes closed, until he felt nearly full. He backed away and opened his eyes. His hand was wet and slimy.

Raef walked to the stream and paused, looking at his reflection in the water. His hair was messy and his chin was dripping with… he did not want to know with what. Raef continued walking until he reached the pool under the waterfall. He removed his robe and knelt on a flat rock by the pool. He did the ritual New Leaf washing, being sure to wash his face and hands well. He then sat cross-legged and closed his eyes. He remained quiet, listening to the water splash into the small pond. After a sufficient time had passed, he stood and put his robe back on. He stared at the waterfall briefly, then turned and walked back to join the others.

When Raef approached the south wall the dragon had returned after its sunrise flight. Dragon Children were crowded around it. Raef walked to the outer edge of the crowd, straining to see over the others in front of him.

"Make way!" boomed the dragon.

The Dragon Children parted in front of Raef. Rail looked directly at Raef, lowered its head and snorted softly. Raef felt himself grin. He walked to his old friend.

"You have been preoccupied, master Raef," said the dragon.

"Yes, I suppose," said Raef.

"You are here at last and have not come to play even once."

"Dragon Children play?" asked Raef.

"Do we play?" came DeAlsím's voice from behind Raef.

DeAlsím rushed up to the dragon's snout.

"Watch this!"

DeAlsím clamored up onto the dragon's snout and lay flat on his back.

"Throw me!" cried DeAlsím.

The dragon tossed DeAlsím into the air with a casual flick of its head. DeAlsím flew into the air, shrieking with apparent joy and flapping his arms. Rail deftly caught DeAlsím, and DeAlsím laughed loudly, clinging to the top of the dragon's fury head. Raef found it very odd to watch a grown man do such a thing.

"Raef, you try!" said DeAlsím.

"Yes, master Raef," said Rail, "show the others what you can do."

As DeAlsím climbed down, Raef pulled his robe off and tossed it aside. He sat and untied the long leather laces wrapped around his calves and pulled his shoes off. He realized that DeAlsím had never seen him play this game with Rail. Raef had been a small youngling when DeAlsím left Fir Hollow. Raef had discovered a new way to fly even higher this season and was very good at it now. Raef stood and scrambled up onto Rail's snout. Instead of laying back as DeAlsím had, Raef crouched on the balls of his feet at the tip of Rail's nose.

"Make me fly!" yelled Raef.

The dragon coiled its neck and flung Raef upwards. At the last moment Raef sprung off with his legs and shot into the sky like an arrow. A collective gasp escaped the Dragon Children below as Raef soared three times as high as DeAlsím had. At the apex, Raef curled into a ball and did two somersaults on his way down. At the last moment, Raef uncoiled and spread his arms like wings, landing belly first on the soft, furry tuft on Rail's head. A great cheer went up. Raef stood and walked to the end of Rail's snout, both arms held high.

"Raef," called DeAlsím, "how did you ever learn to do that? You are amazing!"

Raef smiled broadly then slid down Rail's neck to

the ground.

"I have been practicing a lot since you last saw me," Raef said.

"Even so," said DeAlsím, "how did you ever come up with that?"

Raef shrugged.

"Now, Raef," said Rail, "you finally have friends to show your skills."

Others began to climb onto Rail's snout to show off their acrobatic tricks. One greenling, a little older than Raef, did a back flip, curving up and over the dragon's back in the air. For a moment Raef thought he would hit the ground, but the acrobat landed neatly in the stream, making a large splash. He came up smiling, unharmed. Then a young woman, who appeared to have the same seasons as DeAlsím, climbed up Rail's neck, sitting just behind its head, hanging on to its fur. The dragon shot into the air and flew once around the basin, carrying the young woman.

"We can ride the dragon?" asked Raef. "I guess I have more to learn than I imagined."

"You have much to learn," said DeAlsím, "although, I've never seen anyone fly as high as you. You are going to be something special here, I think."

Raef watched the dragon land and the woman slide off. The dragon lifted its head and roared, then flapped its great wings and flew up and out of the basin. Off to visit someone in one of the villages, Raef supposed. A group of young greenlings walked up to him and clapped his back approvingly. Raef gazed at the spot the dragon had disappeared over the mountain's edge and determined to fly with the dragon soon. He would be the most daring of all the Dragon Children.

Raef and DeAlsím wandered off to the north. Raef carried his robe slung over his shoulder. He left his shoes behind.

At mid sun DeAlsím and Raef saw Rail circling over the basin. They walked to meet the dragon where it was landing. As they approached the dragon lifted off again, but Raef noticed it had left behind a large pile of food. He and DeAlsím picked up their speed a bit.

Raef found the food better than before. He decided it was better new like this, when it still had chunks in it and before it turned all gray. In spite of being more comfortable eating the Dragon Children food, he was still appalled to watch DeAlsím slopping it all down his chest as he ate.

As Raef was eating, a group of greenlings eating nearby caught his attention. While their skin was darkened with grime like all the other Dragon Children, the bits of skin that did show through on their arms, faces and chest was of a color of skin he had never seen before. Raef stopped eating and moved closer. They had very straight hair that was dark as night, which Raef had never seen before either. Their skin was the color of cinnamon, and they had broad short noses. They were quite a bit shorter than Raef, but their faces showed the same seasons as Raef. He imagined they could not have more than thirteen seasons. Two of the greenlings noticed him looking at them and walked over to Raef.

"Oi-aye," called the first greenling, "you are the new one, no?"

"I suppose so, yes," Raef replied.

"I am Toaz," he said, extending his hand.

Raef extended his hand, unsure of how to great the strange looking greenling, and Toaz slapped his palm playfully.

"Is this how you greet each other here?" asked Raef.

Toaz ignored his question and continued, "This is my friend, Mizo."

Mizo extended his hand toward Raef, palm out. Raef put his own hand out and Mizo slapped it.

"Where are you from?" asked Raef, "you do not look like people from any village I am familiar with."

Mizo smiled and stood tall, "We are from Conch!"

"I have never heard of that village."

"Conch is no village," said Toaz, "it is an island. The biggest of all the islands!"

"Islands? What islands?" asked Raef.

"Islands!" said Mizo, "you know, out in the ocean."

Raef had never seen the ocean, though he had heard many tales of it. He had seen islands in the forest lakes at times, but they were quite small.

"How can an island hold a village?" asked Raef.

"They are not small!" said Toaz. "Conch is larger than all of the Great Basin." Toaz spread his arms wide, "Much bigger than all this!"

"Is it very far from here?"

"Very far, yes. When Rail took me here, it flew almost an entire sun's journey to reach Black Rock from my island," Toaz said, "and Rail was flying very fast."

Raef looked at Toaz and Mizo.

"Is everyone on your island, you know, like you?"

Toaz and Mizo looked puzzled.

"No, there are many adults too," said Mizo after a pause.

Raef laughed.

"No, no. I mean, do they all have skin that color?"

Toaz looked at his bronze arms.

"Oh, yes no one is pale like you on our island. I had never seen pale people before coming to Black Rock. Not on any of the islands."

"There are more islands?" Raef asked.

"Of course," said Toaz, "there are many islands. Conch is the largest, though."

Raef tried to imagine what an island would be like, way out in the middle of the vast ocean. He could not.

"How long have you been here?" Raef asked.

"Two seasons already," said Toaz, "Mizo came shortly after me."

Mizo grinned. His teeth looked very bright against his tanned skin.

"Are there others are here from Conch?"

"Oh, there are many, many in Black Rock who are from the islands," said Toaz.

"You are the first I have seen."

"Most stay on the east end of the caldron," said Toaz.

"Caldron?"

"Yes," said Mizo, "this was once a great volcano, thousands of seasons past."

"How do you know so much?" asked Raef.

"About Rail?" Toaz said, "everyone knows about Rail."

"Not where I come from," said Raef, "very few villagers have seen it and almost no one knows its name."

Mizo smiled, "Everyone knows Rail on Conch. Rail is the great prankster! We have statues of it on all the islands."

"You do!" said Raef, finding this hard to believe, "Statues of the dragon for all to see?"

"Yes," said Toaz, "Rail does not visit the islands often, but when it does it plays with us on the beach, and the lucky ones it brings here to live in its kingdom."

"You mean to say, it visited us," corrected Mizo, "now we are here with it, always."

"Oi-aye, Toaz!" called a female voice.

Raef turned to see two greenlias walking their way, licking orange goop from their hands. They had bronze skin as well. Toaz and Mizo held out their hands and the greenlias slapped each of their palms.

"Mina and Shiri, this is Raef, from the pale villages," said Toaz.

"Oi-aye," said one of the greenlia.

Raef tried to smile back, not sure if he should offer his hand to be slapped.

"You are from the islands as well?" asked Raef.

"Of course," said the second greenlias.

"Were you afraid when you came here?" asked Raef.

"Why would we be afraid?" asked Toaz, "we were

with Rail."

"And, you got used to the food?"

Toaz laughed.

"My friend, Mizo, he would not eat it at first. He did not eat for three sun's jouneys! When he finally ate, he was so hungry he got it all over him!"

Raef laughed but noticed that Mizo still had dried food more or less all over him.

"Have you seen the caves?" asked Toaz.

"Yes, but I have not slept in one yet."

All four islanders laughed.

"No, not the sleeping caves, the tunnels," said Mizo.

"I do not believe so," Raef said.

"Oh, it is so wonderful! Come, you must see," said Toaz.

Raef watched the greenling heading for a cliff wall off to the east. He looked around for DeAlsím but could not find his old friend. This was all still too new and slightly frightening. Realizing he did not want to be alone he finally raced after Toaz.

# 4

Toaz lead Raef west along the south wall heading west. When they had left most of the other Dragon Children behind Toaz climbed up a narrow rocky trail. Raef followed and then saw Toaz disappear into a narrow cave opening. Raef hesitantly followed Toaz inside. He was relieved to find it wasn't smelly like the other caves. A cool breeze blew from the deep tunnel that stretched out of sight.

"This place is very…mysterious looking," said Raef.

Toaz smiled.

"Come see inside."

Raef followed Toaz deep into the tunnel. Several spans in the tunnel split into three. Raef followed Toaz into the left tunnel, which sloped down. Soon it was too dark to see well. Raef reached out and took Toaz's arm.

"It is too dark," said Raef, "we will be lost!"

"A little farther," said Toaz, "I know the way."

Slowly, it began to grow lighter. The light was coming from somewhere ahead. As they turned a corner, Raef was amazed to see several crystals the size of his arm growing out of side of the wall. The crystals glowed with light the color of the mid sun sky. Four had been broken off and were lying on the floor of the cave. Toaz took one of the broken crystals and gave another to Raef.

"We will have to return these here before we leave," said Toaz. "If the sunlight touches them, they lose their light."

Raef looked at the glowing crystal in his hand.

"This is the most amazing thing I have ever seen!" he said.

"This is nothing," said Toaz, "come."

Raef followed Toaz through a twisted maze of tunnels.

"This mountain is full of caves," said Toaz, "I want to explore them all."

"Do you ever get lost?"

"I did once, but Rail sent someone to find me who knew the caves. Now I never get lost. Now I help find others who get lost."

Raef grew excited as they crawled down through the rock. He had never been in a cave before, much less one with magical crystals of light. He had thought the forest was an adventure. That was nothing. Black Rock held secrets greater than he had ever imagined.

Toaz stopped and climbed up through a small hole in the roof of the tunnel. Raef followed clumsily. When Raef emerged on the other side, he found himself in a hollow round formation. Man-sized yellow stalactites hung from above and lacey yellow crystals stuck out from the walls, glittering in the soft light. Bands of purple and blue rock circled the domed cave and sparkling red crystals sprouted from the floor like flowers.

"This is beautiful!" said Raef.

"You will not believe me," said Toaz, "but there are caves more amazing than this."

"You must show me!"

"Not now, those places are far inside. It is already after mid sun. We would need to bring extra food for such a journey."

"All right, but you have to promise to take me soon," said Raef.

"Of course, my new friend."

The two sat a while more, admiring the sparkling crystal formations. The mix of feelings inside Raef were less than comforting, even though what was before his eyes was nothing short of dazzling. Being kidnapped, this strange place, the glowing light crystals, this amazing cave, the disgusting food, it was all simply too much to take in.

Toaz took them back a different route, past pools of cool spring water where they paused to drink. When they reached the glowing crystals they left their crystals on the floor of the tunnel and Raef held on to Toaz as he lead him once again to the cave mouth. It was already late sun when they emerged, blinking, into the light. Raef and Toaz walked back towards the more populated area at the center of the south wall.

As they approached Raef saw Rail sitting on the basin floor as a great number of Dragon Children were walking towards it. The Dragon Children passed under the great beast as it bent its long neck over them.

"What is it doing?" asked Raef.

"Marking its children," said Toaz.

"What? What do you mean, *marking?*"

As they drew nearer Raef could make out the dragon's long tongue, licking the full length of the back of each Dragon Child as they passed under it.

"Rail marks us with its scent," said Toaz, "You know, like a wolf licks its pups."

"A wolf *cleans* its pups with its tongue. It does not *mark* them," Raef said.

"Perhaps," said Toaz, "but Rail marks us. So everyone knows we are its children."

Raef paused as Toaz walked ahead. Raef watched Toaz walk directly under the dragon and Rail flicked its ribbon tongue over Toaz's head and down the length of his back. Raef scrunched his nose and quivered at the sight.

"Come," said Toaz, "it is nearly dark."

Raef walked in a broad arc around Rail before rejoining Toaz, keeping well out of the dragon's reach. It did not seem to notice, to Raef's relief. Mizo, Mina and Shiri appeared out of nowhere to join them.

"You can sleep in our cave if you want," Toaz said.

Raef remembered the smell of the cave he had entered earlier.

"No thanks, I think I will sleep out here so I can watch the stars."

Toaz shrugged and continued with the others towards the east. Raef found a place to lie that was not too close to any of the smelly Dragon Children. Using his robe as a matt, he lay out under the stars, the few he could see in the sky. The ground felt warm, which was nice as the air was cool. He was startled when the dragon lumbered up to his side.

"How are you, my friend?" said the dragon.

"All right," said Raef.

Rail leaned close and peered into Raef's eyes. It felt to Raef as if the dragon could see right through him.

"Do not be afraid," said Rail, "you are ready. Do not doubt how strong you are."

Raef felt himself relax a bit. The dragon nuzzled his side. Raef instinctively patted the beast's soft snout.

"I am proud of you, my child," said Rail, "And have no fear, I will be watching and guarding over you all night. You are entirely safe."

"Will you not fall asleep?" asked Raef.

The dragon grinned. "Dragons never sleep."

With that, Rail unfurled his huge wings and lifted itself into the air. Raef watched the dragon fly to the flat rock that overlooked the south ridge. The dragon reclined on its elbows and stretched its wings in a dramatic pose. Raef could just make out a long jet of smoke from Rail's nostrils in the moonlight. Raef looked at the sky, but could see few stars. Perhaps it was cloudy.

Now he knew why the dragon never visited him at night in Fir Hollow. It was here guarding its children. Raef closed his eyes and tried his best to sleep.

Erif lifted a rabbit pelt from a wooden bucket full of water and dropped it into another full of rotten vegetables. He moved his face rapidly away, stirring the fetid mash with a stick.

"Uh, this stuff smells horrid," he said, lifting another pelt from the first bucket of water.

He had lessons on making parchment as an apprentice, but that seemed a lifetime ago. Besides, he had not paid much attention even then, not expecting to need to make his own writing skins. But he had nearly used up his entire stock of parchments recording the visions Zul had shown him in the pools of water. If he ever hoped to record the entire saga, he would need to make more parchment.

Erif left the smelly bucket of rabbit pelts and set out for a rock outcropping he'd seen recently. He was pretty sure he had seen lime in those rocks. He would need that next.

"I have to make this work," he told himself, "The villagers need to know the truth."

# 5

Raef woke the next sunrise a bit later than the sunrise before. None of the other Dragon Children were awake, but the sun was already up and low in the sky.

Raef stood and stretched. He picked up his robe and carried it as he walked to the waterfall. He decided he liked going to the waterfall each sunrise. He watched his bare feet pad across the damp rock. He did not know where his shoes were. He supposed he did not need them any longer. It was a shame, as they were very new.

After his morning rituals he returned to the south wall and had first meal. He had not seen DeAlsím or Toaz, so he set out to find one of them. As he walked through the crowd that had gathered around the food he felt himself bump into someone.

"Oh, I am sorry," said Raef, seeing the man he had bumped into.

The man was as old as Raef's father.

"No problem, brother," said the man. "Are you not Raef, the new one."

"Yes," said Raef.

"You should join us. We are playing tag!"

Raef noticed a dozen or so Dragon Children running and laughing. Some were younglings, two were greenlings like Raef, but several were adults. He had never seen grown adults run and play tag before. He smiled as he watched them playing.

"Perhaps later," said Raef, "I was going to find someone."

Raef left the playing man and walked to the wall. He went up the trails and peeked in all the caves that were approximately half way up the wall. At first it seemed rude to be peering into the homes of people he did not know, especially as Raef saw no privacy curtains in the caves. The Dragon Children he did see sleeping wore their day clothes, or what was left of them. He realized there were no night robes here, so there was no need to change, thus no need for privacy curtains. He looked down at himself. He still carried his robe, but he had never changed his clothing, and it was becoming streaked with grime. There was nothing he could do about that, he decided, so he kept searching for DeAlsím.

By one quarter sun he gave up and decided DeAlsím must be out in the basin somewhere. Raef descended to the basin again and began walking east, the direction where Toaz, Mizo and the two greenlia had gone on their way to their cave. Raef came across Mizo shortly.

"Ho, Mizo!"

"Oi-aye!" said the shorter greenling.

Mizo ran up to him and stuck out a hand. Raef paused, then remembered to stick out his own hand.

Mizo slapped it.

"Where is Toaz?" asked Raef.

"Here at Black Rock."

"I know that, I mean, where in Black Rock."

"It matters not," said Mizo, "he is here and safe."

"Should we find him?" asked Raef.

"There are many Dragon Children, why do you need Toaz?"

"Never mind," said Raef.

"Do you want to come swim with me?" asked Mizo.

"Sure. Where do you want to swim?"

"At the river," said Mizo, "where else would we swim?"

"Well, the waterfall is nicer," said Raef.

"But the waterfall is twice as far!"

"Mizo, it is not that far. Come with me, it will not be as crowded."

"It is not crowded because it is too far to walk!" said Mizo.

Raef walked away and Mizo followed. There was no one at the waterfall when they arrived. Raef was surprised as it was the nicest place in the basin. Well, other than the tunnels, but he needed Toaz to go there. Raef removed his shirt, and he and Mizo swam together in the pool. Afterwards they lay out on the basin floor to dry.

Raef opened his eyes later, realizing he had fallen asleep. He looked to the sky and saw it was three quarters sun. He sat up to see Mizo laying flat on the ground, gazing up at the drab gray sky. Raef realized they had missed mid sun meal. As he pondered this he realized he was not particularly hungry. He shrugged, picked up his shirt and robe, and stood. Mizo stood as well.

"We should eat now," said Mizo.

Three quarters sun was not a time for eating, at least, not back in the villages. But the food piles were always present here in Black Rock.

"Okay," said Raef, "why not?"

They walked back together and stopped at a pile near the center of the basin to eat. A few other Dragon Children were eating as well. As they were eating Toaz happened upon them.

"Oi-aye!" called Toaz.

"Oi-aye!" said Mizo.

"Ho, Toaz!" said Raef.

The three traded slapping hands, then went back to eating. Toaz ate a bit with them, then they all turned towards the south wall. The walk back was quiet except for the sound of soft wind blowing over the smooth rock floor. Raef inhaled the smell of damp moss that drifted across the basin. He found it pleasant.

It was nearing sunset when they approached the south wall and Raef could see Rail busily marking Dragon Children as they walked by. Toaz and Mizo walked right under the dragon and it licked each on the back. The sight did not bother Raef this time, but he walked out of reach of the dragon's long neck and tongue anyway. He followed Toaz and Mizo farther to the east along the south wall. As they had told him, there were several other dark skinned islanders here, but there were other pale villagers as well. Toaz walked to a campfire and sat in a circle that was forming around it. Raef joined him and Mizo sat at Raef's other side. The islanders on either side of him both smelled strongly of dragon breath, but Raef found he did not mind. The Dragon Children around the fire began telling scary stories, each one trying to outdo the last. Raef half listened as he basked in the heat of the fire, looking up at the few stars he could see. He felt older, more independent here. He realized he was not afraid. When the fire died the Dragon Children lay on the ground rather than return to their caves and tents. Raef lay down next to his new friends to sleep. Sleep came easily.

# 6

Raef awoke late the next sunrise. It was his fourth sun's journey at Black Rock. Toaz and Mizo were waking up too. Raef smiled at them. They got up and went to the stream to drink. Raef followed and instinctively kneeled and began his New Leaf ritual washing. Toaz and Mizo looked at him curiously. Raef smiled, realizing his rituals must look odd to them. Raef stopped washing and looked at his reflection in the water. His long hair was tangled and his clothes were dirty. He smiled at his reflection. He looked more like other Dragon Children now. He sat to meditate, and Toaz and Mizo waited patiently.

When Raef was nearly finished he heard a commotion from one of the caves. He stood and the three of them started toward the south wall to get a better look. Raef looked up to see several Dragon Children carrying out a man from a cave. Raef and Toaz went to look closer. The Dragon Children carried the man down from the wall and lay him on the ground. He was an old man, Raef noticed.

"He will not wake up," said a younger man who

had helped carry him.

The shadow of Rail loomed over them and the dragon landed. Everyone stepped away from the old man as Rail approached. The dragon sniffed at the man on the ground. Several Dragon Children looked expectantly at the dragon.

"He is dead," said Rail.

With blank faces, the Dragon Children who had carried the man slowly left. Rail looked at Raef. Raef's stomach grew cold.

"This man has lived well here. I have fed him most of his life. Now he returns the gift to me."

The dragon grasped the corpse with its claws and lifted into the air. Raef looked around to see if anyone else was afraid. Few Dragon Children seemed to pay any attention at all. Toaz had returned to Mizo and they had started walking to the east. Raef looked up. Rail was on the high perch, the dead man now between the dragon's long teeth. Raef felt faint. Even from far below, Raef heard bones snapping as the dragon crushed the body of the dead Dragon Child. Raef wanted to run but he could not tear his eyes away from the spectacle. Only legs could be seen hanging out of the dragon's mouth now. Blood dripped from Rail's chin. Raef was finally able to turn and run.

Raef ran north until he could run no more. Panting, he kept walking until he reached the waterfall. This was the furthest place from the dragon's perch. Raef sat on a rock. His breathing was ragged. He was nearly hysterical. Raef got up and dove into the pool, without even removing his shirt.

The water made him feel better. He swam to the center and let the waterfall beat down on his head. Raef imagined the water driving the memory of what he had seen from his mind.

When Raef finally crawled out of the water, he was exhausted, and he fell asleep on a rock. He awoke later to the sound of others playing in the water. He sat up. A greenlia smiled and waved at him. He waved back at her. Raef knew he should eat, but he was not hungry. Raef sat by the waterfall watching the other Dragon Children swim until everyone had left and it grew dark. He returned to the south rim by moonlight. He slept out on the basin floor alone.

# 7

Several sunsets past and the memory of the dead man began to fade. Raef kept mostly to himself after seeing the man being eaten by Rail, but eventually he began to talk again to DeAlsím, Toaz and Mizo. He swam with them in the river and played under the waterfall. The slimy food no longer bothered him. Memories of Fir Hollow faded. As sunsets passed and the depth of winter descended on the Great Province any snow falling over the Great Basin melted before it hit the ground. The few drops of rain that made it all the way to the basin floor had warmed by the time they hit the ground.

Raef awoke one sunrise, two full moon cycles after he had first come to Black Rock to find the entire basin filled with mist. It gave the place an eerie, mysterious feel. Raef got up and walked through the thick mist. He had never seen a fog so dense. He watched as tiny droplets stuck to his skin. He went first, as always, to the waterfall to perform his washing ritual and to meditate. Afterwards he followed his nose to a food pile and ate a little. He heard some

Dragon Children playing tag so he ran to join them playing in the fog. By mid sun the mist lifted and Raef walked back to the waterfall alone. He noticed that there was a trail beside the waterfall that led upwards. He had seen it before but never bothered to consider where it went. It was steep and very narrow, but he managed to follow it all the way to the top of the north wall. Raef sat on the rock lip that protruded out over the basin, next to the stream cascading over the edge. Raef could see the entire basin from here: cave openings in the walls, the zigzag stream, groups of Dragon Children snoozing, Rail busy marking any it came near. Raef sat for a long time, looking over the Great Basin.

"This is a wild place," he said to himself, "not like home."

Raef held a dirty hand up to his face and inspected it. He grinned, knowing an Intercessor would never be allowed to look this way in the villages.

"This is where I belong."

Raef took a deep breath and stood up. His shirt was now ragged, so he tore it off and dropped it to the ground. He looked down at his grimy feet with tattered ends of his trousers fluttering at his ankles. It made him smile. He no longer carried his robe, but stored it in DeAlsím's cave. Leaving his old shirt, he climbed down the trail to the basin floor and began the journey to the south rim. It was dusk when he arrived and several fires already burned. Rail had not yet gone to its perch above and was marking the straggling Dragon Children as they returned to sleep. Raef walked near the dragon and looked up at it.

"Are you hungry?" asked the dragon.

"I am," said Raef.

Raef walked to a food pile and began to eat. The dragon followed and reclined next to him.

"You were out exploring," said Rail.

"I was thinking," said Raef.

"And what decision has your thinking brought you to?"

"That I am staying here."

"Then you will be mine."

The dragon lifted its head over Raef and the greenling bent his head back and looked up. Raef saw the dragon open its great mouth above him and begin to uncoil its long tongue. Raef looked down at the food pile and reached for a piece of melon. He flinched a bit but held still as the warm, wet tongue ran up his spine, behind his neck and then flicked over his long hair. The strong sent of dragon wafted into Raef's nose, and he breathed it deeply. He could not remember why it had been offensive to him before. Raef glanced up to see the dragon peering down at him, and it gave a low snort. Raef reached into the pile again and drew out another piece of melon and held it to his mouth as he chewed on it. Juice ran down his arm to his elbow, then under his arm to his armpit. Rail nuzzled Raef's cheek with its soft snout, then took a few steps back, and flew up to its perch. Raef felt the melon juice run from his armpit down his side as he watched the great dragon preen its wings on its perch in the moonlight. He wiped his hand on his trousers and walked east to find Toaz.

# PART TWO

## WHISPERINGS

# 8

Erif kicked his foot through the shallow puddle, disturbing the image within it. He looked around him. The ground was dotted with small puddles left over after a rare rain on the dry island. He was afraid to move, afraid that he would see more of what was happening to Raef in one of the other small pools of water nearby. Erif drew his sword and held it out defensively.

"There is more," Zul's voice said out of nowhere.

"I don't want to see more! Why do I have to see any of this?"

"Avoiding the vision will not stop what Rail has done."

"Or what it is still doing!" said Erif, "That foul beast will taste this steel one day, I swear it."

Erif looked down at the puddle near his feet. The water was nearly still again. An image began to form.

"We shall look ahead," said Zul.

"How far ahead?"

"Two full seasons beyond the last vision."

Erif saw Raef waking up in some kind of cave. Raef sat up and wiped the sleep from his eyes. He had been sleeping on the bare ground, and the cave was lit in a blue light that Erif knew could not have come from sunlight. Erif saw a few others laying on the ground, sleeping near Raef. Raef stood and stretched. The greenling would now have fifteen seasons. Raef was tall and had become quite handsome, in spite of his matted hair. Raef had apparently tried to make new trousers, but they were poorly sewn and only came down to just below his knees, as if he had been unable to find enough fabric for his long legs. The trousers were also badly torn in several places and dark gray with grime. Like most of the other male Dragon Children, he wore no shirt and Erif saw that his chest and arms were as thin as they had ever been. He had no facial hair at all, and his face still retained an almost youngling appearance, which was at odds with his significantly above average height.

Erif sheaved his sword and tried to have empathy for the creature before him.

Raef looked down over the four sleeping Dragon Children around him. They had been exploring a deep cave for the last five sun's journeys. At least, they assumed it had been five suns, they could not see the sun here and could only guess when each sunrise and sunset occurred outside. The others had wanted to turn back after three sun's journeys, but Raef was determined to find the end of this very deep cave.

Raef tiptoed over the others and made his way to a small spring-fed pool they had found just before deciding to stop and sleep.

Shortly after Raef had become fully accustomed to Black Rock he had found himself waking early again, as he had back in Fir Hollow. At first it annoyed him to have so long each sunrise alone with no one to play with, but over the moon cycles it had become agreeable that he was the first to rise. He had time to do his sunrise rituals and to survey the basin and all its inhabitants. Only the ever-vigilant Rail was up as early as he.

Raef knelt at the tiny pool and began his New Leaf ritual. Afterwards he paused in silence, as he did each sunrise, to meditate. When he returned, Mizo was sitting up and rubbing his eyes. Raef smiled at the sight. Mizo, as all the island Dragon Children, was quite short but unlike the others had retained a particularly young face. He hardly looked a greenling, much less a greenling with sixteen seasons. Mizo smiled wide when he noticed Raef. Mizo smacked Toaz on the shoulder.

"Oi-aye, Toaz!" Mizo said loudly, "wake, you lazy sloth!"

Raef did not know what a sloth was, but Mizo and Toaz used the word frequently when the other slept too much or moved slowly.

"Leave me alone, you annoying little sand rat," Toaz mumbled, not opening his eyes.

Raef sat, opened the food skin they had prepared for the journey and scooped out a handful. He was a bit worried since there was less than half of the original amount of food left, and they were still going deeper in the cave. Still, he did not want to turn back. Mina came and sat next to Raef, reaching in and pulling out a handful of food.

"Not to complain," said Mina, "but this food is not very good five sunsets old."

Raef looked at the grey mush in his hand. Mina was right.

"Just a little further," said Raef.

"We should turn back soon," said Mina, "or we will become permanent parts of this cave."

"Tunnel," said Raef.

"Cave, tunnel, whatever you want to call this place, I don't want to be a permanent part it."

Toaz finally got up, as did Shiri, the fifth Dragon Child in the party, and ate. Raef became impatient waiting for them to finish eating. After what felt like an ethernity to Raef, the others began tying the supplies to their belts or slinging them over shoulders. It was true that Raef moved a lot slower than he did back in the village, but he had never become quite as lethargic as the rest of the Dragon Children in the Great Basin.

The air in the tunnel had started to get warmer a sunrise past. As they walked down the long tunnel, holding glowing crystals to light the way, Raef felt the air getting even warmer. The tunnel began to slant sharply down, and walking became difficult. At what felt like mid sun's journey, they came to a three way fork in the tunnel. Mizo stopped and dropped the bag of food he was carrying.

"My arms hurt!" said Mizo, shaking his arms

slowly.

"Your arms always hurt," said Toaz.

"We can rest a bit," said Raef, "and we should eat as well."

"I am not sure I *want* to eat food that is nearly six sunsets old," said Shiri.

Everyone put down what they were carrying and started to eat. Raef decided to help save food by not eating. Instead he inspected the three tunnel entrances. Shiri followed.

"Which way looks best?" called Toaz.

"The air coming from this one is hot," said Shiri, pointing to the tunnel on the left.

"Then we take that tunnel," said Raef.

"Raef," said Shiri, turning to face him, "the air is really hot."

"What if something dangerous is in there?" said Mizo.

"You mean, dangerous like a dragon?" said Toaz.

"No, not a dragon!" said Shiri, feigning fear.

They laughed. Raef walked back, picked up his food bag, and began to strap it to his back.

"Okay, enough rest, we should go," he said.

"We just sat down!" said Mizo.

"We go or we will never learn where this tunnel goes," said Raef.

Raef walked to the opening of the left tunnel, and he heard groans behind him as the others picked up their travel bags. Raef entered the cave and felt a blast of hot air hit his face. He began to sweat. They soon came to a place where the tunnel divided again in two. Hot air came from both sides. Raef picked the left tunnel, but it soon divided yet again into three. The tunnel height and width was becoming much larger. Raef picked the center tunnel this time, but immediately another tunnel joined theirs from above, then another from the left. Hot air drifted through all the tunnels around them.

"There are too many tunnels," Mizo said.

"Wait," said Raef.

He walked forward a bit, then returned, then went into each of the tunnels that linked to the one the had been in. Every direction he went opened into new and larger caves. He ran back to the others.

"This is not a tunnel anymore," he said, "there are hollowed out holes everywhere, all connected together."

"Like a sponge," said Mizo.

"What is a sponge?" asked Raef.

"Never mind," said Mina, "it is something from the islands."

"The hot air comes from somewhere ahead, no matter which tunnel you take," said Raef, "so let's just go forward."

The others nodded hesitantly, so he led the way, sometimes turning left and other times right as they passed through the web of holes. The air became almost too hot to withstand.

"What is that smell?" Toaz asked, "I do not like it."

Raef sniffed the air. It reminded him of something the healers used.

"Sulfur," said Raef.

They continued a bit further until the tunnel opened up into a huge cavern that raised up high above them, larger than any Raef had ever seen. On either side they could see dozens and dozens of other tunnels emptying into the cavern. They walked a few steps more, and the ground dropped off in a near cliff. Below them a red river of slow moving molten rock flowed from left to right. The heat rising up from the river was nearly overpowering. On the other side of the molten river was a rock wall. The cavern was very wide, and they could not see far enough in either direction to see where the river came from or where it went.

The cavern ceiling, many spans above them, was made up of thousands of giant dull-black crystals protruding straight down. They were not transparent at all, but were definitely crystals with eight flat sides with flat ends that hung down at differing lengths. Each crystal was at least as big around as a man. Soft red light from below reflected off the black surfaces. They put down their light crystals as the molten river lit the cavern well enough to see.

"What is this place?" asked Shiri.

"What is left of the volcano of Black Rock, I imagine," said Toaz.

Waves of heat rose from the river and blew across their faces as they gazed into the river below.

"Do you think it is dangerous?" asked Mizo.

"If we jumped down there, yes," said Raef, "but I do not think Rail would live here if this river was a threat to the Dragon Children above."

"How would it know?" asked Shrina.

"It is a spirit," said Raef, "spirits know more than we do."

The group continued to gaze at the river and the crystals that hung above. Toaz and Mina stood to look over the edge while Mizo and Shrina walked back and sat just inside one of the tunnels. Raef felt the hot air blowing past his face. It dried his skin out, and he realized he enjoyed the sensation after two seasons in the perpetual dampness of the basin above.

"This is an amazing place," said Toaz, "but we must be getting back to the basin."

"You are right," Raef said, "we need to get back before the food runs out."

They began to pick up their light crystals for the return journey.

"I wonder if we are the first to find this place?" said Mizo.

"I imagine so," said Mina, "no other Dragon Children would have taken the time to pack all this food and take such a long journey."

"And there were so many places where we could have taken the wrong tunnel," said Toaz, "certainly we are the first!"

Raef smiled at the thought of being the first Dragon Child to find this magical place. He waited for the others to go ahead of him to take one last look at the hot river below. Then he turned to follow, but chose a different tunnel opening to return through. He knew they would all come together soon as the holes converged. As he made his way, he came upon a place where someone had made a carving in the rock. He stopped to read the inscription, shocked that someone had been here before.

*Tanla, daughter of Rail*

*Provincial Season IIX*

Raef did not know what to make of it. Provincial Season IIX was nearly 100 seasons past. At first he was disappointed to realize that someone had found this secret place so many seasons before him. But another thought came to him; exactly how long had villagers been living here at Black Rock? How long had there been Dragon Children in the Great Province? He had never heard anyone speak of such things. Raef decided not to tell the others about the carved inscription.

# 9

The return trip was uneventful. Fearful that they would run out of food, they walked quickly and slept less, returning to the basin floor in what they believed to be three sunsets. When they emerged from the tunnel it was dark. They could not tell how long the sun had been set.

"I guess we lost track of the sun's journey down there," said Toaz.

"It does look that way," said Raef, "but at least we are home again."

Mizo, Shiri and Mina lay down to sleep once they reached the basin floor, not even bothering to walk back to their cave.

"I need to wash," said Raef, "I smell so bad I can scarcely stand myself."

Toaz smiled, "We smell bad even for Dragon Children!"

Raef laughed. He had never heard another Dragon Child admit that they all smelled bad. Toaz followed as Raef made his way across the basin floor to the pool under the waterfall. They both jumped in and swam, trying to wash away eight sunsets of sweat. The sun began to rise and they got out of the water and lay on a large boulder, waiting for the sun to dry them. When the light did come, it felt weak.

"The sun will never dry us out like the heat from the underground river," said Toaz.

"Certainly not as fast," said Raef.

"That was truly amazing," said Toaz, "and I had not even wanted to come along."

"You thought you had already seen all there is to see in the tunnels."

"Yes, but now I know you are the new expert of the tunnels, not I."

Raef smiled to himself.

When the sun had risen to one-quarter sky, Raef sat up, deciding he was dry. He pressed his palm to the rock below him and felt the slight moisture that was always present. It had been nice to feel truly dry down in the tunnel.

Toaz was sleeping, so Raef got up and returned to the pool's edge to do his ritual New Leaf washing. He sat for a moment with eyes closed, then stood. He looked at his reflection in the pool. His face, arms and chest were still streaked with black and his long hair hung in matted clumps. He smelled better but looked much the same as before, which was the way he was accustomed to seeing himself. He decided to not to disturb Toaz and began the walk back to the south wall, stopping at a food pile on the way to have first meal.

A few Dragon Children were up and moving around by the time Raef approached the sleeping caves. He began the long walk up to his cave. He had started sleeping in caves after living in Black Rock for three moon cycles. At first he had stayed in DeAlsím's cave, but he had taken his own cave this season. Mizo and Toaz shared the cave with him now, though the former islanders frequently ended up sleeping on the basin floor, too lazy to climb all the way up to their cave.

"Lazy sloths," Raef said to himself.

Raef climbed the narrow trail to the highest cave in the basin, not far under Rail's perch. Raef stood in the entrance and turned to surveyed the basin. It was nearing mid sun, and still many Dragon Children lay sprawled on the basin floor, sleeping. Rail would be returning soon. Perhaps Raef would ask for a ride. He had learned to ride the great dragon, straddling its neck with his legs as it flew over the basin and up and down the mountain range. Rail never took him over the forest or villages, but Raef loved soaring with the great beast. All other games were no longer entertaining to him.

Raef glanced back into this cave. He saw his blue robe folded neatly at the very back. It was still bright and un-torn. He never wore it, but had kept it here, along with his eating knife, protected from damage, all the moon cycles since he arrived.

He heard murmuring from below and turned to face the basin again. Rail had just flown over the ridge, returning to Black Rock. From its talons Raef could see something dangling. At first it looked too small to be a person, but as Rail came nearer Raef could see that it was. A very small person. Raef descended the trail as Rail circled the basin with its prize.

When Raef reached the basin floor Rail had already landed. All the Dragon Children in the area had already begun to gather around the dragon. Raef made his way to the circle as the other Dragon Children parted to make way for him. Standing in front of Rail was a youngling, and a small one at that. He looked to have perhaps nine seasons, quite young for a Dragon Child in Black Rock.

Raef was startled a little by the youngling's appearance. His face and hands were very white. He had medium length hair combed very neatly and wore an expensive looking brown tunic over a well-made linen shirt. He had a wide leather belt and an eating knife with a carved bone handle. His trousers were gray wool and he wore pointed tipped shoes made of light tan deer hide, laced all the way up to his knees. Memories tried to fight their way to the front of Raef's mind. A merchant. This youngling was a Merchant's son, and one who was quite well off. Perhaps a guild master's son. Raef shook his head quickly. He did not want to think about village things here.

The youngling's eyes were wide open and his face wore an expression Raef had not seen in a very long time. Raef could not recall what the expression meant. The youngling retreated to the dragon and hugged its leg. Some of the younglings from Black Rock walked to the smaller newcomer and began to speak to him. The new youngling's eyes widened even more, he covered his nose with his hand, and he hugged the dragon's leg tighter.

Raef turned and began to walk back to his cave. He will be fine, Raef thought to himself. He will make a fine addition to Black Rock. There were not very many younglings so small and this newcomer would be a welcomed friend to the few already here. Yes, he will have friends here, Raef thought. He will have many, many friends.

Toaz and Mizo joined Raef in their cave some time after mid sun. They sat in the cave together, telling stories of their explorations in the tunnels of Black Rock. Near sunset the trio left the cave to eat. When it was dark they found a fire and joined the Dragon Children who had gathered there to try to frighten each other with made up stories. When it was dark, Toaz and Mizo lay by the fire to sleep. Raef left them to return to the cave. Before entering he looked up at the night sky. He counted fifteen dim stars. He thought he remembered there being more once.

# 10

Raef woke the next sunrise, finding himself sleeping on his back on the cave floor. The rock floor was smooth, but hard against his back. He sat up and stretched his back. It ached a bit. He seemed to recall a time when his back did not ache each sunrise. He noticed his blue robe. A memory began to form where he was wearing the robe and was waving fir branches. He stood quickly, feeling a need he could not explain to leave his cave. Raef did not even pause to look to see if the dragon was gone from its perch. He walked quickly down the trail to the basin floor. As was his habit, he crossed the basin to the north wall and came to the waterfall pool.

He walked to the pool's edge and stopped. This is when he was supposed to kneel and do the New Leaf washing. He did not want to wash this sunrise, for reasons he did not understand. Instead, he stared at his reflection in the dark water. The ripples distorted his face, making it look almost sinister. Raef put a finger to his right cheek and watched his reflection as he pressed and ran it across his skin. His finger left a pink trail in the dark grime on his face. He pressed his palm to his cheek and slowly wiped it, pressing firmly. He blinked, not recognizing the pink side of his face in the reflection. It didn't look like him, it looked like...like the small youngling who arrived a sun's journey past.

Suddenly a distant memory flashed in his mind of himself as a younger greenling, looking at his reflection in a ceremonial washbasin in the Keep as he did a New Leaf washing ritual. His face was clean and fresh and his hair was neatly combed and almost regal looking. The vision brought a feeling of panic. Raef felt his body grow rigid and his breathing quicken. The water at his feet stirred and an image of a very old man with long white hair appeared.

"Raef, were have you gone?" said a voice that seemed to come from the water itself. "Why have you left me, my son?"

Raef felt the hairs on the back of his neck stand up and he turned and ran as fast as he could. He followed the river to the center of the basin, his bare feet slapping against flat rock as he ran. Before he had quite reached the center of the basin, he slowed, bent over and put his hands on his knees. He panted hard. He had not run in a very long time. As soon as he could, he straightened up and walked. He wanted to be far away from the pool beneath the waterfall. It was nothing, he reassured himself, nothing more than a mirage.

He stopped at the first food pile he came to. It looked no more than a sunset old. He scooped up something green and held it to his mouth. He paused, and watched as clear liquid dripped off what he held in his hand. Dragon drool. He threw the food to the ground and ran to the nearby river to wash his hand. How could he eat dragon spit? Who could do that, he wondered.

Raef turned at an unusual sound behind him. Standing a ways from the food pile, all alone, was the new youngling. He no longer wore shoes and his tunic was torn. Dried streaks ran from his eyes down his cheeks. His lower lip was trembling. Raef walked slowly towards the youngling. Something about the youngling frightened Raef slightly.

"Ho, youngling," said Raef.

The youngling looked up at Raef and took a step backward.

"Have you seen the tunnels yet?" Raef asked.

The youngling only started and said nothing.

"What are you called?" asked Raef again.

"Rimmel," said the small youngling.

"Rimmel, that is a name I have not heard. Where are you from?"

"Moss Rock, sir."

Moss Rock. So many new ones had come from Moss Rock recently.

"Do not call me sir," said Raef, "we are all children here. Dragon Children."

The youngling stood very still, continuing to stare at Raef.

A greenlia came to Rimmel's side and took his hand.

"Come, you need to eat something," the greenlia said.

She led the youngling to the food pile and scooped out some for him and put it in his hand. The youngling stared at what was in his hand, then looked up at the greenlia.

"Go ahead," she told him, "it is what we all eat here."

Rimmel sniffed what was in his hand then stuck out his tongue as if to lick it. Raef turned away and headed toward the south wall. He saw Mizo and Toaz sitting and talking with other greenling, but Raef turned to avoid them. He found a trail, though not the one leading to his cave, and followed it up. It took time, but he eventually found a way to the very top of the basin rim. He stood and looked over the edge. It was too steep to climb down the other side. Far down below, on the other side, he saw trees, trees that seemed to go on forever. They looked so bright and green.

Raef sat on the rim and looked back and forth between the basin and the trees on the other side. By mid sun the sky began to grow dark with ominous clouds. Raef watched the dragon return and deposit new food piles across the basin floor. He watched Dragon Children gather around the new piles. He could not see from here, but he knew they were eating. He felt his stomach growl, but he did not return to the basin floor to eat.

The sky grew even darker, and it began to rain. The drops of water were cold on Raef's skin. The Dragon Children below retreated into the caves. Raef wrapped his arms around himself in an attempt to stay warm.

Visions began to come to his mind. A kind woman,

his mother, he thought, looked down at him, smiled and stroked his hair. A youngling ran beside him in a large meadow, jumping in the tall grass and laughing. Another youngling with hair cut very short held up a stone to him. The stone had no color, and Raef could see through it. Raef shook his head, trying to drive the visions from his mind.

But the visions came faster now. He was in a large room with many people, all sitting on benches made of logs. Everyone was saying something, over and over, but Raef could not make out the words. Raef was then at the front of the room, and villagers lined up to come by and greet him. Raef was handed a package, and he was very happy. He opened the package and held up a small blue robe. Raef was sitting in a small room on a stool, listening to a man dressed in a red robe, who was explaining a map that hung on the wall.

Raef stood and held his head, shaking it violently, but the visions continued to come. He saw himself as a younger greenling, picking leaves off short plants in a small garden, collecting them into a clay bowl. He was sweeping between long benches. He was practicing writing with a goose quill pen as an older man stood behind him and gave instruction. He was carrying buckets of water through village streets. He was in a building, a little larger than a house, at a table with five other greenlings, eating something very tasty and drinking something from mugs. Waking up on a mattress of straw laid on a raised wooden box and finding several other greenling in similar beds around him. Waiving branches of fir trees over villagers as they passed into the Ceremonial Lodge.

"Stop it! Stop it!" yelled Raef.

The rain had begun to fall hard, soaking Raef and the mountain around him. Raef felt his lip tremble. He breathed in very deliberately, trying to stop it from coming, but he felt hot tears well up in his eyes. A single tear ran down his cheek. He could distinguish it from the rain on his face by its warmth. Then Raef sank to his knees and began to sob uncontrollably.

"Why? Why won't you help me? Why did you leave me out here?" Raef yelled into the sky.

There was no answer. The rain continued to pour down, and the sky grew dark as night approached.

# 11

The next sunrise Raef woke early even though he had been up most of the night before. He stood from the small flat place he had found to sleep on near the rim's edge. He stared out over the basin. He sighed and began the long walk down the wall, then on to the waterfall and pool beneath it. He came to the water's edge and peered into it. The image of Zul was clear. It was as if the spirit had waited since sunrise past for Raef to return.

"Why are you here, Raef?" the image asked.

"The dragon took me here," said Raef, "It's not my fault!"

"You are a Keeper," said Zul.

In the water, beside the inage of the Great Spirit, Raef could see his own reflection. He saw how filthy he was. His long hair, once his pride as a Keeper, was tangled and ratty. He was ashamed.

"Why are you here, Raef?"

"DeAlsím showed me the dragon when I was small. I did not know any better."

"But you kept going to see the dragon, for many

seasons, even after you became a Keeper."

"I could not help it! I wanted to stay away, but I could not."

Raef felt tears rising again. He could not bear to see Zul now, but the image would not go away.

"I want to be…to be like before. I do not want to be, to be like this."

The image of Zul rose out of the water, stepped to a rock next to Raef and faced him. Raef stepped away, feeling his heart begin to race. Zul had never been more than a vision in his mind before.

"You are a Keeper, Raef, you are one of mine. I want you to come back."

"I…I am not a Keeper. I cannot be."

Raef turned to face away from the spirit, but Zul appeared in front of him again as soon as he turned. Raef hung his head.

"I cannot do it. How can I go back after…after all this?"

Zul faded from sight. Raef wiped his tears from his cheeks. He looked at the waterfall. The water looked dark and oily. He had never noticed it before. He wanted to leave. He wanted to go back to Fir Hollow. He saw the trail that led to the top of the waterfall. Above the waterfall was a pine forest. That might lead him back to the villages.

He turned and began to walk back to his cave. Yes, he decided he would try to escape. He had very little hope of succeeding, but he had nothing to lose either. Before he left, however, he needed something first. The sun was higher now, warming the basin after the rain sunset past. He could see others up and walking around as he drew closer. Rail was back and the Dragon Children circled around, begging to play. As Raef passed by the dragon, he looked up at it. It looked oily, just like the waterfall. As he passed he could smell the dragon's foul breath. Rail bent over a greenlia and let down its long tongue, marking her with its scent.

Raef hurried from the scene, climbing the steep trail to his cave. Raef ran to the back and picked up his blue robe. It was now far too small to wear as a robe. He held it up to inspect it. He had learned to make garments, well, trousers at least, as all Dragon Children had to replace their own clothing as they grew or when the old ones wore out. There was plenty of discarded fabric lying around from all the new arrivals who soon adapted to wearing only sleeveless dresses or trousers. But any discarded fabric he might find would be dirty or torn. Raef wanted something nicer.

Raef looked down at his trousers. The fabric was thin in several places, and his skin showed through. He did not want to be seen like this by people outside the basin. The robe was not large enough to make both a shirt and trousers. Besides, he did not know how to sew a shirt anyway. He collected his knife and a sewing needle he and his friends kept in the cave. He did not know where the sewing needles had come from, but most caves had at least one. He would make trousers later, right now he simply wanted to get out of the basin. He was nervous that Rail would catch him before he could escape.

Raef slid down the rock face below his cave to the

basin floor. Rail had flown off again, so Raef was free to escape unnoticed. He ran across the basin floor to the waterfall. Once he arrived at the pool, he jumped in and washed. Not a gentle ceremonial wash this time, but a hard scrubbing. He was amazed at how long it took him to rub off all the dark grime. When he was as clean as he could make himself he got out of the pool, collected his robe, knife and needle, and began walking up the trail that led to the top of the falls.

Raef had only used this trail a few times to reach the top of the waterfall and sit at its edge. When he got to the top, he was briefly tempted to sit and look over the basin once more. Instead he turned away from the basin and began walking alongside the stream. He came to a small pine tree and soon there were more. Before long the trees behind him blocked the view of the Great Basin altogether. Still, he did not feel safe and he followed the stream until the air began to smell fresh, and he heard birds chirping. He realized he had not seen or heard a bird in two seasons.

When he felt safe from Rail's eyes he sat under a tree to begin his work. He carefully split the robe up the middle with his knife, from the bottom, stopping at about where the seat of the trousers would be. He found his knife had not grown dull, he assumed because he had never had reason to use it in Black Rock. He sewed what had been the front edges of the robe to the newly split back, making two tubes that joined at the place he had stopped cutting with his knife. Finally, he sewed the remaining front part together, leaving a hole at the top large enough to pull the trousers on. He left the arms intact.

Raef stood and held up his creation. It looked a bit odd, the old neck opening not really the right shape for trousers, but he removed his old trousers and pulled them on anyway. He had intended to use the sleeves as a tie strap around his waist, but they were positioned a little too low. When Raef tied the sleeves together they did hold everything up, but the end result did not look much like trousers. The legs were fine, but the upper part around his back rode up too high and the tie strap made of sleeves looked quite odd indeed. He folded the part that stuck up too high in back downward over his behind like a flap. He walked to the stream, found a smooth part in the water, and looked at himself. No, it did not look right, but he did not know how to fix it. At least they were clean. He discarded the needle and tucked his knife in his makeshift tie strap.

His thoughts were interrupted by his grumbling stomach. It was now past mid sun, and he had not eaten in over a sun's journey. He looked around and saw nothing he could eat. Would he have to return to the basin after all this, he wondered? Raef began walking in circles, half looking for food, half from anxious frustration after coming so far but feeling trapped. This was Zul's fault, he decided. The spirit had asked him to come home, and now he had no food for the journey.

"Zul!" said Raef, "what am I supposed to eat out here?"

Raef rarely spoke to Zul outside of meditation. He

was not even sure it was possible. Raef knew that Zul spoke through meditation, which only happened at sunrise, during the New Leaf ritual, or perhaps at a village ceremony. Raef did not believe the spirit would even hear him, but he yelled out to him all the same.

"This is how you treat your children? You call me out of Black Rock only to leave me to starve to death? At least Rail feeds its children."

The air grew very still. It seemed even the birds grew silent. Raef felt momentarily afraid. Perhaps he had offended the Great Spirit. Certainly no Keeper would ever speak to Zul in this manner.

No vision or sound came from the Great Spirit as Raef waited silently. But just as Raef was about to walk away, he heard a rustling noise near the ground. He looked to a nearby bush and saw it move a bit. Raef strained his eyes and saw a rabbit in the bush, apparently eating something. It did not seem to notice Raef. His stomach panged again.

Raef searched the ground for something to throw. A fist-sized stone lay at his feet. He slowly bent down to reach the stone, keeping as silent as possible. He had never killed anything before, and he was a little frightened to kill the animal now, but there was nothing else in sight that was edible. Raef stood, arm cocked, for several moments staring at the bush. The rabbit emerged from the left side of the bush, facing away from Raef, grazing on bits of grass. It still did not seem to notice him.

Raef was anxious. He did not want to see blood. The rabbit began slowly moving away from him as it ate. Realizing it would soon be out of reach, Raef threw the stone as hard as he could. The rock struck the rabbit on the back near its hind legs. It leapt into the air as the stone struck it, then tumbled end over end when it landed again. Raef sprang after it, but the rabbit righted itself and quickly sprinted in the opposite direction. Raef followed it as it ran in a large circle, arching away from the stream, then back again. Raef could not catch it until the rabbit ran out onto a slim rock that protruded a full span into the stream. Raef paused at the edge of the large rock, examining the animal. Its eyes were wide as it scampered back and forth at the end of the boulder, trapped between the rushing water and Raef.

Raef was afraid to try to catch it with his hands. He spotted a long stick on the ground, grabbed it, and swung at the rabbit. The rabbit jumped sideways easily evading the stick, but slid down the side of the rock and ended up in a deep pool in the stream. It began to flounder, eyes even wider than before. Raef walked to stand over the pool and watched the animal struggle in the water. Perhaps it was hurt too severely to swim. Perhaps rabbits could not swim in the first place. Whatever the case, the rabbit was not able to get out of the water; in fact it was drifting toward the current and would soon be swept away. Raef gripped the stick more tightly. If he hit the rabbit, it might sink or get knocked into the current. If he tried to pick it up, it could bite or scratch him. He felt foolish for being so afraid of a rabbit.

"Come on," he told himself aloud, "just grab the fool thing!"

He dropped the stick and waded into the pool. He

slowly reached for the rabbit. It thrashed harder, but
could not get away. Raef bit his lip and snatched the
rabbit by the scruff of the neck. As he pulled it up
out of the water, the rabbit went rigid, its back legs
dangling limply. Raef went back to shore, holding the
rabbit away from him.

He looked around for a way to kill it. He thought
about smashing its head with a rock, but that seemed
a little gruesome. Besides, the rock he had thrown at it
had not slowed it down much. He would likely have to
hit it very hard on the head to kill it. As he held the
rabbit, Raef noticed how thin the rabbit's neck was,
now that it was stretched out. He had never thought
of rabbits as having much of a neck at all, but he
could see that this rabbit's neck was longer and
thinner than he expected. Perhaps he could break its
neck. The thought turned his stomach, but at least it
wouldn't be bloody. Raef put his free hand around the
rabbit's neck. He was surprised at how delicate it felt.
The rabbit pulled its back legs up under its stomach
and began to kick at Raef's arm. Its nails slashed long
scratches into Raef's wrist and he quickly pulled his
hand away from its neck. It had drawn blood, and his
wrist stung.

"Damn the spirits!" he said, shaking his hurt arm
in the air.

With his free hand, he grabbed the rabbits two
hind feet and turned it upside down. With the hand
that had been holding it by the scruff of the neck, he
slipped his fingers under its chin and placed his
thumb firmly on the back of its neck. He could feel
its backbone running under his thumb. The rabbit

began to twist violently. It was stronger than it looked. Raef yanked downward on its neck, twisting it to the side while pulling up on its legs. He felt the neck bones snap under his thumb. He let go of its neck and the rabbit's head flopped to one side. Its body contorted a few times, then grew still. It was dead. Raef felt a little sick.

Raef solemnly placed the dead rabbit on the ground. He began pacing around it in circles. His hands were shaking. He had killed something. He stopped and looked down at it. It almost looked peaceful. Raef took a few deep breaths to calm himself. He pulled his knife from his belt and knelt over the rabbit.

Raef had never skinned or cleaned anything other than a fish before. He made a complete mess of the rabbit, getting fur and blood everywhere, even on himself. He had learned to make fire from the Dragon Children, so that part was easy. It was near sunset before the rabbit was done cooking. Raef ate ravenously and found his catch amazingly tasty. It was the first cooked meal, or meat of any kind for that matter, he had eaten in two seasons.

He washed his face, hands and arms after eating to remove the grease and blood that had gotten on him while eating. This was the first time he had washed after eating in three seasons as well. He found a spot on the ground where the dirt was soft and lay looking up at the stars. They seemed a little brighter than usual. He smiled to himself as he noticed how satisfied his stomach felt. He had never hunted anything before. Now he could say he had. It had been a series of unusually fortunate events more than anything, but he could not help feeling a little pride. He was truly on his own, for the first time in all his seasons, and he had caught his own dinner. He fell asleep easily, with the sound of the babbling stream nearby.

# 12

Raef awoke the next morning energized. He was escaping Black Rock. He was really doing it. He had eaten the entire rabbit sunset past, and he did not feel hungry, so he continued his journey right away. He did not bother to do the New Leaf ritual.

He knew the villages lay to the west, so he turned away from the stream and walked away from where the sun was rising. The small pines grew more dense and tall as he walked and by mid sun he had reached the western edge of the plateau. The ground dropped off at his feet the height of several trees to the forest below. The forest seemed to stretch off to the west forever. There was no sign of civilization at all. No villagers lived anywhere near Black Rock, he remembered.

It was slow going climbing down to the forest. The side of the plateau was steep and there was no trail. The ground was dirt, not rock, and he slid several times in the loose soil. Once on the forest floor, Raef felt immediately more at ease. The trees here were green and dense, much like the forest he grew up in.

As he walked further into the forest, he heard birds singing, lots of birds. He stopped to listen. It sounded almost magical. He jumped as he felt something on his toe. It was a beetle. He got on his hands and knees to watch it.

"A beetle! I have not seen a beetle in two seasons."

Raef stood up and looked around slowly.

"What else have I missed all this time?"

As he walked and the sun reached mid sky, the number of pine trees grew fewer and larger fir trees took their place. Ferns began to appear as well as snowberry and other familiar forest bushes. The forest seemed alive with animals. Squirrels were everywhere. A butterfly flew by, nearly hitting Raef's head. He even saw a fawn in the distance once. He felt his heart lighten.

Shortly after mid sun Raef found a small clearing full of berry bushes. The blue colored berries were tart but good, and he was able to eat his fill. Near sunset he found a patch of edible mushrooms that he roasted over a fire. He was still hungry, but decided he did not want to try to hunt and kill anything to eat. He knew he might need to again soon, but not this sun's journey. Sunrise to sunset had been entirely pleasant, and he did not wish to do anything to upset that.

By the third sun Raef began to think about home. Would his parents look older? Would Irah still be living at home? She had been old enough to marry when he left. What about his friends? Would Domik still be the same? Chaz, Kiever and Liet would be Warriors by now. Raef looked down at his slim chest.

What if Chaz was big and strong? What if Domik was no longer timid? Would Domik even want to associate with Raef anymore? Domik knew about Raef and the dragon. Raef felt his smile fade. His heart no longer felt light. He trudged on, shutting off his questions by searching for food. He did not sleep well that night. The ground felt too rough, and he had to fight off unpleasant memories that interrupted his sleep.

Raef lost count of the suns since he left Black Rock and worried that he would get lost. As each sun passed he grew more uneasy, not even sure he wanted to find Fir Hollow again. When he began to recognize hills and smaller forest mountains he knew he was nearing Fir Hollow. It grew harder to keep unpleasant memories of his youngling and early greenling seasons away. To make it worse, food had become harder to find, and Raef was growing weaker. He knew the villagers hunted and gathered food this far from the villages. The game was too skittish here and hard to find. Any he did spot were too far away for any crude weapons he could make to be effective. The fact that he had no training in making weapons did not help.

The sun finally came when Raef recognized exactly where he was. He was due east of Fir Hollow. He pushed through the trees and all at once found himself at the edge of the east meadow. Something kept him from entering the meadow. Instead, he sat behind a tree and peered out over the grassy meadow. This was the same meadow where Raef had first been chased by Rail as a small youngling. The meadow itself was empty, but Raef could make out buildings and a few people on the other side at the village edge. The distant sound of voices rose over the village. Busy people. Important people. The back of his neck felt warm, almost as if a very faint breeze of summer air was drifting by.

"What am I doing here?" Raef thought. "After two seasons, how can I just walk back into Fir Hollow? What will I tell them? They saw the dragon take me. They saw that it knew me."

His heart began to sink. A memory flashed into his mind. He was behind his youngling home, facing the wall with hands pressed against the dried mud exterior. Folor was whipping him for something he had done. Raef's backside stung at the memory, and he rubbed it unconsciously.

"My father will never accept me back. Not after what I've done. I would be an embarrassment to my family."

Another image flashed in his mind: Raef carrying a bucket down the street, shirtless in the hot sun, while Liet and Chaz laughed at him, calling him a walking skeleton. Raef's lip trembled at the memory, but he stopped himself from crying. He wrapped his arms across his bare chest.

"They will be warriors now. Real warriors, not apprentices. When they find out I have been with the dragon, they will…I can not even imagine what they would do."

He recalled Keeper Dimmel teaching him how to do the New Leaf ritual as an apprentice Keeper.

"I will be excommunicated as an apprentice Keeper, probably from the Intercessors as well.

Maybe even the whole village will banish me."

Raef could not stop the memories from coming. His eyes began to tear up but he hardened his face to make them stop.

"No one here cares about me," said the thoughts in his head, "No one here would ever like me if they really knew me."

A great shadow of despair fell over him.

"It is no use returning to Fir Hollow, why even try?"

In great shame, Raef slowly stood, head down, and turned away from the meadow. He was startled to see a dragon talon and paw on the ground immediately in front of him. He looked up to see Rail standing over him.

"Rail, what are you doing here?"

"I was worried about you, so I came looking for you."

Raef sank into the dragon's neck and closed his eyes. Rail gently wrapped a talon around Raef's back.

"I missed Fir Hollow, but I cannot go back. No one loves me, Rail. No one."

"That is not true at all, Raef. I came all the way here myself to find you. Toaz and Shiri have been asking for you, as is your old friend, DeAlsím. You have a home, in Black Rock, and all the Dragon Children miss you."

Raef stood back to look up at the dragon. Rail raised its majestic wings to make a canopy over them both.

"You are a Dragon Child, Raef. You do not belong here."

Stony bronze scales graced the slowly heaving side of the beast. Its powerful tail lay coiled behind, flexing now and then. An ebony talon, sharp as broken glass, still partially encircled Raef. The old excitement of being so close to such power and danger ran up Raef's spine.

"Come home, precious child of mine."

Raef climbed up on the dragon's neck. The dragon snaked through the trees until they were a fair distance from the meadow. Then, with a single thrust of Rail's wings they were in the air.

# 13

Erif sat on a dusty rock, nursing a blistered palm. His sword leaned up against the rock next to him. Sweat dripped from his forehead. He had been practicing hard since the last vision Zul had shown him.

"This is foolish," he thought, "I cannot fight the dragon alone. The Dragon Children are blind to what Rail has done to them. They could very well fight against me when I attack Rail. I will be completely outnumbered. To have any chance of defeating Rail, I will have to convince the villagers to come with me. They will call me crazy! Imagine what they will say when I ask them to go to Black Rock and attack the dragon. They will lock me away."

Erif became vaguely aware of a warm breeze behind him. He ignored it. His thoughts continued.

"No one will ever believe that Rail has prisoners in the mountain. The entire Province is convinced the dragon eats its prey."

Erif let go of his sore hand and allowed his shoulders to slump.

"No one will ever believe me, much less help me. It would take several villages to even hope for success, how will I ever convince them?"

Erif let out a long sigh. He heard the words form in his head, "It is no use, why even try?"

The hair on the back of Erif's neck stood up. This was not right. These were not the thoughts Zul had trained him to think. These thoughts were from somewhere else.

Erif snatched his sword, stood and spun around, arms extended, sweeping his weapon in an arc. The sword glanced off the nostril of a very real dragon. Rail leapt back, clasping its snout with a claw. A large drop of deep red blood fell, hissing when it touched the ground. The cut on Rail's nostril quickly healed itself, completely disappearing. Erif held his sword ready.

"You evil whisperer!" Erif said, "that was you!"

Rail raised a talon, aimed at the man's chest. Erif angled the sword across his body defensively.

"I am not one of those gullible villagers, Rail," said Erif, "I know your voice. And I know your weaknesses."

The dragon lowered its claw and hissed.

"You are nothing," said Rail, "a mere ant to be crushed."

"I am the son of Zul."

"A pathetic outcast youngling he took in. You are no true son of his."

Erif lowered the tip of his sword, pointing it below

the dragon's chin. Erif took one step forward.

"A lie, Rail. I am no youngling, and to Zul I am no outcast."

"It makes no difference. You are here, abandoned, far from the others. You can do nothing to help those you believe are in danger."

"My time here is not forever, Rail, and if you did not fear me, you would never have come. If I were really nothing, you would not need to come here to convince me that I was."

Erif leapt forward, slashing the sword at Rail's neck. The dragon recoiled, avoiding the blow.

"Leave. Now!" said Erif.

Erif took another step forward. The dragon stepped back and coiled itself, then shot into the sky. Erif watched the dragon fly out of sight, heading for the mainland and villages of unknowing people. Erif felt a hand on his shoulder.

"You did well, my son,"

"It was Rail," Erif said, "it whispered those thoughts into my head."

"Yes," said Zul, "Rail is a deceiver."

Erif took a deep breath.

"I am sorry I have been wavering in my confidence lately," said Erif.

"It is part of your training."

Erif looked into the old spirit's eyes.

"You sent Rail?"

"No, I never call on Rail. It is my enemy. But I knew Rail would come. It is very predictable."

Erif looked to where Rail had been standing.

"Sometimes, it feels like I am failing," said Erif.

"Not failing, learning," said the spirit.

—·◇·—

DeAlsím and Toaz walked along side Raef as they approached a food pile. Raef scooped up a large piece of something green and began to eat. He noticed a very small youngling looking up at him curiously. The youngling's face, arms and chest were smeared with dirt and food and his hair was completely unkept. Raef felt a tinge of shock as he slowly recognized the youngling as Rimmel from Moss Rock who had arrived the sunset before Raef had tried to return to Fir Hollow. The youngling was barely recognizable now.

At sunset Raef walked up the trail to his cave. Toaz and Mizo were already there, lying down to sleep. They began telling coarse jokes and making up frightening stories. Raef found he was in no mood to join them. He walked back to the cave entrance and looked out over the basin. It began to rain. Moonlight peeked through a hole in the clouds, dimly illuminating the basin. Everywhere Raef looked there was only black rock. Dull, flat basalt as far as he could see. His depression returned, matching the gloom around him. He remembered little Rimmel; how he looked when he arrived and how he looked now. Raef looked down at his chest. It was streaked with food and grime.

"This is what I have come to," he thought.

He felt tears on his cheeks. He did not want the others to see he was crying, so he stepped out into the rain. The rain disguised his tears.

"I will never get out of here," he thought, "and even if I could, I would never be allowed to live in the villages. I am truly ruined."

Hot tears began to flow faster down his cheeks. He wanted to be alone, far from anyone. He climbed up to the basin rim and began to walk along it, away from Rail's perch. The rain was cold, and he was getting soaked, but he did not return to his cave. He wanted to feel miserable; he deserved it. Sinking into despair, Raef cried out the spirit, Zul.

"Why did you not help me escape? Why did you let the dragon take me back here again?"

Only the rain responded. Raef hung his head. It did not make sense to him. Zul was supposed to help. Raef had been a Keeper, or at least an Apprentice Keeper. He had continued to do the ritual washings and meditations, even here in Black Rock. Why had the Great Spirit abandoned him?

Raef paused and looked up into the dark night. He felt the cold rain on his face. Was Rail was too strong for Zul? Or perhaps Black Rock was beyond the reach of the Great Spirit. These thoughts caused Raef to sink deeper into depression.

Raef felt his chest grow cold as he began to fear a far worse possibility. Perhaps Zul was unwilling to forgive the transgression of his befriending the dragon. Perhaps that was why the Intercessors refused to even speak the dragon's name. What if it was an evil beyond what the Great Spirit would forgive?

Raef sank to his knees and dropped his face into his hands. In desperation, he called out to the sky.

"Why don't you love me?"

No vision or sound came. Raef tensed in pain as he felt something snap inside him. He stopped crying. He felt his face harden. Raef stood silently in the pouring rain and turned to face the dragon's perch.

In the moonlight, Raef saw the dragon's silhouette, reclined on the flat rock, its great paws dangling off the front edge. Raef slowly walked to the perch and sat next to the dragon.

"Why are you here in the rain?" asked the dragon, "Your cave is dry."

Raef did not know how to answer. He felt the dragon's head move over him, its hot breath wash over him.

"You may sleep here with me, just this once, if you like," said Rail.

Raef curled up on the wet rock next to the dragon. He felt Rail's hot tongue run up his back, and the strong scent of dragon enveloped him.

"Yes," Raef said to himself, "I am a Dragon Child."

Then the dragon covered him with one wing and Raef fell asleep.

# PART THREE

## RETURN OF THE DRAGON CHILD

# 14

"Why did you not answer him?" asked Erif.

"Do you not see the fallacy in his reasoning?" answered Zul.

"I suppose a little, but that is not the point. You left him believing you do not care about him."

"But, Erif, it is my point. His beliefs are so warped he is unable to even see truth, much less understand it."

Erif turned to face the Great Spirit.

"Zul, he is in great pain. He is still but a greenling."

"Yet his pain is still not great enough to cause him to let go of the lies he tells himself."

"Those lies are all that protect him!"

Zul gave a soft smile, then placed a hand gently on Erif's shoulder.

"You are becoming wise," said Zul. "You will be a great Warrior yet."

"I am no longer sure I wish to be wise. It feels as if wisdom just brings sadness."

"Only when you limit your perspective to the moment, rather than to all the seasons of time."

Erif shook his head and blew out a long breath.

"This conversation is becoming a bit too cavernous for me."

Zul chuckled, "I agree, enough for now. Let us go to the beach together and enjoy the waves."

"That is a magnificent idea."

Erif joined Zul on the trail leading to the ocean.

"Let us allow Raef to grow up a bit," said Zul, "We shall see what the seasons do with the pain in his heart."

———·✧·———

Raef stood in the entrance of his cave overlooking the Great Basin. A soupy mist floated through the basin making it difficult to see, but Raef could still make out the bodies of several Dragon Children lying out on the basin floor, sleeping in the late morning. His latest cave mates were sleeping as well. Hummel had seventeen seasons, nearly as many as Raef. He had come from Summit City, the ruling city of the entire province. Hummel had told Raef tales of the great city, of streets and buildings made of stone and the regal clothing everyone wore. Raef did not believe Hummel's tales entirely, but he made a good cave mate.

The third in the cave was Rashi, who was still a youngling of eleven seasons. Rashi had come from Fir Hollow, arriving two seasons past and was the youngest Dragon Child in the Great Basin at the moment. Raef took him in as they were from the same village, and Rashi seemed quite lost in Black Rock at first. Raef glanced back at the lanky youngling, hair disheveled, covered in filth with barely a loincloth covering him. The youngling had adapted quickly. Raef doubted his own parents would recognize him now. It was rare for Rashi to come up and sleep in the cave any longer. The youngling spent most of his time exploring the tunnels, gone for several suns at a time.

Raef had long since tired of the tunnels. Every tunnel was only more of the same. Finding a new tunnel felt exciting for a few season until the realization came that one tunnel was just for the most part just like all the others. Some colorful crystals here and there, but otherwise nothing but endless twists and turns that always led back to the Great Basin. Even the molten river in the deepest tunnel no longer interested Raef.

Raef had eighteen seasons now, five of which he had spent here at Black Rock. He was now a full head taller than anyone in the basin. His hair still hung past his waist, as he had never been able to cut it and give up the symbol of an Intercessor. He still wore the remnants of his blue apprentice robe as trousers, although the legs were now too short and they were threadbare, torn, and so soiled one could scarcely tell they had once been blue. They clung to him like the skin of a reptile that needed to molt.

He let out a long sigh. He was tired even though he had not exerted himself in seasons. He felt not entirely present, something he found hard to explain, even to himself. He felt nothing but numbness, as if he were not alive at all. He did not think he could live in this place any longer. He remembered the last time he had tried to escape, three seasons past.

"I made it all the way to Fir Hollow," he said to himself.

He tried to remember why he had not entered the village, but instead had returned to Black Rock with Rail. He wondered if Rail would follow him again if he tried to escape. Raef walked to the back of the cave and picked up his old eating knife. He slipped it under his tie sash, which was really the sleeve of what had been his apprentice Keeper robe. Raef walked out of his cave and down to the basin. He walked through the misty sunrise across the basin floor to the waterfall. He did not pause to wash, but walked up the trail to the top and followed the stream north on the plateau. He remembered the way to Fir Hollow. He knew he would not get lost. He had a bit more confidence he could find food, even kill an animal if he had to. And he was not afraid of what the villagers would say when they saw him. If they killed him on sight it would be better than staying here.

He was curious that he did not feel wonder at the beauty of the forest and its animals as he had before. The colors were as bright as before and the sounds of nature as crisp as he remembered, but none of these brought a smile to his face. He was disappointed by his dull response, but he determined to continue, trudging methodically through the increasingly dense trees.

The suns passed in seeming endless succession as he travelled, eating when he could, until he once again began to recognize hills in the distance. He altered his course toward where he knew Fir Hollow lay and continued his quest. He eventually reached the meadow on the east end of Fir Hollow.

This time he did not hide behind a tree, but marched right out into the thigh high grass. The grass brushing his legs brought strong memories from his past. He stopped in the center of the meadow and tried to recall. He reached down and gently ran his hand over the tips of the grass. This was the place. The very spot where twelve seasons past he had first encountered Rail. Raef tried to remember how he'd felt back then, as a youngling of only six seasons being chased by an ominous shadow. He could not recall. He looked into the sky to where the shadowy dragon had disappeared and to where it had finally carried him away seven seasons later. He recalled being carried over this very meadow, realizing he was being taken from the village, not just for a ride. The feelings of his past tried to emerge, but they could not. Raef blinked, pausing another moment in case he did begin to feel them again.

He looked toward the village. No one was in sight. No one had seen him yet. He could hear voices, busy voices, laughing voices, loud voices. It was so different from Black Rock. He took a breath, and then started walking through the grass, toward the village. He glanced down at himself. His body was covered in large splotches of oily streaks running down his chest and arms and onto his trousers. His feet were bare and filthiest of all. He looked at the village as he approached its edge, and allowed himself to wonder briefly what they might think of him.

He entered the street that led to the heart of the Intercessor sector. His heart began to race as he passed homes on either side of him. A young woman came into sight at the corner ahead of him. She was carrying a large basket and was looking downward as she walked. This seamed odd to Raef until an old memory returned. In the villages, women did not meet the gaze of men or greenling. It was proper for them to cast their eyes down.

But this woman broke that rule. Perhaps she had seen Raef out of the corner of her eye, but now she looked directly at him. At first the expression on her face was one of seeing a ghost, but as Raef continued to walk toward her, she began to slowly smile. Then she threw down her basket and ran to him. Raef froze. Just before she threw her arms around him, he recognized her.

"Raef!" cried Irah, "you…you are back!"

She stood back and looked at him, her smile as wide as he had ever seen his sister wear.

"Raef, you have grown…so tall! I think you are taller than father."

"I…I am older, of course."

It was odd for him to be looking down at his older sister. He tried to calculate the seasons, but he no longer knew how many she had. She had grown quite attractive, he noticed, and was pleased that she had.

"Look at you, my brother. You are…a man now. I never imagined you as a man. Well, of course you are by now but, well, you were barely a greenling when…" her voice trailed off.

Raef tried to think of something to say to his sister, but could not. He tried to smile at her, but his mouth did not seem to want to form that shape.

"What happened to you?" Irah continued, "We all thought you were dead, when that dragon took you away. And now you are all, well, very dirty and ragged. You look worse than a beggar, truth be told, but...but you are lucky to be alive at all, you are!"

She seemed to hesitate a moment, but then Irah hugged Raef again, quite firmly.

"I am so happy to see you."

This was not what he had expected. It was a very nice response, he decided, after being seen in such a state. Yet the joy he knew should be welling up inside him remained dormant. It all felt unreal somehow. He felt his sister dragging him down the street by his arm.

"Come, we must tell the others," Irah said, "Father will be so excited. As will Wren, even though I suppose he does not know you well."

"Wren? Who is Wren?"

"Oh, Raef, of course you would not know, but I am married now. My husband's name is Wren."

They turned the corner and passed the Keep and Ceremonial Lodge on their left. Everything looked much smaller than he remembered.

"Wren is a mason," said Irah, "He is a very good man."

"A mason?" asked Raef, "But you are an Intercessor. Why would you marry a mason? That is a Merchant's profession."

They turned another corner heading east between rows of Intercessor homes. It all looked so familiar.

Raef was surprised how little had changed.

"Raef, there is nothing wrong with a mason. Wren is a good provider and father. He is quite high up in the Mason's Guild."

"Father? He's a father and you…you are a mother now?"

"Well, Raef, of course. It has been many seasons."

They followed the road, looping north and then back west, passing the home where Nilo had lived and then coming to Raef's youngling home. Something about the sight of his old home sent a chill down his spine. It was not a bad feeling, but somehow startling. Irah did not call out to announce herself, but pushed right through the door with Raef in tow. Malta, his mother, was cooking inside. Her hair had gray streaks in it he had not remembered. When she saw Raef, her mouth dropped open, and she let go of the spoon she had been holding, allowing it to fall to the floor. For several moments his mother stood, her mouth moving but no sounds coming out. Then she put her hands to her mouth and began to cry.

"Great spirits of the Province," said his mother, "Zul has brought my son home to me…alive!"

Raef resented the comment about Zul. That old spirit had nothing to do with him returning. Not this time, anyway. His mother walked slowly to him, put her arms around him and hugged her face to his chest. It was very odd to be looking down at his own mother. He realized he should hug her back, so he put his arms around her shoulders.

"Is the pottage ready, mother?" asked Irah, "Raef let me get you something to eat. You look absolutely starving. Just look how skinny you are."

Irah picked up the spoon, wiped it on her dress, and served some pottage into a bowl, which she put on the old family table. The table had a different cloth on it than Raef remembered. His mother loosened her grip on him and walked him to the bench, helping him sit down. The pottage, something he had never been especially fond of, filled his nostrils with an aroma that made his stomach growl out loud.

"Oh, my," said his mother, "it sounds like you are hungry."

"I have not eaten in two suns," he replied.

This was true. On his journey he had eaten perhaps once a sun and not at all since sun's journey past. The pottage tasted better than anything he remembered eating. He ate ravenously, even though he knew his manners were quite rude. He could not stop himself. Just then the door slammed open, and Raef turned to see Folor enter. Raef froze. Folor froze as well, staring at Raef. After a long silence, his father spoke.

"Raef? Is this Raef?"

Raef slowly stood, remembering that he should show respect for his father and the position of Keeper he held. Folor ran to him and put his hands on Raef's shoulders.

"My son! How? How is this possible?"

Raef's father seemed to lose his normally carefully controlled composure. He quickly pulled Raef to him in a short embrace. Raef went rigid at his father's touch. Folor had not shown affection much in the past, and it felt strange. His father let go and stepped back, looking almost embarrassed.

"He was eating, Folor," said his mother, quietly, "he has not eaten in two suns."

"Sit, sit!" said Folor, "Please, finish eating!"

His father moved Raef back to the bench where he sat and slowly began to eat again. Raef was again astounded at how good the pottage was. It even had cabbage and peas in it, and he had never liked either. He had difficulty stopping himself from continuing to eat once he was full.

"Look how you have grown, Raef," said Folor. "I think you are even a bit taller than I. Here, let us see."

Folor pulled Raef to his feet again and stood back to back with him, reaching back to touch the top of their heads. Raef was indeed a bit taller. Folor seemed very pleased by this. Raef stepped away from his father and turned to face his family.

"Enough fussing over me," Raef said forcing a small smile, "I want to know what has happened since I have been gone."

"What has happened here?" his mother said, "Why it is the same as always. We want to know what in all the Province happened to you to bring you back to us."

Raef brushed the question aside. He did not want to talk about where he had been.

"Nothing has changed?" he asked again.

"I told you already that I have married," said Irah, "Oh, I must get Wren and bring him to meet you. I will return soon."

Irah disappeared from the house. Raef was not really interested in meeting him. He tried to remember someone by that name. He could not.

"Here, Raef," said Folor, "you look like you need some clothes. I think mine will actually fit you now! Come and put something better on."

"Can I wash first?" asked Raef.

"Of course, of course," said his mother, "only, I believe you will need more than just a usual washing."

Folor brought Raef a set of clothing as Raef's mother rolled out the wash barrel from the corner. When water had been warmed and the barrel filled, Raef was left alone in the house to attempt to scrub off five seasons of grime. It seemed to take forever, even with a stiff scrub brush. When he dressed, he found the trousers and shirt Folor had lent him were long enough, but quite baggy on Raef's thin frame. He had to wrap the tie sashes around himself twice to pull the waist tight enough. He walked out of the house and found his mother and sister outside waiting. A small female youngling, appearing to have three or four seasons, stood next to Irah. The little one seemed frightened by Raef's appearance and she hugged Irah's leg.

"This is my daughter, Enira," said Raef's sister. "She is a bit bashful."

Raef looked down at the youngling in amazement. It was hard to imagine that he was an uncle.

"You will meet my husband soon," said Irah, "but you are not yet ready to be presented to anyone. He went to help father while we finish getting you ready."

"I do not understand," said Raef, "is something wrong?"

"Well," said his mother, "nothing you could help, I suppose."

The two women pushed Raef back inside the house and sat him on the bench. Enira followed but sat on a stool in a far corner. Irah poured oil over Raef's head and his mother walked behind him.

"This may hurt a bit," said his mother.

With that, they went to work attempting to comb the rat's nest out of his hair. In the end, they were forced to cut off two hand-spans off the ends as it was too hopelessly tangled to comb out. It still hung half way down his back, respectable for an Intercessor.

"You still look quite fine," said Irah, "not as long as father's, but definitely long enough for a Keeper."

"A Keeper?" said Raef, "I just want to be an Intercessor again."

Irah grinned at her mother and the two of them stood Raef up and dragged him outside. When Raef walked out the door he noticed it was already becoming dark. He also noticed that no one was out on the streets, which somehow seemed odd. He tried to remember why that would be unusual. Little Enira hid behind her mother.

"What are we doing?" asked Raef, "and where is everyone?"

"Raef," said Malta, "your father and Wren have been gathering people to welcome you home. They are expecting us at the Common Lodge."

"The Common Lodge?" asked Raef, "but that is only for the gatherings of the entire village."

"Exactly!" said Irah.

"The whole village?" said Raef. "I do not wish to see the whole village right now."

"But, son," said Malta, "everyone thought you were dead. The village saw the dragon take you. That you escaped and returned is an oracle. No one has ever managed such a thing. The village is already calling you a hero."

Raef tried to make sense of what his mother had said, scarcely noticing that his mother and sister where leading him down the road toward the central square. A hero, Raef thought to himself. How could he possibly be a hero? As they approached the Common Lodge on the edge of the square, Raef could see dozens and dozens of villagers arriving from all parts of Fir Hollow.

"They are all coming to see you!" said Irah.

Raef felt very uneasy. The women led Raef into the building, and villagers parted as they made their way to the front of the lodge. They approached Raef's father who was standing next to a stout, stern looking young man.

"Wren," said Irah to the man, "this is my brother, Raef!"

Wren extended his thick hand to Raef. He did not smile.

"It is good to meet the son of Folor," said Wren.

Raef took Wren's hand in greeting. Wren's hand was calloused and solid as rock.

"As it is to meet you, Wren, husband of my sister, Irah."

Folor whisked Raef away from Wren and drug him up onto a platform at the front of the lodge. The crowd grew silent. Raef felt a chill run up his spine. Out of the crowd emerged an older man dressed in a bright red robe. The old man smiled, and Raef recognized him as Prime Keeper Bremen. Bremen joined them on the platform, took Raef's hand in greeting, then turned to the villagers who had gathered.

"Village of Fir Hollow," the Prime Keeper began, "you have been gathered for a momentous occasion. This young man standing by my side is one we all thought to be dead seasons ago."

A murmur moved through the crowd. Raef looked at his feet.

"Many of you witnessed the event," Prime Bremen continued, "when the dragon showed itself for the second time in our generation and seized Apprentice Keeper Raef, the son of Folor, just outside this very lodge, in the village square."

The murmuring grew louder.

"We all assumed young Raef to have been eaten alive by the great beast of Black Rock," said Bremen, raising his voice to a crescendo, "but we should have known, by Keeper Raef's special choosing as a youngling. This is no ordinary young man. This is no ordinary Keeper. The beast was unable to kill him! Keeper Raef, even as an apprentice, defeated the beast and escaped!"

The villagers began clapping and shouting. The lodge became very noisy. Prime Keeper Bremen shouted over the crowd.

"For five seasons Keeper Raef wandered the forests, fought off predators and with the power of the Great Spirit was finally led back to us!"

"Ho! Ho! Ho!" chanted the crowd.

Raef looked out at the villagers of Fir Hollow as they cheered for him. He did not understand. None of what Keeper Bremen had said was true.

The crowd rushed the platform and took Raef upon their shoulders, carrying him around the great hall as they cheered. When they finally returned him to the platform, Keeper Dimmel, Raef's old mentor, and an older Keeper called Chaummer emerged from the crowd and climbed onto the platform. Keeper Dimmel handed a folded red robe to the Prime Keeper. Bremen took the robe and held up a hand to silence the crowd. The noise subsided, but the crowd did not become entirely silent.

"No training the senior Keepers could have given would compare to what the Great Spirit has taught Raef," said Bremen. "Raef, you left us as a young greenling apprentice. You return to us man. As Prime Keeper and overseer of the Intercessors of Fir Hollow, I declare you this sunset to be a fellow Keeper in full standing."

Bremen unfolded the robe and held it out to Raef. Hesitantly, Raef held his arms out as Prime Bremen slid the sleeves over his arms and hung it on his back.

"Villagers of Fir Hollow!" shouted Bremen, "I give you, Keeper Raef!"

The celebration that followed lasted until nearly mid moon. The village inns and taverns brought food. The crowd spilled out into the adjacent village square. People came to greet Raef that he could not recall at all. He felt a strong desire to be alone, away from all the noise and commotion. But he did recognize his old friend Domik when he came to greet Raef. Domik was surprisingly short and still quiet. He had become a scribe, which was a respectable position for an Intercessor. Domik had not married, however, which was unusual for a man of eighteen seasons. Nilo came to greet Raef as well. He had thirteen seasons and was a new greenling, apprenticing in the Intercessor kitchen and living in the dormery.

Raef's old fellow dormers made a point to speak with him as well. Xoh, Mijo, Denol, Breem and Kommel were all grown now, married and working as Intercessors in various positions. They greeted Raef not by clasping his hand but by dipping their heads slightly, showing deference to his position as Keeper. By the time the moon was high it seemed as if every villager in Fir Hollow had passed by to greet him. Except the Warriors, of course. Raef was aware that none of the young Warriors he had known as a youngling had come to see him.

When most of the villagers had gone home however, Prime Warrior Rodon came to the square. Raef instantly recognized his son Chaz as well, who walked beside Prime Rodon. Rodon looked much older than Raef remembered. He walked with a slight limp but looked otherwise as strong as ever. As the two approached, Raef was surprised at how much taller he was than either of them. Rodon, as Prime Warrior, wore a headband covered in medals and honors he had earned. Chaz now had a few medals on his headband as well, and the young Warrior's muscles stood out on his arms. In spite of his height, Raef felt insignificant next to the Warriors.

"Keeper Raef," said Rodon, "I wanted to come see

you when I heard you had returned. You were good to my family and to my son when I was injured. We have never forgotten that."

Chaz was looking at the ground as if he were embarrassed or ashamed. Raef could not understand this. Chaz was so obviously superior to him, already decorated with Warrior honors.

"I am very glad to hear that the old beast did not kill you," said Rodon, "It would have been a great loss."

Rodon bowed stiffly and left. Chaz glanced up at Raef, bowed slowly, then turned and left as well. Raef suddenly wanted to leave very badly. Fortunately, the other Keepers decided to return to their homes since so few villagers were left in the square. Raef waved goodbye to his sister and her new family, then followed his father home. His mother had returned home earlier. He felt apprehensive. He did not want to sleep in his parents' home, but he knew they would not accept him sleeping outside.

When he arrived at his youngling home he entered to find that his mother had been preparing a bed for him. It was in the place where his sister's bed had been, and his mother had secured a new privacy curtain around it.

"Thank you for making arrangements for me to stay," said Raef to his mother.

"We would have it no other way," said his mother.

"We know you will have your own home soon," said his father, "but stay here until you do."

"Of course," said Raef.

He looked around the small room and felt a strong

urge to escape. Everything was so crowded here in Fir Hollow. He missed the vast openness of the Great Basin.

"I am not ready to sleep yet," said Raef. "I will sit outside a bit first."

"Do you wish for me to join you?" asked Folor.

"No, father, I think I need to be alone a bit. I am not used to being around so many people."

"Yes, I understand," said Folor.

Raef left the room and sat on the ground outside, leaning up against the outer wall. He looked up at the sky. The stars were so bright they almost hurt his eyes to look at, and there were millions of them.

Raef heard shoes padding against the dirt road and looked to see the silhouette of a greenling coming toward him.

"Raef, is that you?" whispered the shadow.

"Who is it?" Raef whispered back.

"Nilo," said the voice.

The greenling came close enough for the moonlight to illuminate his face. Even after seeing him earlier that sunset Raef was not accustomed to Nilo's older appearance. The last time Raef had seen him Nilo was a small youngling. Nilo came and sat next to Raef. Raef held his hand out to Nilo, palm up. Nilo wrinkled his nose and looked sideways at Raef. Raef quickly retracted his hand, remembering this was not Black Rock. Nilo shrugged.

"What are you doing up so late?" asked Raef. "The dormeress will beat you if she finds you missing."

"Neena won't care tonight," said Nilo. "She fell asleep long ago before any of us apprentices returned.

She knows we were out at the celebration and told us to put ourselves to sleep. Most of the others are still out as well."

"I see," said Raef.

"Rail had told me you were alive. I was not sure I believed the old beast, but I certainly did not expect to see you in Fir Hollow again."

"Quiet," said Raef, "don't use its name in the open like this."

"I am being quiet. No one near is awake anyway."

Raef leaned back against the wall. It was confusing to be sitting outside his old home in Fir Hollow while speaking of the dragon.

"What did...Rail say about me?" asked Raef.

"It said it took you away to someplace even more secret than our old hiding place."

"It did."

"Then why are you back?"

"I did not want to stay any longer."

The two sat in silence as Raef watched the stars.

"Do you...you know...still go see it?" asked Raef.

Nilo looked at his feet.

"No. I don't do that any more. I am an apprentice, you know."

"Yes, I know. In the kitchen, right?"

"Yes. It isn't much, I suppose, but I was never good at paying attention in lessons, so I was not chosen for a learned position. It is better than working in the stables, at least."

"That it is. So...you must have continued to see the dragon after I was taken."

Nilo looked embarrassed, then looked away.

"When I was still a youngling," said Nilo, "but I have not gone back in...well...a few seasons."

Nilo changed the subject and began to talk about being an apprentice and living in the dormery. Raef clearly smelled the scent of dragon wafting off the greenling who sat next to him. He wondered why Nilo felt the need to lie.

When Nilo left Raef entered his parents' home. He could hear them snoring behind their privacy curtain. He went to the bed made for him and closed the curtain around it. It felt very strange to sleep where he could not look out a cave entrance and see the sky. He felt confined. He woke several times before sunrise.

# 15

Re-establishing himself to village life was quite different than Raef expected. He had expected condemnation and to be treated like an outcast. Instead the villagers gravitated to him in apparent fascination. It was also quite difficult readjusting to village life. He had forgotten how regimented it was. Meals were eaten at very specific sun positions and he often found he was either not yet hungry or wanted to eat too early. He found it annoying that he could not stop and eat when he pleased. The Keepers had new clothing made for Raef, but he found he did not particularly like them. Undergarments, trousers and a shirt, an outer tunic and then his Keeper robe on top of all that. He found it quite stuffy and confining. And shoes made his feet sweat. Raef had also forgotten what it was like to have his schedule determined by others. He was no longer an apprentice, but he was still the youngest Keeper, thus was required to follow their lead. Keeper Chaummer, whom he did not know well, had been given charge over him and his schedule. Raef found himself wanting to leave and wander the village or forest on his own. He frequently found his mind wandering when he should have been focusing on his work.

Keeper Chaummer assigned Raef to the care of the west village, where the Laborers and poorer Merchants lived. His first duty was to assess any needs that had been neglected in that quadrant of the village. He was to search out and discover who was sick and send for the herbalists to concoct remedies. He found families that needed alms and called for almoners to bring food. He found male youngling neglecting lessons and playing in the streets and sent them to the Training Lodge. He also frequently snuck into the forest and simply rested, sitting under the shade of a tree. None of the other Keepers seemed to notice how often he left the village nor did they ask why he went missing from time to time.

Meanwhile, the Keepers called on the Laborers to construct a small hut for Raef to live in. Raef asked to have it built on the farthest eastern edge of the Intercessor sector, on the edge of the East Meadow. It was a very simple hut, made of sticks and a little mud, but he was quite pleased to be able to sleep in his own home rather than with his parents.

On his first night alone in his new hut, Raef sat by the only window and looked over the meadow in the moonlight. He would not need a privacy curtain in his own hut and he planned on leaving the window shutters open every night. Raef's thoughts were interrupted by the sound of a voice outside calling his name. Raef went to the door to find Chaz.

"May I come in?" asked Chaz.

"Of course," said Raef, opening the door for Chaz. Raef was surprised that Chaz, of all villagers, would come to visit him.

"It is not much, but make yourself at home," said Raef.

Chaz sat in one of the two stools in the hut. Raef sat opposite him. The young Warrior appeared nervous.

"This is a fine first home," said Chaz, looking around the small room.

"It is merely a hut, not a proper house. I would imagine you have a much larger home," said Raef.

"Yes, but I have a wife and a son."

"You are married?" asked Raef. "And you have a son?"

Chaz gave a weak smile. Raef looked at the young man before him. Of course he would be married by now. He should not have been surprised. Raef got up and drained some ale into his mug from the small cask on the floor against one wall.

"Have some ale?" asked Raef.

"Thank you," said Chaz, taking the mug.

"I only have one mug," said Raef.

"We can share," said Chaz, "We are old friends, after all."

"You consider me a friend?"

Chaz scrunched his eyebrows, cocked his head, and looked into Raef's eyes.

"Raef, we have known each other as long as I can remember. We went to Training Lodge together. We played together as younglings. Of course you are my friend."

Raef looked at the ground.

"Raef," said Chaz, "I know I was not always kind to you when we were young. But I have always thought of you as a friend, perhaps even more a friend than Keever and Liet. I just did not know how to show it. Warriors are trained to be rough, practically from birth. You were never that way, and I did not know how to act around you."

Chaz drank and passed the mug to Raef.

"It is nothing," said Raef, "We were only younglings."

Chaz was trying to smile, but Raef saw a tear form in the Warrior's eye. Raef was immediately embarrassed for the man, but Chaz allowed the tear to roll onto his cheek.

"My father tried to teach me a better way," said Chaz, "but I wanted to be like the other Warrior younglings."

Raef felt an ache inside him. For a moment he thought tears might come to his eyes, but he sat taller and hardened his face. The ache went away.

"I am glad you returned to us," said Chaz, "I have a question, the kind one would ask an Intercessor."

"Warriors do not seek guidance from Intercessors," said Raef.

"I am asking none-the-less. Raef, I feel I should no longer be a Warrior. I have been thinking of taking my family to another village, where my heritage is unknown, and I could follow another destiny. Would a Keeper bless such a choice?"

"But, you have always wanted to be a Warrior! You excel at everything Warriors do."

Chaz turned away from Raef. His body seemed to tighten for a moment, then he turned back to Raef. His eyes dripped tears.

"Do I? My father was nearly killed trying to protect the village, and still he could not drive the dragon off."

"Warriors do much more than protect the village from the dragon. You enforce the laws in the village. You hunt for us. You settle disputes with other villages or even fight if need be to protect us."

"None of that matters! Raef, the dragon is the real threat. No one will discuss it, but the dragon is the greatest threat to any village, and the Warriors can do nothing to stop it."

Raef had never heard anyone speak so openly of the dragon in Fir Hollow. Perhaps this was some sort of a trap to get him to admit he was a Dragon Child.

"The dragon is rarely seen," said Raef, "only twice in our generation. Why do you think it is such a threat?"

"Raef, I do not know if anyone has told you, but it has gotten a lot worse since you left. Villagers are disappearing frequently. The Nobles make up excuses as to what happens to them, but I know it is the dragon. I have led search parties through all the forests around the village, but I have found nothing, no sign of it. That damned dragon just sneaks in and takes people right under our noses. Two seasons ago a youngling of only nine seasons vanished. Hear me, Raef, only nine seasons! No one is safe."

Raef remembered Rashi back at Black Rock. This must be the youngling Chaz spoke of. He was safe, at least from physical harm, but Raef could not explain that to Chaz.

"But you," continued Chaz, "You know more than we do. I have not forgotten how you frightened the dragon away after it attacked my father. You were still a youngling, yet it left when you called it by name. Raef, how did you know its name?"

"Chaz, I cannot…"

"Never mind," said Chaz, leaning back, "It is probably some secret of the Keepers. The point is, you seem to be able to stop it when no one else can."

"Chaz, that was a very long time ago. Besides, as you remember it did come back for me and took me two seasons later."

"But you escaped. You alone have overpowered the dragon."

Raef stood and began to pace the room. He searched his mind for a way to change the conversation.

"You are different somehow, Raef. You have beaten the dragon before. We must know how to fight it. Defeating the dragon is not found in the ways of the Warriors."

Chaz stood and walked to Raef. Raef tried to meet the Warrior's gaze.

"Teach me!" Chaz said, "I will do exactly as you say. I will grow my hair out. I will wear a robe and meditate. Anything! It is pointless for me to go on as a Warrior. But you know the dragon's secrets."

Raef stood in silence. Yes, he did know some of Rail's secrets, many, in fact. But none of them were good secrets. None could help Fir Hollow.

"Chaz, I do not know what to tell you. I suppose I do know a little about the dragon. But I cannot see how what I know could help."

"You got away! How did you do it?"

It was the first time anyone had asked.

"It is hard to explain. Zul helped me, I suppose." Raef felt his face redden. He was a poor liar.

"Try to remember. I know it was along time ago. Maybe you blocked some of those memories out by now. But, Raef, we need to know."

Raef sighed. Everyone believed he had escaped seasons ago and been lost since then. He could think of nothing to say that Chaz would understand.

"I will leave you now," said the Warrior. "I have disturbed you enough. Just promise you will think on this."

"I will," said Raef, walking with Chaz to the door, "but do me one favor."

"Anything."

"Remain a Warrior. If you do trust me as a Keeper, trust my intuition. You may be right about Warriors not knowing how to fight the dragon, but I feel that you should remain as you are. Perhaps you will play a role in defeating the dragon one season. But I feel fairly certain that it is important for you to remain a Warrior. I do not know why, but I do feel it is the role you were meant to play."

Chaz sighed and hung his head. Raef realized he had never seen Chaz do that before.

"I will do as you say," said Chaz. "The other Warriors reject the Keepers as spiritual leaders, but I feel they are wrong. I do not wish to remain a Warrior, but I will because you have requested it."

Chaz looked up at Raef, and a smile slowly grew across his face.

"I would never have expected you to want me to remain a Warrior. I though you disliked Warriors."

"I do, but I do not dislike you. You are what the other Warriors should aspire to become."

Chaz departed, and Raef watched him walk into the darkness. He had been quite dishonest with his old friend and he felt badly about that. But he realized he had not lied about believing Chaz should remain a Warrior. That had been true. As Chaz had spoken, something inside Raef told him this young man needed to remain a Warrior. In fact, something inside him believed Chaz was destined to do something important. Raef closed the door and brushed the feeling aside. Who was he fooling? He did not have a Keeper's intuition. The village may call him a Keeper, but he knew he was not. He would always be a Dragon Child, even if he no longer lived at Black Rock.

# 16

The next sunrise Raef rose, did the ceremonial New Leaf washing, and went to the Keep to meet the other Keepers as tradition dictated. Together they walked to the Ceremonial Lodge, passing between the young apprentices who waived fir branches over them. Raef stood with the other Keepers as the male villagers passed through the Lodge to give homage and receive the sunrise blessing before starting their labor. Raef then left for the west side of the village as was expected of him. He passed the Healing Lodge and recalled his apprentice seasons there. He took the northern loop in order to pass by the Training Lodge where he spent his youngling sunrises. Groups of the smallest younglings were arriving to receive their lessons. The older younglings would come later. He passed the Common Lodge and walked through the village square, watching vendors and shoppers as they noisily bartered over goods. He took the northernmost bridge over the stream so he could avoid passing by the noisy and smelly shops.

He stopped by homes where he knew no one was

sick or in need, so he could show concern but avoid getting stuck in a home where he might actually have to stop and visit. He had a mission and would let nothing get in his way. When the sun reached one-quarter sky he returned to the Keep, discarded his robe there, and headed due north into the forest.

The old secret trail had been well used and was no longer difficult to find. Chaz was right about more people coming in contact with the dragon than before. But Chaz did not know it was the people who sought out the dragon, not the other way around. Raef was surprised how short the journey was to his old secret meadow. Perhaps it was because he was older and walked faster. Rail was waiting, sitting up and basking in the early sun with its eyes closed. Raef approached the dragon stiffly.

"You are here," said Raef.

"As always," said Rail, not opening its eyes.

"This is when we used to meet. You know, before..."

"Before you came to Black Rock."

"Yes."

"So I am here again, waiting for your visit, just as before."

"I am a little surprised you came again," said Raef. "I did leave Black Rock, after all."

The great dragon opened its eyes and lowered its head to Raef.

"You are a Dragon Child. Leaving Black Rock does not make you any less one of mine. And because you are mine, I will always be here to meet you."

Raef shifted his weight, his face growing stern.

"There is a man with my seasons in this village named Chaz."

"Prime Rodon's eldest."

"Yes. I want you to promise never to harm him. Not a scratch."

The dragon emitted a slow, low-pitched chuckle. "It is presumptuous for you to ask such a thing."

"I thought we were friends."

"He is a Warrior."

"And I am a Keeper!" Raef shouted, "what of it?"

The dragon lifted its head and peered down on Raef.

"He is a friend," Raef said softly.

"Not a good one. I remember the past. Do you?"

"We were younglings then and foolish. Whatever disagreements we had in the past are over now. He wishes to start over as friends. So do I. He is one of the few here who I really know."

"Then bring him here, let us be friends all together."

Raef looked at the ground. "He would never come here. He ... he would never speak to a dragon."

"And still you choose to be his friend?"

Raef did not answer. It was too complex for him to sort out in his mind. He was mixing two worlds never meant to meet.

"All right," said Rail, "I will leave that one alone. I rarely attack villagers anyway. You know that."

Raef looked up at the dragon, "Why did you allow me to come back to my village?"

"I stop no one from leaving the Basin. The others simply do not wish to leave. You, on the other hand, are quite the adventurous spirit. I will have to consider how we can make use of your nature."

The great dragon draped a talon over Raef's shoulder. Though the beast was smiling, Raef thought it looked just a bit worried.

"I must return now," said Raef, "I will be missed if I stay."

The great dragon spread its wings upwards, blocking the sun. Rail bowed slightly, then shot into the sky, the wind nearly knocking Raef to the ground. He watched it disappear to the north, then turned and slowly walked back to the village.

Raef emerged from the forest behind his old home. Nilo was sitting on a stump nearby and watched as Raef came out of the forest.

"Greetings, Nilo."

Nilo did not reply, but scowled at Raef, then looked away. Raef hurried past him and returned to the Keep to fetch his robe.

Sun and moon cycles passed. Fall grew to winter, and light snow began to fall over the village. Raef had to wear a coat under his Keeper robe to keep from feeling too cold. He missed the warmth that always rose from the Great Basin's floor, warming everything and melting the snow before it could settle. He did have to admit, however, that the light dusting of white was a nice change. He had missed seeing it.

He was slowly given more responsibilities from the Keepers until he had very little time to himself. He was, at least, able to determine his own schedule, unlike his seasons as an apprentice. He and Keeper Chaummer were now responsible for caring for all of the western village. The west side of the village was no larger than the east, but it had nearly twice the population, giving the two Keepers more than enough to remain busy. Folor and Keeper Dimmel oversaw the needs of the Intercessor sector and Folor was the only Keeper who oversaw the work at the Healing Lodge. Prime Keeper Bremen oversaw the tiny northern sector where the Nobles and wealthiest Merchants lived in vast multi-roomed mansions. The Noble sector also included the Council Hall on the north end of the village square, which was a small but ornate structure where the Village Council met.

Raef had never been inside the Council Hall before, but he now had occasion to enter when he needed to find Prime Keeper Bremen or relay messages to the Nobles or the Council who met there. As a youngling and even greenling he paid no attention to village politics. As the youngest Keeper, however, it was his role to relay messages to the ruling Nobles. The Nobles kept in close communication with the Keepers as the Keepers oversaw many aspects of village life themselves. The Nobles were also the only class in the village who the Warriors submitted to. Raef frequently met young Warriors in the Council Hall as they came to relay messages from the Warrior sector. The young Warriors would show respect to Raef, but never smile.

Raef also met a Provincial Guard for the first time at the Council Hall. The guard was dressed in a metal breastplate and skirt made of metal chain mail. He wore a short, thick sword and an ornate silver helmet. Raef happened to meet the Provincial Guard in the

Council Hall when the guard was collecting the
Provincial Tax from Fir Hollow.

"I remember hearing adults speaking of taxes as a
youngling," said Raef to the guard, "but I did not
know villages paid a tax to the Province."

"You are a Keeper, are you not?" asked the guard.

"Well, yes."

"How is it a village Keeper could not know such a
common fact?"

"Please excuse him," said one of the village
Nobles, "Keeper Raef became lost in the forest the
season he entered his greenling year. He was gone five
seasons and only now found his way home."

The guard's eyebrow rose as he looked Raef over.

"He missed much education during his apprentice
years," said the Noble.

"You survived on your own in the forest all those
seasons?" asked the guard.

"Yes, sir," Raef lied.

"I am impressed. I suppose with that you are to be
forgiven much."

The guard left carrying a large sack the Councilman
had given him. A small squadron of well-armed
Provincial Guards met him outside the Council Hall
to escort him to the next village.

"We are lucky," said the Noble, "Fir Hollow gets
no trouble from the Provincial Guard. In fact, they
rarely visit us other than to collect the tax. But then,
we strive to be obedient to the Overseers so they have
no reason to meddle with us."

Raef smiled at the Noble and handed him the
written message he had been sent to deliver. He liked

being sent to the Council Hall. He walked outside, and two Intercessor apprentices passed in front of him, bowing as they did. Other than the Warriors, everyone bowed when they passed Raef. Perhaps, he thought, it was not so bad here. No one knew he was a Dragon Child, and he began to believe they never would.

But Raef knew. Two moon cycles after returning to Fir Hollow the desire to see Rail grew too intense to ignore. He began to arrange his schedule so he could visit Rail at one-quarter sun. Not every sun, but often.

On one of his visits he found Domik playing with Rail. Domik acted embarrassed at first to be caught with the dragon. But soon after he and Raef began visiting Rail together, just as they had as younglings. On another occasion Raef entered the secret meadow to find Nilo and a young greenlia playing together with Rail. Nilo acted quite angry when Raef arrived and left with the greenlia immediately. Raef could not understand Nilo's actions, but Rail quickly turned his attention back to itself by offering Raef a ride flying above the trees.

# 17

Spring came and went, and summer arrived along with Raef's first seasonal celebration since returning to Fir Hollow. In Black Rock no one celebrated the passing of seasons. He had even missed his largest celebration of all, greenlings end, when he became an adult. But now he celebrated his nineteenth season at a tavern with the other Keepers and a few of his friends. Even Chaz had come, breaking the Warrior taboo of attending a celebration of an adult who was not a Warrior. Oddly, Domik had not come. In fact, at his celebration Raef realized he had not seen his old friend in several suns.

Half way through his celebration, a woman burst into the tavern, looking distraught. She walked up to Raef, head down, and bowed. She appeared to be roughly the same age as his mother and was obviously quite upset.

"You may speak, woman," said Raef, "what is troubling you?"

"Pardon my insolence, Keeper Raef," said the woman, "but I have been searching for my son,

Domik."

Raef finally recognized her as Domik's mother.

"I have not seen Domik," said Raef, "In fact, I have not seen him the last several suns, which is unusual."

"It is a strange thing," said Keeper Dimmel, "Domik has not come to attend his work in some suns. I imagined him to be sick, but have not had time to stop by his home to check on him."

"He is not sick," said his mother. "I have been by his home every sunrise and sunset the past three suns. He always stops by to see me after last meal, but he has not recently."

She began to weep softly.

"I fear something terrible has happened," she continued, "It is not like Domik to go away without telling someone. I thought perhaps Keeper Raef would know as they are together often."

Raef noticed Prime Bremen glance at him. Raef did not like the look on Bremen's face. He felt his stomach grow cold.

"I...I have not seen Domik in many suns," said Raef.

This was not entirely true. He had seen Domik only five suns past.

"He is probably visiting another village," Raef continued. "Pine Creek or Moss Rock, perhaps."

"What reason would a scribe have to visit another village?" asked Keeper Dimmel.

Raef wished desperately for someone to change the topic. Dimmel went to Domik's mother and began talking with her. Bremen gave Raef another glance, then went to her as well. Chaummer and Folor started up a conversation about fishing and Raef and Chaz joined them. Soon Bremen and Dimmel walked Domik's mother outside and Raef relaxed.

When the celebration ended Raef said goodbye to all, waited for them to leave, then ran to the forest. It was well after sunset and dark but the moon was full enough to light his way to the secret meadow. There in the center of the clearing were Domik's shoes. He would have taken them off before climbing on the dragon. Raef bent down and picked up a shoe, holding it up in the moonlight.

"I wonder how he will like Black Rock," said Raef.

# PART FOUR

## KEEPER

# 18

Raef woke from the light glimmering through the cracks of his shuttered window. He sat up and rubbed his eyes as straw poked softly against his legs. He got up and pulled his trousers over his legs, pulling the tie straps in front of him to tie. He tossed off his night robe and pulled on a shirt and a grey tunic before going to the water basin, which now sat on a corner stool. After performing the New Leaf ritual he cut a slice of bread for first meal, then slipped his knife into its scabbard on his left tie strap. He pulled on his scarlet robe and laced the straps of his shoes up his calves between bites of bread, then left for the Ceremonial Lodge.

Snow crunched under his feet as he walked down the path. Mud marred the white frosting here and there where early risers had walked. Raef pulled his robe around himself more tightly. The novelty of snow had worn off.

"Greetings, Keeper Raef," said a sandy robed greenling as Raef passed under fir branches held over Ceremonial Lodge entrance.

"Greetings to you," he replied.

He did not know the apprentice's name. Inside the Ceremonial Lodge it was marginally warmer. A small fire cracked in a pit at the front of the large hall. Raef had a momentary pang of empathy for whichever greenling had been up before sunrise to prepare the fire. He took his place at the front, chanting with the other Keepers, as the men of Fir Hollow arrived and began passing in front of them. Prime Keeper Bremen touched each on top of the head as they passed, giving a blessing of protection during their labors.

"Keeper Raef," said Keeper Chaummer, after the men of the village had all been blessed, "would you join me on my rounds?"

"I have my own rounds to do."

"We shall do them both together. We see each other so seldom as of late, and we are, after all, assigned to the same sector."

"Of course, Keeper Chaummer."

Raef followed the older Keeper out to the street, then toward the West End of Fir Hollow. Raef felt his chest tense. He did not wish to accompany Keeper Chaummer, following the elder Keeper's schedule. He sighed and followed Chaummer, hoping he would find an excuse to get away before mid sun.

Raef was careful to slow his steps so as to not overtake Chaummer's plodding gate. They maneuvered their way through the throng of vendors in the village square, passed the clanging smithery and crossed over the central bridge, entering the fetid streets of the Labor sector.

"What a lovely sunrise," said Chaummer, "Is it not a marvel how the snow covers the drab of winter?"

Raef's shoes squished in the shallow mud of the street as he eyed the sludge sloshed on what little snow was left lining the road.

"Snow simply accentuates the dirt, if you ask me."

"Look at the trees and rooftops, Raef. The Province is unsoiled if you just lift your eyes up a bit."

Raef eyed the trees and homes dusted in white.

"It is still too cold."

"This is nothing, young Raef. You should visit the mountains in winter. The snow is much deeper, up to your knees or higher."

Raef pulled his robe tighter still around himself and remembered the warmth of Black Rock. A robe or jacket was never needed there.

"It is cold enough here for me," said Raef.

They turned left and passed through the southernmost street of the West End. Keeper Chaummer stopped to visit with the sick, elderly, and mothers caring for infants. Chaummer talked very slowly with each family. Each visit felt like an eternity. Raef fidgeted and grumbled to himself.

Out on the streets again Raef continued to look out over the snow, trying to see what Chaummer saw in all the frigid whiteness. Eventually they entered the northern streets, the part of the sector Raef was charged with. Looking along the rooftops, he could not help but notice a dark spot interrupting the void.

"Chaummer," said Raef, "that roof over there has a hole in it. A large one at that."

"Ah, yes it does."

"But, this is winter. How could anyone sleep in such cold?"

"Certainly they have blankets," said Chaummer, continuing to saunter along.

Raef looked further and noticed three other roofs perforated with gaping black mouths. He wondered how long they had been like this. He had never noticed this before.

"Chaummer, wait."

The older man stopped and turned to face Raef.

"Keeper Chaummer, I do not think we should leave these families in such a state."

"What do you mean?"

"We should fix their roofs!"

"The Keep has limited coffers, Raef. We do care for the poor, but we cannot fix every broken roof in Fir Hollow."

"But surely we can do something."

Chaummer folded his hands and lifted an eyebrow. Raef looked back at the disfigured roof on the house nearest him.

"Apprentices!" said Raef, "We could ask Merchant or Labor apprentices to do the work. The materials are only mud, grass and saplings. Those have no cost."

"Greenling Laborers do not apprentice," corrected Chaummer, "they are put directly to work."

"But this is winter. The fields are too hard to plow yet, so certainly there are field Laborers who can be spared."

"I suppose you may be right," said Chaummer, "I know little of farming. But even so, is this not an issue for the Laborers to take care of themselves?"

"Look at these houses! We are Keepers. We are to look out for the village. This is my sector to care for. I will not leave it in such a state."

A smile slowly crossed the older man's appearance.

"Very well, my enthusiastic young Keeper, go speak with the Village Nobles and see what you can arrange. I once had fire like you. I will not stop you from trying."

Raef left Chaummer and walked swiftly back to the square and the Council Hall. A young Noble apprentice received him at the entrance and showed him to the Council Chambers. To his surprise, the Council allowed him to present his case without making a future appointment. He decided the Council must have little to do at the moment.

As he explained the situation in his sector, he began to worry that he would be found foolish. He was still young and was asking for something out of the ordinary. But after his presentation, the Village Council members smiled to each other and sent a messenger for the Prime Reever, overseer of the Labor class. The Prime Reever himself returned. After hearing Raef's plan, he granted the use of three greenling and one Laborer skilled at roof repair. When it was settled, the Council even sent one of their own apprentices to retrieve the Laborers.

Raef sat on a bench in the entry of the Council Hall to wait for the apprentice to return. As he waited, a young woman entered. Raef stood and bowed very slightly in her direction. She glanced at him from the corner of her eye, came closer, looked up and smiled at him. Soft waves of straw locks bounced over her shoulders.

"Keeper Raef!" she said. "What brings someone like yourself here?"

Raef stepped back in surprise at her boldness.

"You speak as if you know me."

"Of course I know you. I see you walking by my home nearly every sunrise."

"You are from the West End?"

"Oh, yes."

He looked down at her, waiting for an explanation.

"I am sorry, but I do not remember you," he said finally.

"I am Naan."

She remained in front of him, beaming up at him. Raef could not help but smile back at her. Her eyes were the color of the sky.

"I see," said Raef, "And what brings you to the Council Hall?"

"I am commissioned here."

Raef studied her. Her dress was like spring grass, embroidered with flowers. Not formal, but nothing a common Laborer would wear either.

"Commissioned? Do you mean a maid servant?"

"Maid servant, spirits no. I am an Artisan."

"Artisan? Here in the Council Hall?"

"I am apprenticing under Matik. I know it is hard to fathom, but yes, *the* Matik!"

"The who? Wait, *apprenticing*? But...you are far too old...well, I do not mean *old*, but apprentices are younger...you know, greenlings and greenlias."

Naan laughed freely. Raef looked around to see if

anyone was watching. A Noble who happened to be standing on the far side of the entry glanced up at him and smiled before disappearing back into the Council Chamber.

"Artisans apprentice longer than the rest of the village. Our work may not seem very important, but it takes nearly a lifetime to become a Master Artisan."

Raef tried to gather himself.

"Here," said Naan, "let me show you."

She walked quickly away and down a dark hallway. Raef followed and was surprised at how fast she walked for her diminutive stature. Naan led him to a half-hidden back room. It was littered with dusty tables and old parchments, but in the center was a canvas the span of both his arms on an easel.

"What do you think?" asked Naan.

Raef looked at the painting. It was obviously not finished, but even what was done was merely a confusion of color and patterns. Raef imagined it might indeed be fashionable, but he was not sure what to make of it. He could not determine if it was meant to actually represent anything.

"It is my first commissioned work. The Council is paying me to do it. It will hang in the entrance of the Council Hall when it is complete."

"It is lovely," he said.

"It is a painting of the village square. Can you tell?"

Raef looked again at Naan. What was it about her that drew his attention? She looked up at him again, and he felt his smile grow bigger than he wanted it to.

"I am glad you like it," she said. "You, being

educated and all."

"It is amazing," he said, his eyes not leaving her face.

"Thank you. Matik says I am one of her best apprentices."

"Matik? You mentioned her before."

"You do not know of Matik? She is a Master Artisan. The most important Artisan in all of the Great Province!"

"And she lives in Fir Hollow?"

"Spirits, no. She lives in Midland. I went to Midland to study with her as an apprentice, but returned to stay with my mother when the the Nobles of Fir Hollow requested me to do my first commissioned piece for them. Master Matik comes and visits now and then to oversee my work. She stays in one of the Noble households when she visits."

"She stays in a Noble's home? I always thought of Artisans as, well, you know…"

"Poor? Not Matik. She is known throughout the Great Province and is quite wealthy. Wealthier than anyone in all of Fir Hollow, to my recognizing. She has done works for Summit City and Krellit and for the Province Overseers. It is amazing that I was selected to apprentice for her."

"You must be very skilled, then."

"I suppose. I have a long way to go to be anything like Master Matik, however."

Raef stood awkwardly, looking back and forth between the dazzling canvas and Naan.

"I suppose I should get to work," said Naan. "I need to mix more pigment."

"Of course," said Raef, "and the Laborers I sent for are likely waiting for me in the entrance. It was good to meet you, Naan the Artisan."

"And you, Keeper Raef."

Raef turned and walked back down the narrow hall. He smiled to replay in his mind how casually this Naan woman spoke to him. He had heard that Artisans paid little attention to social norms. He did not know if this was acurate, but it was certainly true of Naan.

He found the Reever, three unkempt but strong-looking greenling and one odiferous older man waiting for him in the entry hall. One of the Council Members stood behind them.

"These Laborers will repair the roofs you mentioned, Keeper Raef," said the Reever.

The older Laborer twisted his hat in his hand and glanced sideways at the Noble.

"You shall all be paid your normal wages," said the Noble. "I will see to that personally."

"Sir," Raef said to the Councilman, "I did not mean for the Nobles to pay for this."

"Keeper Raef," said the Noble, "your concern is caring for the poor, mine is to oversee the village coffers. You were right to bring this to our attention."

The Councilman nodded to the Reever, who dismissed the Laborers, bowed to the Noble, and left himself. When the entrance door to the Hall scraped shut, the Councilman turned to Raef.

"It is the Reever's job to oversee the Laborers' work, but he has much else to attend to and this is not a project he had expected. It would be good if you could discretely monitor the work, being careful not to offend the Reever, but to be sure it is done well and in a timely manner."

"Of course."

"Just seeing your presence now and again should be enough to motivate the workers to attend the job well."

"I will be discrete."

"Thank you, Keeper Raef,"

The Councilman bowed, turned and walked to one of the inner rooms. Raef smiled as he left the Council Hall, but his mind was more on the woman he had met than how well his request to the Council was received. The sun was straight up in the sky, so he went to his hut for mid-sun meal.

# 19

Winter slogged on, and Raef used much of his Keeper's allowance to purchase more blankets and additional layers of clothing. He was still not accustomed to seeing his breath in the air and having goose bumps on his arms and legs at mid sun. He longed for spring.

"How did I tolerate this as a youngling?" he asked himself.

He became rather fascinated watching the Laborers repair the four roofs in the West End. He watched them remove broken or cracked poles, cut saplings to length then lash them in place and cover them with mud and grass. The grass was the hardest for the greenlings to find, being winter. Raef watched the older man showing the greenlings where to tie the new poles and how to pack the mud properly. Raef knew it would not be proper for a Keeper to climb up on a roof and repair it, but by the fourth home he wished he could join the Laborers. He was certain he could do the repairs as well as they.

But far more fascinating was the always cheerful

Naan. Raef began finding excuses to stop by the Council Hall, always sure to take time to go to the back room and visit Naan as she painted. He even met the Master Artisan, Matik, a few times. Matik was a thin old woman with a bright smile and hair the color of salt and pepper which brushed the top of her shoulders. Matik had a habit of holding Raef's hand with twiggy fingers when she spoke to him and patting his arm when she was excited about something. Naan, he found, may have been from the Labor class, but she was well traveled and quite intelligent. She seemed wholly unafraid to offer her opinion on any matter with Raef, which, as he was not only a man but an Intercessor and a Keeper, was most inappropriate. Raef found this secretly delightful.

"Raef," said Keeper Chaummer one drizzly sunrise, "you have been sneaking off to see that Artisan woman for nearly a moon cycle now. When are you going to get the nerve to ask to court her?"

"Court her? But...she is an Artisan. I am an Intercessor, even a Keeper."

"You are a man, she is a woman. Your sister married a Merchant. It is not as if this never happens."

It was true, what Keeper Chaummer was saying.

"I suppose I never thought about courting."

"You, young man, were away too long. Come with me," said Chaummer.

Raef followed Chaummer to a small, seedy tavern deep in the West End. The older Keeper bought them mugs of ale and then sat across a table from Raef.

"Raef, you were gone a very long time. You missed

much. You would have been married and had at least one youngling by now had you not been taken from us."

Raef looked down into his mug. He had never considered that.

"You have not even been home a full season. I know you must not yet feel fully accustomed to returning to village life. But I think courting Naan would be good for you. It is not good for a man of your seasons to be alone so much."

"Courting," said Raef. "I never think of myself that way. Sometimes I still feel like the greenling I was when I…when I was taken."

"You are not a greenling anymore. The rest of us see that, it is time you do as well."

Keeper Chaummer smiled up at him until Raef had to turn his gaze away. It was uncomfortable meeting Chaummer's eyes. Raef wondered why he had never thought about courting all those seasons at Black Rock. No one courted at Black Rock. No one was married at Black Rock. Courting and marriage had never even crossed his mind while living among the Dragon Children.

But Keeper Chaummer was probably right. Raef was well beyond the age of courting and marriage. He felt a momentary wave of shame, wondering what others might think of him, still living alone at nineteen seasons. The thought of marrying was worrisome, however. He cherished the amount of time he had alone, to wander about where he pleased.

But this Naan, she was unlike any woman he had met. She was…more fun. He really did like her. In his distant past, he had always imagined marrying a quiet Intercessor woman, which Naan was nothing like. But, as he pondered it, he would much rather marry Naan than a reserved, well-kept woman from the Intercessor sector anyway. If Chaummer thought it was okay, perhaps he should not be concerned that others might not approve. Chaummer was a Keeper, after all.

# 20

The next sunrise, after the sunrise homage at the Ceremonial Lodge, Raef made his way alone to the far side of the West End. Naan had told him which home was her mother's. Raef approached a tiny hut painted in the colors of spring grass and sunflowers, completely out of place among the other drab houses. Raef smiled as he looked at the hut from the street. He had passed this home many times before he knew who lived here, laughing at the absurdity of such a spectacle. It had to be the work of Naan. It must have taken a season or more for Naan to collect the plants needed to make so much pigment. The hut itself, on the other hand, was falling apart, brightly decorated though it may have been.

"Yamrah, mother of Naan!" called Raef.

In a few moments, the door creaked open, and a short woman peeked her head out, smiling broadly.

"Who is it? Oh, a Keeper. You must be that Keeper Raef my daughter goes on about."

"Yes," said Raef, "I am he."

"Come, come," said Yamrah.

Raef walked the short path from the street and entered the tiny home, having to bend over to get through the doorway.

"I am unable to make the trip to ceremony much any more," said Yamrah, "so I don't know you by sight, but you are tall, just like Naan said you were."

"I suppose," said Raef.

"Suppose nothing, you are as tall as a tree, you are. Let me get you some tea. It is cold out, and tea is just the thing for the cold."

Yamrah retrieved a kettle hanging by a wire over the central fire and poured into a pair of worn leather mugs.

"Here you are, Keeper."

Raef took a mug and drank. It was a bit rancid. He could not tell if the taste was off due to old tea or a sour mug. To be polite he drank anyway.

"I have come to ask you for something," said Raef.

"What in all the Province could an old Labor woman like myself do for a Keeper?"

"I understand your husband is gone."

"Yes. I'd wish to tell you he died, but the bastard left for another village with some younger woman. Left me here with little Naan half a lifespan ago, he did."

Yamrah spit on the floor.

"Sorry to be so coarse, Keeper. I'm just an old commoner who knows no better."

Raef smiled, "Do not mind me."

He knew what he came to ask next. Raef felt himself shiver, and his stomach clench tight. He summoned his courage and took a deep breath.

"Yamrah, I would like to ask your permission to court your daughter."

Yamrah cocked her head back, looked up at Raef, lifting her eyebrows.

"Your daughter, Naan," Raef repeated.

"You want to court Naan? Why dragon spit, Keeper Raef, you can marry her sunrise next of you like. She's all grown; don't need my permission to live as she pleases."

Raef felt his own eyebrows pop upward, and his face grow very hot. He tried to think how to respond.

"Yamrah," he said, finally, "I want to court Naan as is proper. I am an Intercessor and a Keeper. I must maintain the formal tradition of the Intercessor cast."

"My Naan, courted by a Keeper," said Yamrah, gazing up to the bits of straw and mud dangling from the ceiling, "Never imagined such a thing in all my seasons."

"I would like your blessing before courting your daughter."

"My permission? Oh, you have that, all right. A Keeper. My grandbabies will be Intercessors!"

At the mention of grandbabies Raef felt himself blush again. After a short and awkward visit, Raef returned to his duties. That sunset Raef returned to Yamrah's home just before last meal. He called for Yamrah from the street who answered promptly and let him in. Naan was cutting trenchers for the table. A pot of something quite nice smelling was boiling over the fire.

"Naan, a nice young man is here to see you," said Yamrah.

"Raef! What are you doing on the West End at sunset?"

"Naan," said Raef, fighting to keep from stumbling over his words, "I have come to make a request."

Naan wiped her hands on the apron she was wearing and came to face Raef.

"Naan, daughter of Yamrah, would you give me the honor of courting you?"

Naan stood as if stunned for several moments. Then she burst into a smile and held her hands to her face.

"Raef, I would like to court you very much indeed!"

Raef was invited to stay for last meal, which was much nicer than he had expected, and afterwards went on a late walk with Naan. Yamrah followed from behind at a discrete distance, as was proper, even though Yamrah had complained that all this formality was not necessary. Raef had insisted.

"I am so surprised you want to court me," said Naan.

"Why? You are a beautiful, intelligent woman."

"I don't know. Life has been so hard since my father left. I had only thirteen seasons when he left us. We were outcasts even here in the West End after that."

"Only because they did not see your potential."

"That is quite nice of you to say, Raef. I always imagined I would simply run off with some young man one sunset."

"Well, I am glad you did not."

"I worry what your Keeper and Intercessor friends

will think of me."

"First of all, it was a Keeper who told me I should stop gazing fondly at you and court you. Second, the only friend I really have left is a Warrior, not an Intercessor."

"A Keeper befriended by a Warrior? That is something. You really are different."

"So are you, Naan."

They walked in the moonlight, Raef wrapping his robe tightly around him to keep from freezing completely. He felt anxious inside. Next to such a pure woman his secrets seemed magnified within, eating slowly at him. It was a risk, but perhaps if he shared with her just a little he would feel better. His heart spead up as he dared to share a small part of himself.

"Naan, it is only fair that you know that I am not really like the other Keepers."

"What do you mean? That you befriended a Warrior?"

"Not that."

He exhaled a foggy breath into the cold air and gathered himself.

"You know I was gone a long time."

"Yes, the dragon took you. The entire village knows that."

"But I was away from the village a long time, five seasons. The village does not know that I did not escape right away. The dragon, well, kept me part of the time. I don't know how to explain it, but it had some power over me, almost like it controlled me for a while."

It wasn't the whole truth, but a bit of it. His feelings eased a little.

"But you are back now," said Naan.

"Yes, and it has no power over me any longer."

He knew this was a lie. A moon cycle had not passed since returning to Fir Hollow that he had not visited Rail two or three times. Sometimes more.

"I have not told the others about what happened when I was away, not even the Keepers. But I wanted you to know."

"Raef, I don't care what happened to you or what you did when you were gone. You are still an Intercessor and a Keeper. I think you are the only Keeper that really cares about the rest of us."

Raef reached out and took Naan's hand as they walked. It was good to have told someone a little of the truth. He felt closer to her than ever.

# 21

Next sunrise word spread quickly throughout Fir Hollow. The sun did not set before Raef was unable to walk anywhere without someone calling out to him about Naan.

"Blessings on your courtship, Keeper Raef!"

"May the spirits give fortune to you and Naan!"

Nearly every sunrise afterward Raef stopped by to see Naan and nearly every sunset he came to walk with her after last meal. He did not tell Rail about Naan, however. He could not mention her when he was with the dragon. He realized he would need to stop seeing Rail before he married, but not yet. Not quite yet.

———·◇·———

Erif walked down the dusty path, returning from a workout. Muscles bulged where there had once been only weakness. The seasons on the hard island had changed him. It was evening, but the sun had not set.

He rounded a corner and froze. A short distance a head lay a small deer. A kill. Standing over it was a sand-colored cat. He had heard of mountain cats but had never seen one before. He had not imagined one to be so large. The one before him was at least as big as he. Fresh blood dripped from its chin. Erif's stomach grew cold. Erif wanted to run, but he knew it would not be wise. Mountain cats, so he had been told, attack anything approaching their kill. He eyed its ropy legs. No, he could not outrun that. He slowly drew his sword and began to back away.

The cat let out a low, menacing growl and crouched to jump. Erif tightened his grip on the sword. He had hoped the cat would let him go. That did not look likely now. Erif lowered his hands and angled his sword across his body defensively.

"I must be insane to fight this thing," he thought.

He eyed the bloody claws and daggered fangs. He exhaled a long breath to ease his nerves.

"That is a lot of knives against my one sword. You don't play fair, do you kitty?" Erif said.

The cat leapt at him, front paws extended and claws bared. Erif jumped to his right and slashed at the cat's side as it passed. The blow knocked Erif down, but the cat stumbled as well. It turned back and let out a piercing shriek. A long red slash slowly appeared on the cat's shoulder. Erif felt himself shaking. That was no good. Relax.

"Didn't work out quite like you thought, did it?"

The cat leapt again and came down over Erif. Erif forced the long sword up, felt contact, and swept it to the left. The animal's foreleg impaled on the sword in the process. It wrenched free with a howl. Ears back, it hissed and flashed its fangs. Erif pushed his doubt

aside and readied his sword again. The mountain cat
lashed out with a paw. Erif stepped away while
slashing back hard with his sword. He felt his sword
contact just before he felt the cat's other paw slash his
right shoulder. The cat jumped back, one paw now
dangling, half severed. Erif tried to ignore the
blinding pain in his shoulder and stepped toward the
big cat, thrusting his sword at the animal's neck. The
cat sat back on its haunches and tried to swipe Erif
with its good paw, but Erif held up his sword to block
it. He felt the blade strike bone. The impact threw
Erif to his back. He spun up to his feet to find the cat
yowling as it attempted to stand on two nearly severed
front paws. The mountain cat stumbled and fell to
one side. Erif swung his sword down with all his
force, trying to keep his legs out of reach of the cat's
hind legs. The blade swept across its throat. Dark
blood stained the ground as the big cat kicked. Erif
backed farther out of range.

As the mountain cat slowly grew still, Erif found
his own legs shaking so badly he could barely stand.
He hobbled over to a boulder and sat, dropping the
heavy sword to the sand. His shoulder began to throb.
Erif dared to look at his wound for the first time.
Rivulets of blood ran from three knuckle-deep
gashes. His vision became fuzzy and he fought to
remain conscious. He would have to get back to camp
soon to clean and bandage it. This would take
considerable time to heal. Erif became aware that
someone was standing before him. He looked up to
see Zul.

Erif gave a wry smile, "I suppose you found that

entertaining."

"Not at all, I do not watch battles to the death for sport."

"But you watched."

"I see everything. I cannot choose to do otherwise simply because it is unpleasant."

"Mere mortals call it closing our eyes," Erif said, grimacing at a flash of pain.

"Spirits do not have that option. Call it a price of immortality."

Erif laughed and then winced again in pain.

"I do not suppose you have it in your spirit soul to fix my arm up for me. Or at least stop the pain?"

Zul smiled slowly, "Sorry, the pain will do you good."

"Do me good? How about just this once I will be generous. You take away the pain, and I'll pass on the good it would do me to someone else."

Zul came closer and smiled softly. "Erif, you spent a life time running from pain. That is why you are here on this island in the first place. You must learn to endure. Yes, it is unpleasant, but it will not kill you. You need to learn that, to know that. You cannot let the fear of pain frighten you from what you need to do."

"Yeah, yeah, old lesson," Erif said as he warily stood up. He picked up his sword, but leaned on it like a cane. "So, old man, will you at least walk back to camp with me?"

"Of course, son. Oh, and by the way, when you have patched yourself up you might want to come back for this deer. Deer are good eating, you know."

"I just might do that."

"But I would leave the cat," Zul continued, "those things are kind of rank."

Erif barked a laugh, making him wince again. "Ow, ow, stop already."

The pair walked off into the evening, both of them chuckling.

# 22

Raef heard his name being called from the street early one sunrise. He peeked out his window to see Chaz. He threw on his robe and opened the door, expecting his old friend had come to give his courtship his blessing. Raef was surprised to see Liet and Keever standing alongside Chaz, all of them in armor breastplates and carrying spears.

"Chaz, what brings you here so early?"

"A report has come from Moss Rock. The village has turned dark."

"Turned dark?" asked Raef, "What do you mean?"

"The village has run off all their Keepers and have allowed the dragon to enter the village."

"They did what?"

"The dragon entered the village," continued Chaz, "it apparently took some villagers away, to eat them I suppose, but now it comes back and just rests in the village streets. No one lifts a finger to stop it or to drive it away. The reports say it is as if they want the dragon to live among them."

"How did you…who told you this?" Raef asked.

"The Keepers of Moss Rock. They said they tried to get the villagers to drive the dragon away. Instead, the villagers drove the Keepers out. The Keepers went to Pine Creek after being run off, but there are too few Warriors in Pine Creek to help them. The Keepers from Moss Rock arrived in Fir Hollow mid moon."

Raef's mind spun. He had never heard of anything like this. What was Rail doing being so bold? And why would the villagers of Moss Rock run off their Keepers?

"What about the Warriors in Moss Rock?" asked Raef.

Raef saw Liet drop his gaze to the ground.

"The Keepers of Moss Rock said that the Warriors had...had befriended the dragon," said Liet.

Keever spit on the ground.

"I do not believe it myself," said Keever, "I would have to see that with my own eyes first."

"How could this have happened?" asked Raef.

"The Keepers of Moss Rock are with our Keepers now, trying to determine this very thing. All the Warriors of Fir Hollow are assembling. We leave for Moss Rock this sunrise. The Keepers have asked us to summon you to speak with the Keepers of Moss Rock, but I was hoping to persuade you to come with us instead," said Chaz.

"Wait one moment," said Raef, "the Keepers asked the Warriors to summon me? Has the entire Province turned upside down?"

Keever stepped forward, "The Keepers summoned the Warriors before dawn. The Prime Warrior and

Prime Keeper have been in discussion ever since."

"Every Warrior in Fir Hollow has been roused and is ready for battle," said Liet.

"We were waiting for instructions when the Keepers began asking about you," said Chaz, "you live furthest from the Keep and are the only Keeper who has not already woken from all the commotion. I offered to summon you."

"One moment," said Raef.

He dashed inside and put on his trousers, shirt and tunic, not even stopping to perform the New Leaf ritual, then left with the three Warriors for the Keep.

"You said you hoped I would come with you," said Raef, "come with you where?"

"To attack Moss Rock," answered Keever.

"What?" said Raef, "I am an Intercessor, not a Warrior."

"You know the dragon," said Chaz, "you could help."

"I never fought the dragon," said Raef, "I just escaped from it."

"Still, you might know some of its weaknesses."

Raef could not think of anything that would help the Warriors fight Rail. He could not risk going with them in any case. No one could see Rail speak to him as a friend, and Rail would certainly do that if Raef went.

"You need to see what they did to their Keepers," said Chaz, "It is as if the villagers of Moss Rock have lost all sense of humanity."

Raef looked for the other Warriors and Keepers as they approached the Keep. Not a single villager was in sight.

"Where is everyone?" asked Raef.

"In the village square," said Chaz, "there is not enough room here."

They passed the Keep and Ceremonial Lodge and walked around the Common Lodge to the central square. Raef saw an entire squadron of fully armed Warriors filling the square. Sunlight glinted off their armor. Raef made his way to the red robes of the other Keepers. Prime Rodon was speaking to Prime Keeper Bremen.

"Keeper Raef," said Bremen, "the Warriors are about to leave for Moss Rock. We are summoning all the Intercessors to beseech the spirits for their safety as they battle Moss Rock."

"Battle Moss Rock?" asked Raef, "I thought they were going to battle the dragon."

Rodon turned to Raef, his face like stone, "Keeper Raef, you should visit the Healing Lodge to see what the villagers of Moss Rock have done to their own Keepers. Whatever has happened in Moss Rock has turned its villagers to savages. We go with heavy hearts to battle our own kind."

Raef looked back and forth between Rodon and Bremen.

"Keeper Bremen, what in all the Province is happening?" asked Raef.

"Prime Rodon is right, Raef. You must visit the Healing Lodge to understand."

Bremen hung his head and left with the other Keepers toward the Ceremonial Lodge. Rodon gave a battle cry, and the Warriors left in rank, following the road north toward Pine Creek and Moss Rock.

"Keeper Raef!" called a small voice.

Raef looked down to see a young one looking up at him. He had the face and stature of a youngling but wore a sand colored apprentice robe indicating he was a greenling. The robe looked newly made so he must have only recently reached his thirteenth season. The greenling's hair hung half way down his back indicating he was an Intercessor. Raef finally recognized him as Keeper Dimmel's son.

"Keeper Raef," said the small Intercessor, "I have been asked to bring you to the Healing Lodge."

"Lead on," said Raef.

Raef followed the small greenling as the Warriors clanged off to the north and the older apprentices called through the streets to gather the Intercessors to the Ceremonial Lodge. Villagers burst out of their homes, pulling on robes and tunics. It was all somewhat dreamlike and unreal.

As they reached the Healing Lodge Raef could already hear the groaning. Once inside Raef found four men, Keeper robes folded next to their beds, being attended to by Healers. The Keepers of Moss Rock had battle wounds, some quite severe. Raef went to the closest Keeper and knelt at his side. The young apprentice who had fetched him kept close to Raef, his eyes wide as he gazed down at the gashes in the man's side.

"Who did this to you?" asked Raef.

"You are a Keeper?" asked the injured man.

"Yes, the youngest in Fir Hollow, but I have the unfortunate experience of having faced the dragon before."

"Your Keepers told us of you."

"I apologize for asking again, fellow Keeper, who did this to you?"

"My own village. For nearly a moon cycle we begged them help us send the dragon away. When we became insistent they turned on us."

"Your Warriors did not defend you?" asked Raef.

The Keeper winced as a Healer bandaged a long wound in his side.

"The Warriors are who did this to us. They defended the dragon from us."

"Warriors attacked the Keepers?" said Raef, "That is beyond belief."

"It is true."

"Then, the entire village turned against you?" asked Raef.

"Not the entire village."

"Tell me what happened, Keeper…"

"Keeper Frenell. I am Prime Keeper of Moss Rock."

"I am Keeper Raef, as I said before, the youngest Keeper."

"Very well, Keeper Raef," said the older man, "Our youngest Keeper came across the dragon, sunning itself outside our village. He reported to us and we spoke to our Nobles about it. We were shocked at their lack of surprise. We later came to believe the villagers were aware of the dragon's presence long before we were. We have no idea how long it has been among us."

"Since the dawn of the Great Province," Raef

thought to himself.

"We beseeched the villagers to stay far from the side of the village where the dragon had been seen. We implored them to join us in meditation to call upon Zul to save us. They acted as if they were concerned. They would spit at the mention of the dragon. But then we began to find many of them outside the village, basking alongside the beast itself! Keeper Raef, it was a most shocking sight."

Frenell closed his eyes and lay back on his mat. He began to tremble and wince. A younger Keeper lying on the next mat, bearing a deep gash across his chest, resumed the story.

"No matter how we warned the villagers, or how vehemently they appeared to agree, the villagers would simply go home and take no action at all. Finally, we were desperate, and we called on the Warriors. We asked them to drive the dragon away. They assured us they would, but not one of them took action. Even the Warriors began to be seen lounging in the sun with that, that foul beast!"

"Chaz did not tell me that," said Raef, "it is... unbelievable."

"And the younglings," said another Keeper, "younglings were out there, actually playing with...I can still scarcely believe it now...playing on the dragon itself! Climbing all over it as if it were a beloved uncle. The parents were right there, allowing this to happen right in front of them."

Keeper Frenell opened his eyes and took a slow, ragged breath.

"We knew it was over by then," said Frenell, "The

problem was beyond anything the Intercessors could resolve. Villagers began to go missing. Sometimes we watched as the beast carried them away. No one seamed in the least concerned. The beast carrying off our own villagers, men, women, even younglings to feast on, yet no one seemed to care."

The Keeper winced and tightened his eyes. Raef tried to imagine the scene the Keepers had described.

"Then, they invited it in," said the younger Keeper, "The dragon came into the village and lay in the square, surrounded by our own villagers. We demanded the village help us drive it out. That is when the Warriors took up arms against us. One of our Keepers was murdered, along with three apprentices. It was unspeakable."

A silence fell over the Healing Lodge. Raef felt himself tremble. It was beginning to unravel, and he could not let that happen. He knew no one had been eaten; they would all be at Black Rock now. He imagined the villagers back in Moss Rock knew that too. That would explain their lack of concern over the disappearances. But what if further investigation by the Warriors of Fir Hollow led to the discovery of the Great Basin in Black Rock? Would everyone then realize where Raef had been all those seasons? How could he protect the villagers of Moss Rock and his own secrets at the same time?

"You said that not all of Moss Rock had helped the dragon," Raef said.

"Yes," said Frenell, "there were a few who remained terrified of the dragon. Mostly common Laborers, they are. They would not fight it, for they were not Warriors. They hid in their huts most of the time. We had to flee for our lives quite suddenly. I imagine those families are still in Moss Rock hiding. That is, if the dragon has not eaten them by now."

Raef tried to make sense of this. He was fairly sure the dragon would not bother any who were afraid of it, much less go looking for them. The villagers who had befriended Rail might, but not the dragon.

Raef stood and took a step back and felt himself bump against someone. He looked down to see the son of Keeper Dimmel, still waiting patiently. The small apprentice was staring at Frenell's wounds, his face pale as milk.

"Keeper Frenell," said Raef, "I must inquire of our Prime Keeper to see what I can do. I will leave you in the hands of our Healers."

Raef turned and walked for the door.

"Come, apprentice," said Raef.

The apprentice turned to follow, mouth agape and gazing blankly ahead. Raef walked quickly to the Keep where he found the other Keepers, his father included, deep in discussion in the inner room. Dimmel looked past Raef at the greenling behind him.

"Sit there, on the bench," Keeper Dimmel said to his son.

"Come, Raef," said Bremen, "sit with us."

Raef took a seat on one of the benches surrounding the center table.

"What is going to happen to Moss Rock?" Raef asked.

Bremen cast his eyes downward.

"Our Warriors will drive the dragon out," said Folor, "Anyone standing in their way will be driven out as well."

"If Moss Rock decides to fight?" asked Raef.

"That will be a terrible thing," said Keeper Dimmel, "as far as we know, the Warriors of Moss Rock are still there. It could be a hard battle."

"Fighting our own kind," murmured Keeper Chaummer.

"From what Prime Keeper Frenell told me," said Raef, "I suspect the Warriors of Moss Rock will be of little threat. It sounds like they are all just lying around. They may have been a threat to the unarmed Keepers, but in their relaxed state I do not think they would be a match for a squadron of fully armored Warriors."

"Raef is correct," said Folor.

"Perhaps, perhaps," said Keeper Bremen, "but I do not wish to even contemplate such things. I cannot bear to imagine a battle between villages. Such a thing has not happened in generations."

"Should we not do something?" asked Raef. "The others, the ones Keeper Frenell spoke of who are hiding from the dragon. Should we not make preparations to go help them? After the fighting is over, of course."

"Yes, yes, that would be good," said Keeper Bremen.

"I will attend to the preparations," said Keeper Chaummer.

Chaummer stood and left the inner room. Folor stood and followed him. Bremen stood, looking weary, and left as well. Dimmel had gotten up and was speaking to his son at the side of the room. Raef stood and walked to join his old mentor.

"Raef, this is my son, Daz," said Dimmel.

"We have met," said Raef, "although he failed to tell me his name."

Daz smiled sheepishly. The color had returned to his face.

"Daz celebrated youngling's end only two sunsets past," said Dimmel, "He has yet to be assigned a tutor, or even an occupation for that matter."

"Your father was my mentor when I was an apprentice," said Raef, "He was a fine teacher."

"You were a youngling apprentice," said Daz. "I wish I could have skipped lessons last season to be an apprentice."

"Raef was an exception," said Dimmel, "you are doing fine."

"I don't care about doing fine; I just wanted to skip lessons."

Dimmel turned to Raef and smiled wryly, "Such is my son. Doing his best to keep me humble."

Dimmel patted his son on the head, who swatted his father's hands away before following him out of the inner room, into the entry hall and outside.

Raef stood silently for a few moments, trying to make sense of all that had happened. It was not even mid-sun, yet he was already tired. He sighed and left to find Keeper Chaummer so he could assist him.

# 23

Reports came back from Moss Rock every sunset. The Nobles and Keepers met at the Council Hall when each messenger arrived. Raef began waiting on the road from Moss Rock to meet the messenger to get a private report before the others heard. So far, the Warriors of Fir Hollow had not discovered any of the secrets of Black Rock. The villagers of Moss Rock had put up a strong resistance when the Warriors arrived, more than Raef had expected. The dragon itself had flown off immediately at the sight of armed Warriors. This confused the Keepers, Raef included. Raef did not understand why Rail had not stayed behind to protect its children. It was certainly powerful enough to have done so. The Warriors, however, were proud to have finally routed the beast; something there was no record of happening before in the Great Province.

Those in Moss Rock who resisted the Warriors of Fir Hollow, and there were many, were slain. The Warriors of Moss Rock had kept weapons with them, but not armor. Those who were not Warriors apparently had fought as well, but they could not stand against the well-trained Warriors of Fir Hollow. Other villagers of Moss Rock had reportedly run into the forest to escape the Warriors from Fir Hollow. And, just as Raef had predicted, the Warriors did find a few families hiding from Rail in their homes, still unharmed. The oddest report from the Warriors was that among those who had been with the dragon, no younglings had been found anywhere in or near Moss Rock. The Warriors had begun a search for missing younglings.

In the mean time, Raef spent as much time as he could with Naan, comforting her from the horrible reports that came nearly every sunset. He did not go to visit Rail. He was too busy in the first place but he was also not sure he wanted to see the dragon after what had happened in Moss Rock. As the suns passed the Warriors concluded that the younglings must have been slain and eaten by the dragon. The Keepers of Fir Hollow came to the same conclusion. When a messenger from Moss Rock returned four suns later, Fir Hollow learned that the Warriors, incensed that Moss Rock had allowed their own younglings to be sacrificed to the dragon, had pursued those who had escaped into the forest. By the end of the moon cycle a report came that the Warriors had found those who had fled. They were found all together, scurrying toward the mountains to the east. In a fit of rage, the Warriors had killed every one of them. The report indicated that it had been a gruesome blood bath. None of those being pursued had weapons other than eating knives, so it had been more of a slaughter than a battle.

The Warriors returned to Fir Hollow on the turn of the next moon cycle in a solemn mood. This did not feel like victory to anyone. The villagers of Moss Rock were just as dead by the sword as they would have been by the dragon's talons. All of Fir Hollow mourned. The sunset after the Warriors' return, Chaz came to visit Raef in his hut after dark.

"It was terrible," said Chaz, fighting back tears. "I have never killed anyone before."

"It was necessary," said Raef, "You know as well as anyone that we could not let it go on. They could have come to Pine Creek, and Fir Hollow next, bringing that beast with them."

"Bringing? How would anyone bring that dragon anywhere? I saw it fly off, it was enormous."

"I meant, that if the villagers of Moss Rock had come here, the dragon would have followed."

"Why would the dragon follow them? And why would they have tried to come here?"

Raef realized his mistake. No one in the villages understood Rail. Rail wanted more Dragon Children. Why, Raef could not say. It was almost like it collected them, like one would collect treasure. But Raef was fairly certain that whatever had happened at Moss Rock would have spread to Fir Hollow through the villagers of Moss Rock. Perhaps the slaughter really had been necessary. Raef did feel badly about one thing; that everyone was mourning the loss of all the younglings in Moss Rock. He wished he could tell them, but he could not. They were, most certainly, all safe at Black Rock. Rail would never have allowed them to be harmed.

Raef shook his head and attempted to recover from his mistake.

"Sorry, Chaz, I am speaking as a crazy man. This whole thing has left me unable to think clearly. All that matters now is that we help those families who had been hiding from the dragon. Have they all been removed safely from Moss Rock?"

"Yes, they are all in Fir Hollow now. We are fairly sure we found them all. We searched the village three times. The only problem is, none of them want to go back. Even with all those bewitched by the dragon gone, they are afraid of their own village."

"They can stay here as long as they need," Raef said, "The Keepers will make arrangements."

Raef put a hand on Chaz's shoulder. He could see the young Warrior's grief.

"I do not want to do this anymore," said Chaz. "Those villagers, the ones who ran into the forest, they looked, well, they did not look evil."

"What do you mean?"

"It was tolerable to fight…to kill the ones who attacked us when we entered the village. You could see the hate in their eyes. But the ones who were running from us, they were different somehow. They looked so…so desperate."

"They were afraid."

"Yes, but the thing is, they were not afraid of us, Raef, it was something else."

Chaz paused, his lip quivering. Raef looked away. He felt badly about those slaughtered in the forest. There had been no need to kill them. They would have simply gone to Black Rock, if Rail had not come back for them first. But Raef could not have explained this to the Warriors. They would wonder how he knew such things. Raef turned back to Chaz, who now had tears running down his cheeks.

"Raef, some of them looked as if they wanted to die. Some of them just fell to the ground and rolled onto their backs so we could kill them. One young man, he was no older than you or I, he fell to his back and said, 'Forgive me,' and spread his arms. He watched me impale him. Raef, I have never seen anyone look at me like that. What did the dragon do to those villagers?"

Raef knew exactly what Rail had done to them. Perhaps he should have gone with the Warriors after all. Maybe some of those who had befriended Rail could have been saved. But Raef couldn't be sure about that.

"I am so sorry, Chaz."

Chaz stayed with Raef until the moon was at its zenith. Raef walked with his friend to his home to comfort him. It was odd being in the Warrior sector. He had not been in this part of the village since he was a youngling. The long, multi-roomed homes with rounded roofs looked foreign. Raef stood outside Chaz's home in the street and listened as his friend greeted his wife and son, who had apparently waited for his return. Raef walked home under the silence of the moon.

# 24

The next sunrise the Keepers met with the Village Council and Prime Rodon after homage. Raef was with them.

"We need to understand what happened in Moss Rock," said one of the Nobles.

"This is a matter for the Keepers," said Prime Bremen. "These are matters of the spirit world. It is important we understand what has happened."

"Then go," said Rodon, "I saw what happened, and I do not wish to see any more."

"I should be the one to go," said Raef.

All eyes turned in his direction. Raef chose his words carefully.

"I am the only one who was taken by the dragon. I have seen it more than most."

"More than any," said Rodon.

"Perhaps," said Raef, "My point is, it may be that I can recognize something in Moss Rock, some clue to what happened."

"Agreed," said Dimmel, "and I will accompany you."

"We must send Warriors as well," said the Councilman.

"There is no need for that," said Raef, "the dragon is gone. There is no further danger."

"I will not allow a delegation to go without protection," said the Councilman.

"Nor I," said Keeper Bremen.

"Very well," sighed Raef.

"I will send two Warriors, but no more," said Rodon, "We need to rest and clear our minds of the atrocities we had to commit. We are preparing now for our cleansing ritual, which will last seven suns."

"And the two Warriors for this delegation?" asked Bremen.

"They will complete cleansing when they return," said Rodon.

The discussion lasted until mid-sun, but all was finally settled. Two suns later Raef was sent to Moss Rock, along with Keeper Dimmel, three assistants and two Warriors, to see what they could learn in what was left of Moss Rock. Chaz would not come as he had seen too much fighting and needed cleansing. Raef said goodbye to Naan, who was quite distressed over his leaving.

"I will be fine," Raef said to her.

"It took you once. I do not want to lose you now."

"I also escaped once. I am not afraid of the dragon."

The Keepers and assistants rode on a long cart pulled by two horses. The Warriors rode on horseback, one in front and one behind. The journey was longer than Raef expected. It was a sun's journey just to Pine Creek, where they were put up in homes of their own cast. Moss Rock was another full sun's journey.

When they arrived, they found Moss Rock desolate and silent. Raef found it chilling to ride through an entire village and not hear a sound other than the hooves of their own horses. The Warriors led the delegation through the village and out the north end where a creek ran beside a field of spring grass. Raef got out of the cart and looked out over the field. Ruddy smudges soiled the green waves from one end to the other.

"What in all the Province?" said one of the Warriors.

"What happened?" said the other.

"What do you mean?" said Keeper Dimmel.

"The bodies," said the first Warrior. "The bodies are all gone!"

"What sorcery is this?" said the second Warrior, "This field was littered in bodies when we left. Even if some had been dragged off by animals, there would still be at least some left."

Keeper Dimmel and the Warriors talked together, trying to make sense of the empty field. Raef ignored them and paced out to the center of the grass. He understood.

They searched the village but found nothing helpful. Raef had questions of his own, but he would find no answers with the others here with him. He would have to return alone, but he did not know how he could arrange that. They did not sleep in Moss Rock, but camped down the road toward Pine Creek.

Keeper Dimmel said that it was forbidden to sleep where so many had died this soon after battle. It was not an edict Raef was familiar with, but he did not know all the Intercessor decrees as he had never finished his apprenticeship. The Warriors, who do not follow the laws of the Intercessors, did not protest Dimmel's insistence that they leave. They apparently did not wish to stay in Moss Rock any longer than necessary.

When the delegation returned to Fir Hollow, Raef went immediately to meet Naan. He found her in the square, and they sat together to catch up. Villagers nodded at the pair as they passed by.

"How was the search?" asked Naan.

"There is no one left."

"No more survivors," said Naan, "That is so sad."

"No, I mean, there were no bodies left."

"What happened to them?"

"I didn't tell the others, they would not have believed me. The dragon must have come back for them."

"What in all the Province for?"

"To eat them."

Naan shuddered. Raef put his arm around her. He did not know why he was risking telling her more than he told the others.

"Sorry," said Raef.

"How…how do you know this?"

"I was with the dragon, remember. I told you I didn't escape right away. I learned things about it. It eats dead villagers, never the living."

"Oh, Raef, that is so very awful. Why would it do

such a thing?"

"Naan, it is not pleasant to speak about the dragon. It brings back memories. I have never told anyone even what I just told you."

Naan leaned into Raef.

"You can tell me. You can tell me anything. I cannot imagine what you went through all those seasons, out there alone in the forest."

Raef felt her warmth against him. He decided it was time.

"Naan, we have been courting for three moon cycles. I have never felt this way about anyone."

Raef moved Naan to sit upright and took both her hands in his.

"Would you marry me, Naan, daughter of Yamrah?"

"Raef, I would!"

She hugged him tightly, then sat up, beaming at him.

"Excuse me, I suppose I should say something like, 'Raef, son of Folor' or do I have to say, 'Keeper Raef, son of Keeper Folor?'"

"Enough with all that. I do not care about formalities. I only know I want to be with you."

"As do I."

She kissed him.

"We should wait until summer," said Naan. "We could have a grand wedding in the summer."

"Summer it is. I will tell the Keepers."

# 25

The word spread like fire throughout Fir Hollow. The coming wedding was welcome news after so much sadness over Moss Rock. The village buzzed with excitement.

The Keepers of Moss Rock continued to recover, no longer needing to stay in the Healing Lodge. The families who had escaped Moss Rock unharmed, there were only five, were staying with families in Fir Hollow. The Keepers of Fir Hollow checked on them often.

Raef did not go to visit Rail after the Moss Rock incident. He was too conflicted, even a bit afraid. He did dream of the dragon; of riding it up in the sky, so high he felt he might be able to touch the clouds. At sunrise he would try to shake the images from his mind. They would never entirely leave. In spite of his upcoming marriage, Raef began to grow dark and quiet, keeping to himself whenever he was not with Naan.

One full moon cycle after their visit to Moss Rock, a messenger called on Raef, requesting he go to the

Keep. Raef entered the Keep just before mid-sun, dismissing the messenger who had fetched him, and walked into the inner room. Keeper Dimmel was at the center table and Daz, his son, sat on a bench against the wall.

"Keeper Dimmel, was it you who called for me?"

Dimmel stood and approached Raef.

"Yes, Keeper Raef. I have an important request of you. It is a request from all the Keepers, but is perhaps more important to me than to the others."

"As always, you may request anything, Keeper Dimmel."

Dimmel smiled and lifted his hand high to rest it on Raef's shoulder.

"You are so tall, like your father. I remember when you were small, when you were my apprentice."

"I remember as well."

"My son Daz has the seasons of an apprentice but has yet to be taken by a mentor. He is not sure, nor are we as Keepers sure, that he is to be a Keeper. The Great Spirit has not made that clear. But Daz has a keen mind and a fair interest in Intercessor traditions. Prime Bremen, Folor and I have decided that Daz should apprentice under a Keeper. We have also decided that you should be the one to mentor him."

"Me? You want me to take on an apprentice?"

"If you will have him."

"But I...I have been a Keeper for less than two seasons."

"Raef, we all recognize something special in you. The entire village does. You are ready to mentor an apprentice. I had only a few more seasons when I mentored you."

Raef stood silently, then felt a smile slowly cross his face.

"Apprentice Daz," said Dimmel.

"Yes, father...I mean Keeper," said Daz, rising and coming to Dimmel's side.

"Keeper Raef will be your mentor. You will be his apprentice. From now on, you will report to Keeper Raef and him alone."

"Really? I mean, yes, Keeper Dimmel, of course."

Dimmel smiled at his son, and Daz smiled back.

"My last order to you, Daz, is to return to the dormery for mid-sun meal. Then report back here to Keeper Raef."

Daz half-bowed and quickly left.

"Keeper Dimmel," said Raef, "I am honored that you want me to mentor Daz, but I do not know what to teach him."

"Each sunrise, after homage, teach him the history and traditions of the Keepers and Intercessor clan, just was you were taught. Teach what you know in any order you wish. After mid-sun meal, send him to work with the different Intercessor masters. He should spend one moon cycle learning each skill, just as you did. If he has difficulty with any skill, he should remain for a second moon cycle before moving on."

"I can do that, I suppose."

"Suppose nothing," said Dimmel, "You are a Keeper, called by the Great Spirit himself. Simply do what you were born to do."

After mid-sun meal, Raef returned to the Keep and waited in the inner room. Shortly afterwards, he heard the door open, and Daz burst into the room.

"Your servant has arrived!" said Daz, bowing deeply.

"You are no servant," said Raef, laughing.

"Apprentice, servant, is there a difference?"

Raef smiled and shook his head slowly.

"So, master Raef," said Daz, "what will you teach me?"

"It is 'Keeper,' not 'master' and more than anything, I will assign you to work."

"Told you I was a slave."

"Well then, slave, you will be happy to learn that I will wait until mid-sun next to send you off to labor. Since this is your first sun with me, I want to start with something more pleasant."

"I don't care what I have to do, as long as you are my mentor."

"You *want* me to be your mentor?"

"You are the only Keeper who is not dull as dirt. I will tell you a secret: I don't even want to be a Keeper. I can tell my father thinks I will be one, so I have not told him."

"Being a Keeper, or anything else for that matter, is not a matter of choice."

"I know. But whatever I am to be, you are the one I would wish to apprentice under."

"Then let us get started, apprentice Daz."

Raef led Daz out of the inner room, down a short hall and into a small room with a silver bowl of water on a pedestal in the center.

"To begin with, I will teach you the New Leaf washing."

Daz learned quickly and had a sharp memory, though he fidgeted and his mind seemed to wander frequently. The following sunset was New Moon ceremony, so Raef had Daz arrive early to arrange the candles in the Ceremonial Lodge. It was Raef's turn to lead ceremony, so Raef stood in the center up front, flanked by Folor, Dimmel, Bremen and Chaummer, all in long red robes. The spring air was cooling when villagers began to arrive at sunset.

Raef watched for Naan. When she arrived she smiled brightly at him. Her eyes sparkled even in the dim light of the Ceremonial Lodge. Raef began chanting as the apprentices, including Daz, began waving fir branches as they walked up and down the sides of the room.

Raef began the New Moon chant. He had memorized it before he had eleven seasons as an apprentice. Raef had watched the Keepers chant as an apprentice, eyes gazing blankly ahead as if in a trance. Now Raef looked over the villagers in front of him as he recited the words that welcomed a new moon cycle. The dull faces, the vacant eyes, looked to him as their Keeper, their Intercessor to the Spirits.

Raef stumbled over a word. He stuttered, trying to continue the chant. He went cold as his mind became blank, no words coming to him. The chants of the Keepers were in an ancient tongue. None of the villagers really understood what was said. Raef stood frozen, gazing into space while trying to retrieve a word, anything, from his memory.

"Say anything!" his mind screamed at him, "Even the wrong words, the villagers will never know the difference."

Out of the corner of his eye he saw Naan smiling at him.

"The Keepers would know, as would most of the apprentices, if he said something nonsensical."

Raef spat out a couple of words, ancient ones, probably not the right ones.

"What am I doing?" he said to himself, "No one here is fooled! They know I am a fraud. I am no Keeper; I have no place here at all, much less standing up front pretending to Intercede for the village."

Raef felt his face grow hot. He closed his eyes. Some words came to him, ancient words to a chant. He began to speak them and they flowed easily. Then he realized that these were the words to the chant of sunrise homage, not to the New Moon ceremony. Everyone, the men and greenling who attended sunrise homage at the very least, would recognize them and know they were not the words for this ceremony. Raef stuttered, trying to remember the correct chant. He continued to chant the sunrise homage as he searched his mind for the New Moon chant. He stuttered and came to a stop. Then he remembered and spat out the final verse of the New Moon chant. He opened his eyes to find the entire village staring at him. Most faces were smiling.

"Let us begin meditation," said Keeper Bremen, "opening our minds to the Spirits of the Province."

Raef lifted his head and closed his eyes. He was supposed to have said that. Keeper Bremen had taken over when he failed. Raef felt his face burn. He tried to focus but all that came to his mind were the words he had forgotten. As Raef tried to concentrate, images did come to his mind, but not images of the spirits. The first was of the villagers smiling up at him from their benches as he had seen moments ago. Then of Keeper Bremen interrupting and speaking for him. Next came a very old memory of his father throwing a bench against a wall and yelling. Another old memory came of Keever and Liet laughing at him and calling him weak. Why were these images coming to his mind? Then he saw Rail bend down over him and nuzzle his head. Raef was trembling as the silent meditation continued. He tried to see the spirits in his mind. The only image that came to him was that of Rail.

# 26

Erif rubbed his chin as he watched the image of Raef. Zul stood nearby, twirling Erif's long sword high in the air and catching it by the handle when it fell.

"Quit showing off," said Erif, glancing back at the spirit.

"I would do something far more impressive if I was showing off," said Zul.

Erif chuckled, then looked back at Raef.

"He really does not understand, does he," said Erif.

"Not in the slightest."

"He wastes so much energy for their approval."

"Yet they already approve of him. They love him, in fact."

"Even the Keepers?"

"Yes, Erif, even the Keepers love Raef. The entire village can see his frailty. They do not know where his weakness comes from, yet they see his potential and are content to be patient with him."

Erif looked at the image of Raef in the flowing water. The meditation was over and the villagers were leaving. Raef stood alone in the front, his face like stone, staring ahead at nothing. Keepers Bremen, Chaummer and Dimmel came to Raef's side, smiled and patted his back. Raef did not seem to notice them.

"He thinks they are patronizing him. He thinks they see him as no more than a youngling."

"Yes, Erif, but even if it were true it would not matter. It is irrelevant whether those windbags approve of Raef, and he should not waste his time seeking their approval."

"You are speaking of the Keepers?"

Zul stopped twirling the sword and looked at Erif.

"Yes, Erif, the Keepers. They are all irrelevant. What is important for Raef is that I approve of him, the only one who knows every dark secret of his life."

"But, how will he ever find out that you do?"

"He has not yet lost enough. When I am all that he has left, then perhaps he will seek me out."

Erif watched as Raef waited until everyone, even the Keepers, had left the Ceremonial Lodge. Raef hung his head and slowly walked down the side aisle to the back and exited.

"It is so tragic to watch."

"But Erif, it is not! You have seen all those so-called Intercessors perform their silly rituals, hoping it will make them become acceptable to me. The Keepers cannot even see the vanity of their pride. Their attempts at interceding are worthless. Not so with Raef. He knows he is broken. He is nearly ready to meet me."

"But, has he not met you already?"

"He has seen me, hardly met me. He knows nothing of my nature."

"Still, it is hard to watch his suffering."

"Not so hard when one knows what is possible because of it."

——·◇·——

Next sunrise Raef found it hard to make himself get up and do his New Leaf washing ritual. The memories of his mistakes sunset past flooded his mind, interrupting his attempts at meditation. When he had finished and eaten some bread for first meal, he sighed deeply, gathering courage to face the Keepers after his public failure.

The spring air stung his face when he left his hut, but Raef felt the sun begin to warm his skin as he walked. Daz and the other apprentices were waiting, fir branches held high, when Raef arrived at the Ceremonial Lodge. He bent under them and walked inside, not looking at any of the apprentices in the eye. He was glad Keeper Bremen always lead the sunrise homage. He was not ready to try leading a chant again any time soon.

After the homage was over and the villagers were off to their labors, Raef took Daz to the Keep and watched him practice the New Leaf washing before beginning lessons on the history of the Intercessors. At mid-sun he released Daz, telling him to report to the stables after mid-sun meal. Raef thought it best to get the worst Intercessor post over with right away.

Raef walked to his hut, cutting between houses rather than take the streets, so to avoid contact with anyone. He ate bread and dried meat for mid-sun meal, took a short rest, then returned to the Keep. When he arrived he was surprised to find none of the Keepers present. He walked outside and saw an apprentice and asked where the other Keepers were.

"Keeper Bremen and the others are in the village square," said the greenling, "There is a big commotion of some kind."

Raef thanked the apprentice and walked swiftly through the streets to the square. When he arrived he was surprised to see a large entourage of strangers dressed in violet robes, the edges of which were trimmed in the colors of wildflowers. These men were surrounded by a small squad of Provincial Guards. Horses and carriages, the finest Raef had ever seen, lined the square. A few of the village Nobles, including the Prime Noble, as well as all the Keepers were in the square speaking with the finely dressed strangers. Beside them was Prime Rodon, the village Guild Prime and the Prime Reever. Raef had never seen all five village Primes in one place before. Raef caught Dimmel's eye, and his old mentor left the group and came to Raef.

"Who are these men?" asked Raef.

"Overseers from Summit City."

"Why are they in Fir Hollow? We are a quiet village."

"They are asking about the Moss Rock incident."

Raef watched the group of strangers. They were speaking agitatedly with the five Primes of Fir Hollow.

Prime Rodon's face turned red and he yelled something back at them.

"What are they arguing about?" asked Raef.

"The Overseers are from a large city. Cities are not like the villages, Raef. They do not have Keepers or even Intercessors. They do not acknowledge the spirit world."

"Not acknowledge...I did not know such a thing could exist. But, even so, why are they angry?"

"They believe we are lying about what happened in Moss Rock. They do not believe the dragon exists."

"Does not exist? How could anyone...but our Warriors, all of them saw it! All of Fir Hollow saw it attack Prime Rodon. All of Fir Hollow saw the dragon take me!"

"Raef, before the attack on Rodon, no one had seen the great beast for over a generation, perhaps longer. There are no records, not even ancient ones, of the dragon ever being seen in one of the larger cities. To these city dwellers, the dragon is a fable. They see us as simple minded villagers who believe in myths."

"That is so ignorant! Who are they to call us simple?"

"Quiet down, Raef," said Keeper Dimmel, "your anger will not be helpful."

Raef watched as his father, Keeper Chaummer and Prime Bremen walked away from the Overseers and came to stand with he and Dimmel. Keeper Bremen wore a dark face.

"The Overseers are speaking with the Warriors," said Bremen, "They seem to believe we are hiding something. I fear they believe we attacked Moss Rock deliberately."

"Fir Hollow attack another village?" said Raef, "How dare those pompous city dwellers even suggest such an insult!"

"Raef, you are speaking too loudly," said Folor, "the Overseers may hear you."

"Keeper Raef," said Chaummer, "these are our superiors, the overseers of the entire Province. It is not ours to question them. They command an army that outnumbers our village. We dare not irritate them."

"But we cannot sit quietly as they condemn our village unjustly!" said Raef.

"Keeper Raef," said Bremen, "know your place. The safety of the Great Province outweighs that of Fir Hollow. If the Provincial Overseers see fit to punish Fir Hollow in order to restore serenity to all of the Province, we must not stand in the way."

"What are you saying?" said Raef, "We must remain silent so these overstuffed foreigners can punish us for what the dragon did?"

"Raef!" said Bremen, "Do not speak of the Overseers in that way again."

Raef shrunk back at the Prime Keeper's remarks.

"Raef," continued Bremen, "we will not sit back and do nothing. We will attempt to reason with them, but we must do so diplomatically."

"Young Raef," said Dimmel, "I know you mean no harm, but you do not know the Overseers as we do. You will bring harm to all of Fir Hollow with merely a disrespectful glance."

Raef looked among his fellow Keepers. Even Keeper Dimmel had nearly twice his seasons. When Raef's eyes met those of his father, Folor looked away.

"Keeper Dimmel is correct," said Chaummer, "it will take a number of suns to find means to make the Overseers understand. It would be best for you to keep far from them during their stay."

"They are staying?" asked Raef.

"They brought tents and attendants," said Bremen, "It appears they will stay until they decide the matter is resolved."

Raef's anger melted as a plan formed in his mind.

"I have an idea," said Raef. "Fir Hollow needs me to stay away from the Overseers. I am still not satisfied with the little we know of what happened in Moss Rock. There was not time for thorough investigation on our last trip. I should go to Moss Rock, alone this time, to learn what I can. The other Keepers can stay here and tend to the Overseers. Then I will be away from the Overseers."

"Go alone?" said Keeper Chaummer, "That would be very dangerous."

"In what way?" asked Raef, "There is no reason for the dragon to return. No one is left in Moss Rock. Everyone is afraid to return, as if the village has been cursed. Moss Rock is probably the safest village in the Province at the moment."

"It would ease my mind if you were, well, away for a bit," said Bremen.

"Are you serious?" asked Folor, "Send a Keeper on a mission alone?"

"We would send assistants, of course," said Bremen.

"No, no assistants," said Raef, "they would only get in my way."

But Raef was unable to persuade them. In the end he was given an apprentice Intercessor who had nearly reached greenling's end and a young scribe about his own seasons. When Prime Rodon learned of the plan, he insisted there be protection for the mission and requested that two Warriors accompany them. Chaz volunteered, as he had completed his cleansing some suns past, and he selected a lower ranking young Warrior to go with them. Raef said goodbye once more to Naan and left with the small band of travelers on his second mission to Moss Rock.

The journey itself was uneventful, taking two sun's journey as before. As they neared the abandoned village, Raef stopped them and pulled Chaz aside.

"Chaz," said Raef, "I know you are here to protect me, but it is important that I enter Moss Rock alone."

"Keeper Raef, that is where we fear the danger lies, if there be any."

Raef paused and looked into the face of his oldest friend. He knew Chaz was only trying to do his job.

"Chaz, we have known each other as long as I can remember. I need you to trust me. I need complete silence in Moss Rock. The slightest sound will keep me from finding the clues I am looking for."

"What you are looking for? Why would you require such silence?"

"It was you who said I know things about the dragon that others do not. You are right. It is not pleasant to recall such things, but now I must. Trust me, please, Chaz when I say I cannot find any clues the dragon left behind unless I am alone."

Chaz remained silent, gazing at his feet.

"I will return for you and the others when I have done all I can alone, and you may all come and see what I have found."

"As you wish," said Chaz, "you are an Intercessor and Keeper of Fir Hollow. What you ask goes against my training, but I will do as you ask."

Chaz turned to the rest of the troupe who had been waiting.

"We shall wait here while Keeper Raef enters Moss Rock alone. We can rest here until he requests our assistance."

Raef continued down the road on foot. He breathed a sigh of relief that they had allowed him go alone, yet he hated that he had lied to Chaz. The spring sun glowed gently down on him. When he was out of sight of the others he removed his red Keeper's robe and carried it under his arm and untied the upper laces of his tunic to cool off. It was a bit further to the village than he had expected, but he decided that was best. The others would not see or hear what was to happen. He entered Moss Rock from the east side and passed rows of huts and houses on either side. It was two moon cycles since the battle, yet the scent of dragon was still strong. It had been here a long time before the Keepers had been aware of it, Raef realized. He was not surprised. As he approached the central square, a shadow passed over him. He did not look up, but waited at the edge of the square for Rail to land in front of him.

"Why?" said Raef.

"Master Raef," said the great beast, bowing its enormous head low before Raef, "is this any way to greet me after so long? You have not come to visit for two cycles."

Raef came close to the beast until he could feel its hot breath on his face.

"You killed nearly an entire village."

"I killed no one," said the dragon, "that was the doing of your Warriors. Including that one you call a friend back on the road."

"Rail, are you mad? A dragon cannot saunter into a village as you did and not expect it to end badly. Very, very badly."

Rail raised its head skyward, shadowing Raef's body.

"You, of all the villagers, should know that is not true. Surely you have not forgotten your fellow Dragon Children, Toaz and Milo. They have told you themselves how I am welcome in any of their villages on Conch, any time. That has been true for generations."

"This is the Great Province, not some vulgar island far out at sea."

"You are calling your brothers and sisters at Black Rock vulgar? Villagers here in the Province run their frantic pace, wearing themselves out to keep fed and warm. All is strife and envy. I offer peace, rest and the glow of bliss as all your needs are tended for. Conch came to its senses long ago. Moss Rock only wanted my harmony. Your Warriors came in and slaughtered them. Which of the two is uncivilized, I ask you?"

"Do not be sly with me, Rail. You have betrayed me."

Rail tilted its head and gazed down on Raef. It slowly moved a claw behind Raef and gently wrapped a talon around his waist.

"Raef, my son, I have shown great trust in you allowing you to leave Black Rock and return to the villages. You must trust me as well."

"I thought you said anyone could leave Black Rock."

"Anyone I truly trust."

This did not seem to square with what Rail had said when he was living in Black Rock, but he began to feel weary of arguing. Raef's head went a bit fuzzy, and he leaned back against Rail's talon. At the dragon's touch, warmth washed over Raef's body. Raef closed his eyes for a moment and drank in relief.

"Rail," Raef said quietly, "are you not even sad at the loss of so many? Were they not your children, those here at Moss Rock?"

The dragon lowered itself to face Raef again. Raef smelled its sickly sweet breath.

"They were becoming my friends, and yes, it is sad. But you know well once someone is a true friend, I take them back to Black Rock to live in the Great Basin with me. That is where they become my children."

"Except me."

"Yes, except you. You are a Dragon Child living in the villages. And we all miss you."

Raef stood up and shook his head, trying to clear

the fuzziness away.

"The villagers, here at Moss Rock, they were not yet ready to go to the mountain?"

"Some were, and I had taken them away already. When I saw the Warriors coming, still a sun's journey away, I began taking all the younglings. Even if they were not yet ready, I could not bear to see them left here."

Raef tried to imagine a youngling, not yet completely used to Rail, being deposited in the vast gray of the Great Basin. He dismissed the frightful thought quickly.

"And those left here?"

"They were still torn between the cares of the village and what I offered them. They simply waited too long, and were caught by those murderous Warriors."

"Why would they fight to the death if they were not yet ready to leave?"

"Raef, you are wise, but I am a spirit. Some things are too deep for you to understand."

"But you could have saved them. You could have fought off the Warriors."

Rail paused, appearing deep in thought, then very slowly grew a smile.

"What of your friend, Chaz, and his father, Rodon, whom you made me swear not to harm? How could I protect the villagers of Moss Rock and drive away the Warriors of Fir Hollow without harming Chaz and Rodon?"

The dragon moved an eye directly in front of Raef, still holding its smile. Raef felt himself grow cold.

"You mean, you had to abandon Moss Rock because of me?"

"Raef, I am truly sorry, but I saw no other way to keep my promise to you."

Raef felt his stomach sink, and he faltered in his step. Rail caught him gently with a talon before Raef hit the ground. Raef pushed away and walked several paces from the dragon. He began shaking his head.

"I am so sorry, master Raef. It is not my wish to burden you with sorrow."

"No, Rail, this cannot be."

"Raef, do not feel too much sorrow. They had not fully chosen me, perhaps they never would have."

"But they are all dead now! An entire village!"

"Not all, Raef. Black Rock has many new Dragon Children from Moss Rock. The Basin is alive with new men and women, greenlings and greenlias, and happy younglings scampering about."

Raef sank to his knees and stared at the distant dark mountain. He tried to remember what it was like.

"You took the bodies," mumbled Raef.

"Too many to eat at once," said Rail. "I took them all, of course, to store at Black Rock. My strength will be great for some time with the supply their sacrifice made. When the bodies are gone, I will not need to feed again for a season or more."

Raef realized knowing Rail was eating all those bodies should bother him. He had lived at Black Rock too long. Rail was right; Raef was more a Dragon Child than a villager. Raef felt the warm, soft nostril of the dragon nuzzle the back of his head and neck. He leaned back and closed his eyes.

"My child," said the dragon, "Do not be sad. These kinds of things only happen when Warriors get involved, and you are not a Warrior."

Raef leaned his head back and felt dragon breath down on his face. Rail's nostril nuzzled him, and Raef tried not to cry.

"I missed you as well," said the beast.

Raef returned to Chaz and the others before the sun began to set, reporting they could now enter Moss Rock with him. They put their packs back on the horses and made the short journey together. Chaz, who usually rode horseback, rode in the cart with Raef instead.

"What were you able to discover?" asked Chaz.

"The dragon had indeed been all through the village, not just on the outskirts."

"No disrespect, Keeper, but I do not see why knowing such a thing would be important. The beast destroyed the village whether it entered it or not."

Raef searched his mind for a something to say. He thought of nothing he could tell Chaz that the Warrior would find important. He needed to find something to say to explain his need to go alone.

"It walked into the heart of the village without being challenged," said Raef.

"What of it?"

"That means that most of the village, the Warriors certainly, were already familiar with the dragon before it ever entered the village."

"You are certain of this?" asked Chaz, "how would the Warriors, or anyone else, have become familiar with the dragon before it came into the village?"

"It had been meeting them out in the forest in secret. Probably for some time."

"I cannot even imagine," said Chaz, "and you are certain?"

"I will show you."

When they entered the village streets, Chaz gazed at the empty houses as they passed.

"I see no sign a dragon was ever here," said the Warrior.

Raef stopped the cart, got off, and walked to the side of the road and began searching the bushes.

"What are you looking for?" asked Chaz.

Raef pulled something from a bush and walked to Chaz, holding a long strand at arms length in front of him.

"What is that?" asked Chaz.

"A dragon hair," said Raef.

He handed the glinting fiber to Chaz, who backed away.

"It cannot hurt you," said Raef. "It has no more power than a strand of your own hair."

The Warrior cautiously took the thick cord from Raef, holding it up to the sun as it glittered in the light.

"It seems alive somehow," said Chaz. "It is eerie, an evil thing."

He tossed the hair to the street.

"No wonder villagers are lured to the beast, if it is made of such magic as that."

"It is not magic," said Raef. "Perhaps it would want us to think it is."

Chaz shivered, then looked down at Raef who still

stood in the road.

"Come," said Chaz, "I want to see the battlefield. The Warriors who came with you the first time told me the bodies were all gone. I must see that for myself."

Raef returned to the cart and they rode to the square, then beyond to the north edge of the village. They stopped and looked over the field of grass, still marred with dark smudges where bodies once lay.

"I did not believe it," said Chaz. "There were so many bodies here. They are all gone."

Chaz got out of the cart and began to search the grass for hidden bodies. Raef leaned back against the wooden back of the seat and watched as his friend searched the grass and stream bank. Raef could still sense dragon scent wafting off the warming spring grass. Chaz searched until the sun began to set and found nothing.

"Now I will show you," said Raef, getting out of the cart.

Raef went to the far side of the field and followed what scent of the dragon was left. Chaz followed as they wandered through the trees over faint trails. They came to a break in the trees where a large flat boulder, the span of six houses, still radiated the spring sun's warmth. Raef knew it must have been this place. He searched the surrounding ferns and quickly found a strand, sparkling in the dim light.

"Here," he said, bringing it toward Chaz.

The Warrior backed away, refusing to touch it. Raef dropped it, wiping his hand on his trousers for Chaz's benefit. He felt a secret pang of shame from all the times he had hidden a dragon hair under his mattress, to take out and admire at night.

"It was here," said Chaz.

"And villagers found it here, coming to visit, telling their friends, until so many knew it they welcomed it into the heart of the village."

"Unthinkable," said Chaz, "I want to leave this evil place."

It was not easy, but Raef convinced the troupe to stay the night in Moss Rock in spite of their concern that the village was cursed.

"The dragon has been gone two cycles," said Raef.

"The curse is gone, and we are safe here. There is no need to camp out somewhere on the road with all these homes we can sleep in."

# 27

The following sunrise Raef performed a homage chant and blessing for the apprentice and scribe. He was surprised that Chaz attended as well and allowed himself to be blessed. Then they searched the village and surroundings for other clues. Raef pretended to search with them, but he had already found the answers he came for. Raef remained deep in thought all sun's journey, playing Rail's words over in his mind.

Was all this his fault? Had the dark spirit abandoned Moss Rock so Rodon and Chaz could remain unharmed? His chest carried an ache that would not go away. His mind danced between memories of Black Rock and Fir Hollow, of Rail and Naan. He wanted both and neither.

At sunset they regrouped for last meal. It was decided they would begin the journey home the following sunrise.

"Did you find all you needed to find?" asked Chaz, as they sat around a fire after eating.

"I found all there is to find."

"It is odd," said Chaz, "this place is different now.

Without the bodies, it is simply lonely and sad. Before, after the battle, it was gruesome and dark."

"There are no bodies left," said Raef, "no disfigured men and women, no decay. This place is ready to be inhabited again, I believe."

"Do you know what happened to the bodies?"

Raef sat still a moment. Perhaps he could trust Chaz with a little. The others in the troupe sat a few spans away. Raef did not think they would be able to hear.

"The dragon. It came back after our Warriors left. It ate some and took the rest to eat later."

"What a terrible thought. How are you sure? What makes you even think such a thing would happen?"

"It took me too, remember? I could not escape immediately. I saw it...I saw it eat a dead person, Chaz. It was horrible."

"I cannot imagine. But why would it take them all?"

"What other explanation is there?"

Chaz sat in silence several moments before speaking again.

"How evil is this beast?" asked Chaz. "It tricks an entire village, or most of it, to welcome it and later to fight for it. Then it flies away when they are attacked, only to return and eat them when they have lost the battle."

Raef shifted uneasily on the log he sat upon.

"Such a dark thing, this dragon," said Chaz.

# 28

They returned to Fir Hollow two sunsets later. They met messengers waiting on the road a quarter sun's journey outside the village. The messengers, upon seeing they were all safe, raced on horseback ahead to tell the village. When Raef and the troupe entered Fir Hollow, a small band of Warriors and Intercessors were waiting. Naan and Daz ran to greet Raef. Raef saw his mother waiting further down the road.

"I am so glad you are home!" said Naan, wrapping her arms around him. "I was so worried for you."

"Master Raef," said Daz, "I have continued my duties and assisted Keeper Chaummer while you were gone."

"You are a good apprentice, Daz. Now return to the dormery, and I will see you first thing next sunrise."

"Aw, Master Raef, I truly do not wish to return to the dormery quite yet. You are a Keeper, and can order me to assist you a bit longer."

Raef shook his head at the greenling's impish grin.

"Very well. Apprentice Daz, attend to my bags and

deliver them to my hut. Then stable this horse. Report to me when all is done."

Daz took the horse by the reigns, tied it to a tree, and began loading Raef's bags from the cart onto the horse. Raef took Naan's hand and led her toward her home. She smiled up at him.

"He is quite taken with you, you know."

"Who, Daz?"

"Yes. He came by to check on me every sunrise, reporting all he had heard about your journey, which was nothing, I suspect, but he was always sure to make something up."

"And how have you been, my love?"

"I have been well. My painting for the Counsel is finished, and it will be unveiled in a ceremony, which is very exciting because I never expected that, but not until after the Overseers have left."

"The Overseers are still here?"

"Oh, yes, they have caused quite a stir. They set up kind of a court, right in the village square. They displaced all the Merchants, who have had to move their booths into the village streets, which no one wants. And the Overseers hold open interviews, that get quite personal if you ask me, of the Warriors and Keepers, both ours and the ones from Moss Rock."

"That sounds terrible."

"They call them interviews. More like interrogations if you ask me. It is as if they are accusing us for what happened."

Raef and Naan passed through the village square and in the low light of the setting sun Raef saw a tall table or bench, long enough for four or five villagers to sit at, with tall stools behind it. A shorter platform stood before it with a single, low bench, obviously for someone to sit on.

"Where did all this come from?"

"They made a Merchant surrender his booth, told all the woodcrafters in the village to cease their work and turn his booth into this. It cost each craftsmen a full sun's labor, and the Merchant lost his booth."

Raef shook his head, "For the good of the village, I suppose."

"The good of the Province, say the Overseers."

"I will speak to Bremen, perhaps he will plea to the Village Council to recoup the losses of the woodcrafters and this Merchant."

As they reached the home of Naan and Yamrah, Raef turned to Naan, bent down and kissed her.

"I will be so happy when all this is behind us," said Raef, "Then we can begin making arrangements for our wedding."

"Yes, I can scarcely wait to be married, but I want all this to be over first."

He kissed her again and began the walk home. As he neared the stream dividing the village, he saw Daz walking in the street toward him.

"Daz, you should not be out this late, especially on this side of the village."

"Master Raef, I am a greenling, not a youngling. Besides, I am well liked, no one would harass me."

Raef came to the greenling's side, put his arm around him and directed him back to the east side.

"The greenlings on the West End rove about unsupervised at night and can be menacing."

"Not to me!" said Daz, walking taller.

"You are impossible. Did you finish all I asked?"

"Yes, Master Raef. The horse is bedded down and your bags are in your hut."

"Very well, you may return to the dormery."

"Master Raef, please, I do not wish to return so soon. I will only have to go to bed."

"As well you should. And don't think calling me 'master' will get you any favors."

Daz hung his head but Raef sent him to the dormery and then returned to his own hut.

# 29

The next sunrise Raef woke feeling well rested. He completed the New Leaf ritual, had some bread and cheese for first meal, then put his red robe on and walked to the Ceremonial Lodge. Daz and the other Intercessor apprentices were in their sand colored robes holding fir branches in an arch in front of the door. Chaummer arrived along with Raef and they walked under the fir branches and into the lodge. A small fire was burning at the front of the lodge for warmth and incense was burning on two small tables at either end of the raised front platform.

Bremen began to chant when everyone was in place and soon the men and greenlings who were Nobles, Intercessors, Laborers and Merchants began entering the lodge. They walked down the right isle, passing the rows of benches, then crossed in front of the Keepers. Prime Bremen chanted ancient words of protection and fruitful labor as he touched each on the head. The men and greenlings then passed down the left aisle and out again to begin their labors.

When no one else came, the Keepers stopped

chanting and Prime Keeper Bremen led them out. The Intercessor apprentices entered the Ceremonial Lodge to put out the fire and incense candles, but Daz followed Raef as he was an apprentice to a Keeper. Together they all walked to the village square, which was already surrounded with guards from the Provincial Army, shining in their armor and holding colorful flags. Four men sat behind the grand bench dressed in pompous, billowing garments colored like the sunset. Provincial attendants in inky robes with flowery collars fidgeted at the sides of the bench.

"Do they know how ridiculous they look?" Raef asked Dimmel.

"Raef, this is why we sent you away in the first place," replied Dimmel, "do you need another mission to attend to?"

"I shall endeavor to behave myself."

"Just endeavor to be silent," whispered Keeper Bremen.

One of the men at the bench lifted a round, polished stone the size of a large apple and crashed it down on a square wooden plate. The resulting crack silenced the crowd that had gathered in the center of the square. Raef wondered if anyone at all was left to attend to labor in the fields.

"The inquest will continue," said the man with the stone.

"Who is he?" Raef asked Dimmel quietly.

"Overseer Drumon. He is the Prime Magistrate. The others at the bench are magistrates as well, all Overseers from Summit City."

"The Overseers of the Great Province require the

investigation of Keeper Raef, son of Folor," said Drumon.

Prime Bremen's face grew pale.

"Me?" said Raef, "They want to inquire of me?"

Prime Keeper Bremen turned to Raef and took him by the sleeves.

"Keeper Raef," said Bremen, "your words curse or bless us all, the entire village. This is not a time for your arrogance. The welfare of the village is of prime importance, not you. Mind yourself, young Keeper."

Raef stepped away, a bit stunned at Bremen's reprimand, and passed between two of the Provincial Guards. The word 'arrogance' played over and over in his mind. An attendant of the Overseers intercepted him and led him onto the low platform and seated him on the bench. Raef felt the eyes of the Province on him.

"You are Raef?" asked Drumon.

"I am."

"You returned from Moss Rock sunset past?" said the Prime Magistrate, glaring at Raef with steely eyes.

"What? How did you…"

"You were on an investigation of some sort apparently," continued Drumon, "I find it odd, Keeper Raef, that the Keepers of Fir Hollow would select you, the youngest and lowest of them all, to represent them. Yet you were charged with leading an investigation into the greatest tragedy that has come to the Great Province in three generations."

Raef felt his mouth slowly droop open.

"Can you explain how you came to be chosen for such a critical investigation?"

"I...I...I was not in charge of anything. The Keepers and Warriors had already been to Moss Rock. I simply went…"

"Why would you go at all, Keeper Raef?"

Raef sat silently, unsure what to say.

"And the two Warriors, they were attending you? Since when in this great province have Warriors attended Intercessors? Warriors, young Raef, attend village Nobles and Overseers, not Intercessors."

"They came just for protection in case…"

"In case of what, young Keeper? What were you expecting to find in Moss Rock?"

Raef was silent. The entire square was silent.

"Villagers of Fir Hollow," said Drumon, straightening up, "this entire affair smells of the worst kind of trickery. This village has had very little attention from Provincial Overseers, and I am beginning to believe that was unwise of us. What we believed to be a peaceful, untroubled village is looking more like one with evil intent on its neighbors."

There was a long silence. Raef could not look to either side, for fear of meeting the eyes of his fellow villagers.

"*Keeper* Raef," said Drumon, "I understand that the bodies of all those who were butchered in Moss Rock are now absent. What do *you* believe happened to those bodies?"

"I certainly do not know."

"Was it not your own theory, *Keeper* Raef, that a dragon, a spirit of some sort, ate them?"

Raef went cold. How had the Overseers heard this?

"I...sir...I supposed I did say that in passing."

"Why in all the Province would you tell someone such a tall tale? How could such a thing even be possible?"

"Overseer Drumon, the dragon has great powers, powers we do not fully comprehend."

Drumon's face darkened, "Do not presume to educate me, young Keeper. I am a learned man, from a city of knowledge. You are but a young thing from a small, superstitious village."

Raef felt his face flush.

"You are a keeper of superstition, interceding to nothing but using your influence to cloud your dark intentions. There is no beast, no dragon, no spirit. Only villages like this one keep such fables alive."

Drumon looked to the other Keepers, standing outside the village square.

"You keep the village in the dark, you keep fables alive, all to control the weak minds of the Laborers and Merchants while you collaborate with your Warriors to do your evil deeds."

The village began to murmur. Drumon looked into the square at all those gathered.

"What have you done! What did Moss Rock have that you wanted badly enough to kill them all? Is it a mystery that only the Keepers of Moss Rock survived? Collaborators of secrets, keepers of lies!"

The village stirred. The Provincial Army collectively put hands to the swords they carried.

"Overseer Drumon," Raef said, "with great respect, Prime Magistrate, I do not understand how you do not believe the dragon exists. I myself was taken by this dragon as a greenling, in front of the entire village, right here in this very square. I was able to escape, not right away, but before it could eat me, lost in the forest until I had eighteen seasons. To this moment I have spoken little of what happened when I was taken, as it is too painful to recall. But I feel the moment has arrived for me to reveal what I saw, for the benefit of this assembly."

Drumon's eyes darkened as he glared at Raef.

"When the dragon took me, again which all those of Fir Hollow here saw happen, it did not try to eat me right away. When it landed, there was a body nearby. The dead body of a man. I do not know where it came from. The dragon ate the dead man before my eyes. I was able to escape some suns later, but not until I had been made to view that terrible sight."

"I am expected to believe you were bodily removed from this village by a flying dragon?" said Drumon. "What kind of fool do you take me for?"

"We all saw it!" yelled someone from the crowd.

"It was right here in this village square," yelled another, "five seasons past!"

The village erupted in testimony.

"Silence!" yelled Drumon, banging the round stone on the wooden plate.

The village slowly quieted as Provincial Guards drew their swords.

"Why would you tell such a fable?" asked Drumon.

"The dragon eats dead bodies," said Raef. "It must have returned when our Warriors left to retrieve the bodies after the battle in Moss Rock. For food. It explains the mystery."

Drumon looked over the crowd. One of the other Overseers whispered in his ear. Drumon then turned to the other three Overseers, and they spoke together in a huddle. When the Prime Magistrate turned back to face the village, he motioned to the Provincial Army, and they sheathed their swords.

"I will cease arguing whether a dragon exists in the Great Province. Yes, there are tales, even in Summit City, of a beast that preys on those who wander out alone. Some of our historians claim there is evidence that such a beast existed long ago, though most learned villagers scoff at such nonsense. Let me state that no sighting of this beast has ever been proven true in any of the cities in all of the Province. The historians of Krellit, the city of learning, are certain that whatever ancient beast these fables are based on, if it ever lived at all, is long dead. I, the Prime Magistrate of the Great Province, member of the Overseers, resident of Summit City, believe this entire affair to be a conspiracy of Fir Hollow to have Moss Rock for yourselves. You are all extremely fortunate that not all of my colleagues with me agree. We can find no motive for such an atrocity, and there is still the great mystery of the vanishing bodies of an entire village. Your wild story, young man, is unconvincing.

"However, we have questioned members of every sector of this village, young and old alike, for five sun's journeys, and it appears every last one of you uneducated villagers firmly believes this entire event is a result of some ancient, dark spirit. Who has fooled you all, I cannot say. Who did this to Moss Rock, we have not found. For the peace of the Great Province we will not punish this village. You are all mislead, but we cannot find who among you is lying."

The village stirred, and Drumon raised his hand to silence them.

"Mind you, we will find who did this. We will leave, but we will appoint a Provincial Inquest to look into the matter. We have great resources in Summit City for such endeavors. When we do find who is responsible for the death of Moss Rock, they and all their family will be put to death. Be certain of that."

A slight ease fell over the village. Drumon raised the polished stone and crashed it onto the wooden plate.

"This inquiry is officially over."

The village erupted as the Overseers turned and were lead away by their attendants. The Provincial Army quickly surrounded the Overseers and attendants as they walked toward the camp they had set up outside the village. Raef got off the bench and walked swiftly to the other Keepers.

"How dare those pompous city dwellers speak to us in such a manner!" said someone behind Raef.

"Keeper Raef," said Daz as Raef approached, "I believe you."

"We do not need to believe Keeper Raef," said Prime Keeper Bremen, "most of us saw him taken with our own eyes."

"That was when Keeper Raef had no more seasons than you," said Dimmel to his son.

"I do not understand how they refuse to believe," said Raef.

The other Keepers circled around Raef as the villagers mobbed around the Keepers.

"I should explain to you, Raef," said Bremen, "these city dwellers frequently do not believe in the spirits at all. Not any spirits, good or evil."

"How…how is that possible?" said Raef, "Zul, the Great Spirit, spoke to me. I have seen the Great Spirit, not often, but I have seen him."

"We know," said Folor.

"Father," said Raef, turning to Folor, "you studied in Krellit. You are a man of learning."

"And I know the spirits are as real as you and I," Raef's father said, "I too have seen Zul and saw you taken by the great beast as it flew over Fir Hollow with you in its talons. Men who gain learning do not like to admit there are things beyond what they can control. The spirit world is beyond us. It comes in contact with us from time to time, but we cannot control it. Much learning requires much humility, which is something most city dwellers refuse to submit to."

"So they cloud themselves to the spirit world to maintain the importance they seek," said Raef, "Father, you are truly a wise man."

"Keeper Raef," said Bremen, "you take after your father."

"Here, here!" shouted someone from the crowd that thronged around them.

Prime Keeper Bremen raised a hand and requested the village gather at the Common Lodge, men and women, young and old alike. The Keepers entered first, standing on the platform at the front as the rest of the village was gathered. When everyone save the Warrior cast had arrived and the Common Lodge was full, the Prime Keeper of Fir Hollow silenced them with a hand. Keeper Bremen said ancient words of blessing over the village and then spoke in language they could understand to intercede to the Great Spirit Zul for protection from the great beast. Raef realized the Prime Keeper's wisdom in calling the village together to ease their minds after the harsh treatment from the Overseers. After the blessing and calming words from Bremen, it was time for mid-sun meal. The villagers were released to their homes. On the way to his own hut, Raef came upon Chaz, waiting in the road.

"Ho, Raef!" said Chaz.

Raef smiled at the youngling greeting from his old friend.

"Greetings, Chaz."

"I wanted to speak briefly to you. I was present when the Overseers questioned you in the square. The Warriors are appalled at the disrespect the Overseers showed Fir Hollow. We are all subject to Summit City, you to the Overseers and Warriors to the Provincial Army, but we did not understand previously in what low regard they view us."

"It was a revelation to me as well."

"My father says it was not surprising to him," said Chaz, "perhaps the older Warriors knew, but I did not realize how the ruling cities view the villages."

Chaz walked alongside Raef on the way to Raef's hut.

"Raef, I do not feel it is an insult to follow your

lead, even though I am a Warrior. You know that, don't you?"

"I am only sorry anyone imagined I was leading you, or any other Warrior, for that matter."

"But we do follow you, Raef. A few of us know you are the only one who knows how to defeat the dragon."

"I wish you would stop saying that. I have no wisdom the village Nobles do not have."

"You are humble, as Intercessors are taught to be, but I know the Warrior tradition of ignoring the Intercessor clan is wrong. At least in your case. We need what you know. You can refuse all you want, but I will never face the dragon again without your assistance."

"I am not sure I want to be known as an expert on dragons," said Raef, "but I thank you, I suppose."

Chaz smiled and slapped Raef's back.

"I must return to my duties. Good sunset to you."

"And to you."

Raef watched his friend turn and disappear around a corner, heading south to the Warrior sector. He could not imagine being with both Rail and Chaz in the same place. That would be disaster. He was fairly certain the dragon would not show itself again, now that it had what it wanted from Moss Rock, but he vowed to do everything in his power to prevent any Warrior from ever seeing him in the dragon's presence.

# 30

Shortly after mid-sun meal, a messenger came to deliver a message to Raef. A greenlia messenger, which was something Raef had never heard of.

"Master Matik has returned to Fir Hollow," said the greenlia, "Master Matik has rented an Inn to prepare a private meal, and she requests you and Artisan Naan accompany her for last meal."

"An inn? An entire inn just for the three of us?"

"It is as you say, Keeper Raef."

"This woman, Matik, really is something, is she not?" said Raef to the young messenger who had delivered the message.

"As you say, Keeper Raef," the greenlia said.

Raef smiled at her.

"You may tell Master Matik that I will be there," said Raef. "And tell her she is more surprising each passing sun, hiring a greenlia as a messenger."

"Again, with all respect, Keeper Raef, it is less surprising in the city. But to be sure, Keeper Raef, it is an honor to serve Master Matik."

"I have no doubt. I will be most pleased to join her

and Naan this sunset."

Raef continued to smile as he watched the greenlia leave. She walked with dignity, but without arrogance. Matik had chosen well. He walked to the apothecary where he found Daz grinding herbs as an older herbalist watched over his shoulder. The herbalist looked up and bowed as Raef entered.

"Apprentice Daz has a talent in the medicinal arts, Keeper Raef."

"I see," said Raef. "I hope he has caused less trouble than he did in the kitchen."

Daz turned red.

"Quite the opposite," said the herbalist, "he works hard and is quick to learn."

"I had difficulty learning the herbs," said Raef, "much less remembering how to make these concoctions."

"Remedies, Master Raef, not concoctions," said Daz.

Raef raised an eyebrow to the herbalist, "I am corrected by my own apprentice."

The herbalist laughed nervously.

"I would like to borrow my apprentice," said Raef, "He missed much in the suns I was absent."

"Of course, Keeper Raef. I will finish here."

Raef turned to leave as the herbalist bowed and Daz followed.

"Thank you for saving me," said Daz.

"I thought you liked working in the apothecary."

"I do, actually it is my favorite of all the Intercessor trades so far, but I would rather be with you."

"I do not know whether to feel flattered or taken

advantage of, you little imp."

"It is not my fault I am small," said Daz, "and don't call me imp. You know I am your favorite too."

"Out of all one of my apprentices."

Daz laughed.

"Come, let's make a quick pass through the West End then go do something fun," said Raef.

They walked through the northern part of West End, which Raef was responsible for, checking quickly on the sick and greeting anyone who was not out laboring. Then Raef took Daz to the Keep where they discarded their robes.

"Where are we going?" asked Daz.

"I will show you."

Raef led Daz to the Training Lodge, where Daz glanced nervously at Raef.

"You are not going to make me return to lessons, are you Master Raef?"

Raef only smiled and continued past the lodge and into the forest. Daz followed close behind. They walked deeper and deeper into the forest, not using any trail, until the trees grew dense, and the ground was covered in thick fern and deep moss.

"It's kind of spooky here," said Daz.

"You have not been this far out in the forest before?"

"I have hardly been in the forest at all," said Daz.

"How can that be? Our village is in the center of the forest."

"My father says it is dangerous."

Raef paused and looked up at the treetops high above.

"This is an ancient place," he said, "full of mystery. I used to love to come out here as a youngling."

"You went in the forest alone as a youngling?"

"All the time."

Daz walked up to a fern bunch. They brushed against his chest.

"Look how tall these ferns are!"

"I know where there are ferns taller than you," said Raef.

"Can you show me?"

"Not this sun, there is not time."

They sat together on a fallen log under the shade of a great fir.

"I wish I could explore the forest more," said Daz, "to learn to find food, go places I've never been."

Daz paused and looked up at Raef.

"Do you know how to find food out here?" Daz asked.

"I had to when I was alone in the forest. You know, when I was finding my way home."

Daz's eyes grew, "After you escaped from the dragon, you mean."

"Yes," said Raef, "you know about that?"

"Everyone knows about that," said Daz. He seemed to ponder something for a moment before speaking again, "Where did it take you, the dragon?"

Raef paused a minute to think how best to answer.

"Far away, to a place I do not think anyone knows about."

"But then you escaped."

"I am here, am I not?"

Daz grinned, "Was it kind of fun, to be all by

yourself out in the forest for so long?"

"It was an adventure, that is for sure."

Daz was silent a moment, looking up into the dark trees. Daz did not move his gaze as he continued to speak.

"Some villagers say you know secrets about the dragon."

"Secrets? What...who says that?"

"Just some villagers. They say you won't tell anyone because it's too terrible, and we'd all be scared."

Raef did not respond. Daz continued to look up into the shadows.

"That would be amazing if you did know secrets about the dragon," said Daz, "Then you could tell me. I've never even seen it before. The last time it appeared in Fir Hollow I was in the Training Lodge and didn't get to see it."

Raef paused before speaking.

"I do know some secrets about the dragon."

"Tell me some."

"It is like you heard, I do not speak of them because it is too frightening."

Daz sighed and hung his head dramatically.

"Too frightening for most villagers, that is," said Raef.

"I would not be scared!"

Raef closed his eyes, a strange warmth coming over him.

"Before I was a greenling," said Raef, "I already knew some of the dragon's secrets."

"I thought you were an apprentice Keeper when the dragon took you."

"Well, first of all, you are forgetting that I became an apprentice Keeper with only ten seasons, but you are correct, I had thirteen seasons, just like you, when the dragon took me. But I knew about the dragon long before then."

"How did you learn?"

"An older friend. He was an apprentice Intercessor, just like you, and I was a youngling. He was my friend."

"So, you saw it, the dragon, when you were just a youngling?"

"Daz, these are things I do not speak to others about."

"Master Raef, I would never tell anyone secrets about the dragon. Not even the other apprentices. They are dull of mind anyway, not really my friends."

"Daz, you are an apprentice to a Keeper."

"What of it? Could you teach me just one secret now?"

Raef opened his eyes and looked down at Daz. The greenling was wiggling as he sat on the log next to Raef. The warmth in Raef's chest seemed to spread.

"The dragon's name is Rail."

"I thought no one was supposed to say his name!"

"I was taught that too. But my friend showed me that if you call the dragon by its name, it will not hurt you."

"Wait, that actually makes sense! The old story of how you called it by name when it attacked Prime Warrior Rodon. You called it by name, and it flew away and left you alone."

"Correct."

Daz stared up into the sky, "That is so different than I expected."

"Almost everything you've been taught is wrong. Rail is totally different than any of the stories you have heard."

Daz stared blankly upward into the shadows.

"Rail," said Daz, "the dragon's name is Rail."

Raef and Daz returned to the Keep as the sun began to get low in the sky. Raef handed Daz his apprentice robe then headed for his own hut. Along the streets a faint dragon scent wafted past Raef's nostrils. He paused, shaking his head. Was it a memory from Moss Rock? He had not seen the dragon since and did not understand where it came from. A pair of greenlings walked by, laughing together, and the scent grew stronger until they passed.

Back in his hut, Raef cleaned off the last bits of dirt and fir needles he had picked up in the forest. He stood, looking down on his clothing once more before leaving for the Inn. He wanted to appear well kept to Naan and Matik. He walked to the Inn as the sun touched the edge of the sky. A wonderful aroma met him as he neared the Inn.

Entering the Inn he was met with music and the scent of seasoned slow-cooked meats. He smelled lamb, beef and venison, and it smelled like sausages as well. The room had been cleared of all but one table, where Naan sat. Matik skittered toward Raef, her young attendant at her side.

"Master Raef, Master Raef," said the petite, smiling

woman, "how very good to see you again."

"Keeper Raef, actually, and it is so very nice to see you again, Master Matik."

Matik took Raef's right hand between her hands and patted with her slim fingers.

"Just Matik to you," she said, "let us do away with formalities all together, shall we?"

"Of course," said Raef, bowing slightly.

Matik, still holding his hand in hers, drug him to the table and sat him across from Naan. She sat next to Naan and made a gesture without taking her smiling eyes off Raef. Trays of meats were immediately brought to the table. An attendant of the inn placed wooden circles in front of the three diners.

"What are these?" asked Raef.

"Plates, my dear," said Matik, "I had to have them made since Fir Hollow is apparently not familiar with their use."

"What are they for?"

"For placing ones food on to eat from," said Matik.

"Why not use trenchers?"

"Eating off slices of stale bread is for commoners," said Matik. "None of us here is common."

"Well, if you mean none of us act in common fashion," said Naan, "then you are entirely correct."

Raef laughed.

Raef found the meal delightful. He had not eaten so much variety or quantity at once in his life. Matik was a marvelous host, entertaining and inquisitive. Raef soon realized this woman could easily run a city on her own, and likely had the pedigree to do so, but had chosen to be an Artisan instead. Her work must be amazing, Raef realized, because it had made her immensely wealthy. No one in Fir Hollow could have rented an entire inn and purchased so much food just for a meal for two friends. He glanced at the minstrels playing harps and violas. They were not familiar and were dressed finer than minstrels he had seen. He wondered how far they had traveled and how Matik knew of them. He returned to eating and laughing with Matik and Naan. Even after a long meal, there were mountains of food left over.

"Naan has told me about your wedding," said Matik as the meal came to a close, "Her first commission is finished and will be unveiled in two sunsets. I will be returning to my home in Midland, but will return for your wedding. I absolutely insist."

Raef watched the woman's fine fingers drum her mug.

"We are honored, of course," he said.

"It is such an exciting thing, a Keeper and an Artisan marrying. I know neither of you have many possessions to speak of, so I have a gift for you. I am leaving funds with the Prime Noble to pay for your wedding party. I have left instructions with him as to what he must do. It will be the grandest wedding Fir Hollow has ever known."

"Matik, I am speechless," said Naan.

"Matik, it is too much," said Raef.

"Nonsense," said Matik, "it is an honor for me. I will return one moon cycle from now to make final preparations."

They stood to part, and Matik hugged them both.

Then she turned to her attendants.

"Wrap this food up and take it to the Labor sector," said Matik.

"Master Matik," said Raef, "your generosity is excessive."

"It is nothing. We have no more use of all this."

She waved and the attendants began wrapping meat and bread in linens. Raef and Naan hugged Matik once more and left. Raef walked Naan to her house, kissing her before he left her. He floated on his way home, passing joyous families who were receiving gifts of elegant food from the visiting Artisan. He waved to them as he passed. He almost did not want to enter his little hut when he arrived. He was too excited to sleep. It had been a strange but wonderful sun's journey.

# 31

Raef woke early next sunrise. He leapt off his bed to do his New Leaf washing, pausing briefly to meditate. He ate a mouthful of bread and left, pulling his robe over his shirt as he walked down the path. He smiled at Daz as he walked under the arch of fir branches outside the Ceremonial Lodge and walked lightly to the front once inside. His mind floated during the chanting, to the forest, to Naan and the amazing meal sunset past, to flying through the sky somewhere in his past.

After homage Daz followed Raef on his route through the West End. They started on the northern most street, working their way west until the road curved south at the forest edge. Three figures burst out of the trees, looking to be near youngling's end, laughing and pushing each other as they ran by Raef and Daz. A familiar scent washed over Raef as they passed. Raef paused a moment, thinking it was awfully early in the sunrise, but then realized if Rail visited as many as it claimed it did, certainly it must start early somewhere.

Daz looked questioningly up at Raef.

"Master Raef, is something the matter?"

"Nothing at all, young apprentice. Let us continue our route."

Raef visited three sick villagers and had Daz commit three families to memory for the almoners to add to their list of those to receive alms. Raef looked at the sun and saw it was passing one-quarter sun.

"Daz, let us return to the kitchen and speak with the almoners."

At the kitchen, Daz gave the names of the new families to receive alms to the almoness, then Raef took him to the Keep where they left their robes.

"Where are we going?" asked Daz.

"To show you something truly amazing." said Raef, "Assuming, of course, you are ready."

Daz smiled, "I knew you were more exciting than the other Keepers."

# 32

The image of Raef and Daz faded and washed down stream. Erif sat back and watched the clear water return the murky color it had been before Zul began the vision.

"This is so hard to watch," said Erif.

"Yes," said Zul, as a tear slid down his ancient cheek, "and I have had to watch it happen to each one of the Dragon Children over the generations."

"You saw them all?"

Zul looked sadly at Erif in response.

"I suppose you do see all of us. I keep forgetting you are a spirit."

Zul smiled, "You speak as if you feel sorry for me."

Erif grinned as he stood up. Zul began walking along the stream, and Erif followed. Erif surveyed the muddy stream winding through boulders, sand and dry sedges.

"I do not think they could have found a drearier

place," said Erif.

"An island of banishment is not intended to be a scenic destination."

"Then the Great Province chose this island well."

"But you find it hard to keep heart in such a desolate place, do you not, Erif?"

"At times, yes."

"I am not giving up on you, Erif. Do not give up on me."

They continued their walk along the muddy stream. A light breeze picked up, and Erif felt the simple pleasure of it against his face.

"Zul, is not your plan somewhat of a risk?"

"A risk?"

"You are wagering success on me. I am an outcast, the last person the villagers would want to follow, especially on a mission to fight the dragon. And there are so many things that could go wrong, not the least of which, I could fail miserably."

Zul grinned, "It is best not to think like that. You are defeating yourself before you have begun. Besides, there are several things you do not yet know that change the situation."

"But, Zul, it is too risky! We could all die!"

Zul stopped, his soft eyes peering into Erif.

"Yes, Erif, this is risky and extremely dangerous."

"Then why are you taking such a risk to save the Dragon Children? You know most of them will not leave Black Rock even if we are able to free them. They are too deep under Rail's spell. Besides, it is not as if anyone forced them to befriend the dragon. All of them were warned to stay away from it."

"Daz is scarcely more than a youngling, and you know where he is going next. You would have me ignore him and all the others who followed the beast before they could understand what it would do to them?"

"They grow older and understand, yet they stay."

"And I would risk everything for the chance to save them."

"Even after they ignored you for so long?"

"I am a spirit. My heart is deeper than yours. I cannot bear to see them suffer."

They resumed walking.

"I will not lie to you," Erif said, "I am afraid. I may be well trained, but I still shiver at the thought of attacking the dragon in its own realm."

"And the possibility you may be hurt tears at my heart. But this is a battle over human choice. Over such things spirits have little sway. It is up to you, and any you can convince to follow you, to intervene or not."

"What if I am too afraid when the time comes?"

"You must love the Dragon Children more than you fear the possibility of injury and pain."

"Sometimes I have little pity for them. I am not entirely sure I will be able to do it, when the time comes. I do still have a family, you know."

"And that is why you are not yet ready. That is why you must continue to watch what Rail has done."

Erif sighed and looked again at the murky stream.

"I am ready to see more."

Zul turned to the flowing water and looked into it. The water grew clear and smooth as glass, even as it continued to flow by. An image began to form in the water.

Daz stood at the opposite side of the clearing, eyes wide.

"It will not hurt you," said Raef, patting the dragon's neck.

Rail lifted its head and snorted softly.

"It looks wild," said Daz.

"Oh, it is," said Raef, "but only to its enemies, those it does not like."

"Does it like me?" asked Daz.

Rail lowered its head and looked directly at Daz. "Of course I do," it rumbled.

"The dragon can talk!" said Daz.

Raef laughed.

"Of course I can," said the beast as it reclined, curling its claws under its chest.

Daz slowly approached.

"It is…so huge!" he said.

Rail chuckled, "Come, Daz, I will not harm you."

"It knows my name!"

Raef watched as Daz approached and slowly reached out a hand toward the dragon's side. His hand flinched when it touched a glassy scale, but then Daz smiled and began to glide his hand over its surface.

"It looks to be covered in slime, but it is not," said Daz.

"No, it is not," said Raef, "Here, Daz, let me show you something."

Raef untied the lacing on his calves, pulled his

shoes off and climbed onto the dragon's snout. He lay down, and Rail flicked him into the air. Raef did a simple somersault in the air before landing softly on the dragon's hairy head.

"Ho, Raef, that was amazing."

"You want to try?"

"Well…okay, I will try it once."

Daz removed his shoes as Raef climbed down. Daz climbed carefully up the dragon's neck and onto its snout, smiling wide but trembling a bit.

"Here goes!" said Daz.

Rail expertly dipped and flicked its snout, flipping Daz head over heals once before catching him on its head. Daz laughed out loud.

"Okay, that was really fun. Can I do it again?"

By mid-sun Daz was already doing back flips high in the air. Raef had to drag the greenling off the dragon so they could return in time for mid-sun meal.

"Bye Rail!" called Daz as the dark beast flew from sight.

"What do you think?" asked Raef.

"Rail is awesome. Are there more secrets about the dragon I can learn?"

"Oh, yes, lots more."

Before entering the village, Raef paused to brush any stray dragon hairs off himself and his young apprentice. He then sent Daz to the dormery to eat while he returned to his hut for mid-sun meal.

# 33

Two sunrises afterward was the unveiling ceremony for Naan's painting. When Raef arrived in the village square for the ceremony it appeared nearly the entire village was present. Even the Village Council from Pine Creek had come to attend. The large painting had been put in the square, covered in linen, and was unveiled by Naan on one side and Matik on the other. Minstrels played, and a dance troupe entertained the villagers who attended. Yamrah appeared most pleased, standing next to her daughter. Folor and Malta made a point to greet Yamrah, as did Raef's sister, Irah, and her husband, Wren. Matik left immediately after mid-sun in a large caravan of carts covered in rosy drapery.

The shock of the Moss Rock incident faded away as the suns passed, and the village slowly returned to its normal calm routine. The Keepers and remaining villagers of Moss Rock even began to plan their return home. Prime Bremen had blessed them, saying it would be good to reclaim the village from the dragon.

Raef and Daz began making frequent trips to see Rail, always just after one quarter sun and sometimes lasting past mid-sun meal, making them late for their duties. All the while Raef and Naan's wedding was quickly approaching.

"Greetings, Keeper Raef," said Naan, approaching Raef in the square one late sun.

Raef had been speaking with two Intercessor attendants. He quickly sniffed his shoulder to make sure the dragon scent was not strong. He had seen Rail not long before. He turned to hug her, noticing she was a bit stiff in response.

"And to you, my love."

"I see you exist after all," said Naan, "I was beginning to wonder if you were a figment of my imagination"

"What do you mean?"

"It feels like I have not seen you in suns."

"I see you nearly every sun."

"Every other, at best, and for the briefest of time."

"That is not true!"

"Let's not argue," she sighed, "What are you doing?"

"Seeing our visitors from Moss Rock off. The Keepers and remaining families are finally returning home. I am sending attendants to go with them and stay until everything is settled."

"Are you going as well?"

"No, there is no need."

"Well, I hope it is all over now. It feels as if I have hardly seen you since the incident first happened."

"Well, I suppose I was busy for a while with

matters related to Moss Rock."

"But even after you returned, I could never find you. We used to visit before mid-sun meal or take the meal together."

"Yes, well, the life of a Keeper can be busy."

"Doing what? You seem to be missing from the village much of the time."

"Are you looking after my affairs now?"

Daz approached, carrying a parchment rolled and tied with string.

"The manuscript you asked for, Master Raef," said Daz.

"Thank you, Daz. You can take it to Prime Keeper Frenell. He is in the second cart from the front."

"I know which one he is," said Daz, running down the row of carts.

"And that greenling," said Naan, "he never leaves your side. You spend more time with him than with me."

"Naan, he is my apprentice. It is his role to be by my side."

Raef felt his face burn. Naan looked up at him, then looked down and leaned against him.

"Raef, I am sorry," said Naan, "It is just, well, something does not feel right. I feel like your mind is somewhere else all the time."

"Moss Rock has been quite an ordeal for the Keepers. It is over now, so perhaps I will return to normal."

"I hope so," said Naan, "I need you back."

Raef swore silently to himself he would not see the dragon again. It was beginning to disturb his life, especially his future with Naan. He was a Keeper and was about to be married. He must be done with such youngling nonsense now. Raef and Naan waved as the villagers of Moss Rock began their journey. Then Raef sent Daz to the scribes, where he was currently assisting after mid-sun.

"Come, Naan, I can put off duties the rest of sunset. Let us visit. The taverns are usually quiet this early."

They spent a quiet time together until the sun grew low. Raef walked Naan to her mother's home afterward. When he returned to his own hut for last meal, Raef removed his robe, tunic, and shirt and knelt before his ceremonial washbasin. The Broken Stem ritual of sorrow and remorse required tears. He had not cried in seasons, but he squeezed his eyes tight over and over until wetness ran down his cheeks. He hung his head over the basin, letting drops fall into the water. Shame overwhelmed him as he thought of all his visits to the dragon since he had been made Keeper. He vowed again to never visit the secret place he shared with the evil beast.

# PART FIVE

## THE SIGN

# 34

Raef celebrated the arrival of his twentieth season feeling unsoiled and with a sense of determination. It had been nearly a moon cycle since his last visit to Rail, and he was not going to fail again. It was, he decided, a new start. His celebration was small, as is tradition for adults. A simple meal with Keeper Chaummer and Chaz, an odd pair to celebrate with, Raef realized.

Summer Solstice came, and Raef was able to assist more with the village celebration than in the past. He still had not led a chant at one of these larger celebrations, but he knew he was still young. He was content to lead a short meditation for the blessing of the crops.

As summer warmed the village Daz began to ask to visit Rail more frequently. Raef said he would not go. Daz continued to ask, nearly every time the sun reached one-quarter sky, but Raef always refused. One late sun, before sending his apprentice to work with the scribes, Raef noticed the strong scent of dragon floating off of Daz. Raef sent him to the scribes without saying anything to the greenling.

Raef turned his attention to his wedding, now only a few suns away. Matik had returned to Fir Hollow with a large troupe of assistants. She rented the entire Common Lodge for several suns, which had never been done before. Matik said it was to have a place to practice in private. Raef and Naan could not determine what there would be to practice, as wedding ceremonies were fairly simple. But each sun different villagers from every sector were called to the Common Lodge to see Matik. They would leave with large grins but would say nothing of what had happened inside. The entire village began to buzz about what this wedding might be like.

Raef visited with Naan every sun, taking mid-sun meal with her at her mother's home or at his old youngling home with his father and mother. Yet even with the Moss Rock incident over and the happy occasion of his wedding impending, he found himself feeling agitated often and had a difficult time focusing on his duties as Keeper. He forgot words during chants and forgot who was sick in his sector that needed visiting. Two suns before the wedding, Keeper Chaummer pulled Raef aside.

"Young Keeper Raef," Chaummer said to him, "I am concerned for you."

"Thank you for your concern, but I am fine, Keeper Chaummer."

"I do not think you are. You should rest. Perhaps the strain or excitement of your wedding is clouding your mind."

"Perhaps," said Raef, not agreeing, but glad to have

an excuse for his poor performance.

"I am officially excusing you from your duties until after your wedding," said Chaummer, "I think it best."

Raef paused. At first his heart sank in despair over his recent failures. But he brushed those feelings aside when he realized this would give him two entire suns free of duties.

"As you wish, Keeper Chaummer. I thank you."

Raef bowed to his elder and returned to his hut, shedding his robe. He spent the rest of the sun with Naan, who had nothing to do either as she had no new commission to work on. They sat along the stream just north of the village and watched the water.

"You seem distracted," said Naan.

Raef shook his head. He realized she had been talking to him and he had not heard what she said.

"Sorry, just excited."

She leaned against him, and he hugged her.

"We cannot see each other tomorrow," said Naan.

"The sun before our wedding," said Raef.

"Silly nonsense, not seeing your spouse-to-be the sun before a wedding," she said, "I don't always agree with our traditions, but I suppose it does add a bit of anticipation, which is fun."

Raef smiled at her, "Yes, I have no issue with it either."

"Of course not, you're a Keeper. Keepers are all about tradition."

Raef laughed a little, then changed the subject, "What do you think Master Matik is planning?"

"I have no idea, but I am sure it will be grand."

# 35

The sunrise before Raef and Naan's wedding, Raef woke almost late for homage. He even skipped his ceremonial washing and meditation to arrive in time. When he walked to the front, Chaummer whispered to him.

"I told you to stay home," said Chaummer.

"I can't miss sunrise homage. That would feel too strange."

After homage Raef returned to his hut and removed his robe. He heard someone calling for him from the street. He opened the door to find Daz waiting.

"What is it, my apprentice?"

"My Master is not working, and I have nothing to do."

"How inconsiderate of your Master to not have given you something to do ahead of time."

"And what am I to do, then? I have work after mid-sun but nothing this sunrise."

"I do not know, my little imp. Come, come sit with me."

Daz entered Raef's hut and sat on the bench opposite Raef. Raef handed him a mug.

"I don't really like ale," said Daz, "I never even liked weak beer much as a youngling."

"You don't have to drink it," said Raef, "I am just being cordial."

Daz gazed out the window, looking toward the meadow. Raef followed his apprentice's eyes, watching the yellowing grass wave in the early summer breeze.

"That is where it happened," said Raef.

"Where what happened?"

"When I first met Rail."

"Out there in the meadow? This close to the village?"

"Yes, it is odd. I was very small, only six seasons, and was playing in the meadow, which my parents had strictly forbidden. And I saw something dark dive out of the sky at me. I ran from it, and the wind from its wings knocked me to the ground."

"I have never heard of such a thing," said Daz.

"I know. No one ever believed me. No one saw it. I still do not know why it came after me."

"Because it knew it would like you, probably."

"Well, all it did was frighten me."

They sat in silence, Raef recalling peering up over the grass and seeing the dark shadow in the distance glance back at him before shooting into the sky.

"Raef, I know it is not yet one quarter sun, but do you think the dragon will be in our meadow?"

"Daz, I cannot go out there now."

"Why not? You cannot see Naan, and you have no duties."

Raef sighed. His chest tightened as he recalled his recent mistakes as a Keeper, his impending wedding and worry that Naan would find him dull once she really got to know him. Raef put his mug down, walked to the door and opened it. Daz remained seated. Raef paused, squinting in the sunlight. He had been good a long time. He had followed every ritual of the Keepers for nearly a full cycle, including staying away from the beast. His chest relaxed. Yes, he did deserve to get away, just once, before he married.

They did not return until well after mid-sun. On the way back to Raef's hut they stopped by the Keep to tell the scribes Daz would not be assisting, then took their meal together at Raef's hut. They stayed up until well after dark, sharing stories about the dragon. Raef discovered Daz had been visiting Rail alone quite often and had stories of his own to tell. Raef returned Daz to the dormery after the other apprentices were asleep. The dormeress smiled, wishing Raef luck and fortune in his marriage.

Raef walked slowly down the dark streets to his hut. His chest began to tighten again, and now his stomach began to feel nauseous and clench in a hard knot. When he came to his hut he hurried inside, shut the door, sank to the floor and leaned back against it.

"What have I done? What have I become?"

He closed his eyes, imagining the Great Spirit looking down on him. It seemed right that he should cry, or at least shed a tear. He found he could not. He wearily removed his clothing and fell onto his mattress. He looked out his window to see the moonlight. The moon was dull and he could make out few stars. He wondered if there were clouds blocking them. It felt like Black Rock.

# 36

He did not know how he fell asleep, but sunrise came as a glaring light through his open window. He heard a familiar, older voice calling his name from the street. He searched the floor for a shirt and pulled it on, then peeked his head out the window. His father stood in the street, calling his name.

"A moment, Father," he called.

He scrambled for clothes and dressed. He stood and opened the door.

"Father, why are you here and why so early?"

"It is, perhaps not as early as you might think. Homage is over, but do not worry, no one expected you the sunrise of your wedding. I am here to take you to first meal. Allow me to share in your last meal as an unmarried man."

"Oh. Of course Father. That would be nice."

Raef joined his father and followed him into the village. His father did not turn toward his house, and Raef pulled up short.

"Are we not going to your house?" Raef asked.

"Your mother is tending to Naan and all the

preparations for the women. I have made arrangements at the tavern for breakfast."

"Oh," said Raef, "that does sound nice."

When they arrived at the tavern the proprietor was waiting outside for them. He opened the door and waved Raef and Folor inside.

"To Raef!" yelled a crowd of men in unison, lifting mugs of malt.

"Surprise, my son," said Folor from behind him, "all your friends are here."

The small room had four long wooden tables at which sat many familiar faces. Chaummer, Dimmel and Bremen, of course, but also his old apprentice mates, Xoh, Mijo and Denol, who he had seen only rarely since returning to Fir Hollow. The current intercessor apprentices, Daz among them, were there, as well as his oldest friend, Chaz, who looked a bit out of place as the only Warrior in the room.

"This I was not expecting," said Raef.

His father smiled and showed Raef to a seat next to Chaz. Folor sat across from Raef. Trays of food were brought out and put before them, meats and sugared breads usually reserved for last meal feasts. Chaz started to extend a hand to Raef, and Raef quickly reached out and slapped Chaz's palm. Chaz paused and looked at Raef, scrunching his eyebrows and cocking his head to one side.

"Oh," said Raef, pulling his hand back to his side, "sorry."

"What was that?" asked Chaz.

"Nothing, just…just being silly I guess."

Chaz shrugged and began to eat. Raef sighed and

looked at his father.

"Yes, this is a surprise," said Raef.

"It can be hard to surprise you," said Folor.

Raef looked at his food. He realized he should say something nice to his father, but he did not know what to say. He glanced at his father, who looked as uneasy as Raef felt.

"It was a good spring," said Folor, "Plenty of rain, and the clouds left just in time for the crops."

"I…I suppose," said Raef, "I do not know much about farming."

"I have done some farming," said Chaz.

"You?" said Raef.

"Yes, Warrior apprentices are taught basic farming. We must learn all we need to know to survive alone as Warriors, in case it is ever needed that we do so."

Raef looked questioningly at Chaz.

"Of course," said Chaz quickly, "I do not see a time coming when the Warriors would leave the village. It is just one of our old traditions."

"How is your father, Rodon?" asked Folor.

"My father is well, thank you Keeper Folor. A Warrior's life is hard, so we try to keep him from going out on many expeditions so he will last longer."

"He has been an excellent Prime," said Folor.

Folor turned back to face Raef. They smiled at each other and resumed eating. After a long first meal, Folor excused himself to return home and assist Malta. The other Keepers left as well, but Raef stayed with Chaz and visited until nearly mid-sun meal.

"I must go now," said Chaz.

Raef stood with Chaz.

"Of course. You will be needed in the Warrior sector."

"Not this sunset," said Chaz. "I must report to the Common Lodge. Master Matik is expecting me."

"Matik? Why would Matik want to see you?"

"Myself and many others. It is for your wedding."

"A Warrior in an Intercessor wedding?" asked Raef

Chaz only smiled, gripped Raef's forearm, then left. Raef shrugged, wondering what in all the Province Matik had planned, and left for the Keep. It was mid-sun, but he was not hungry after such a large first meal. When he arrived, he was surprised to see Keeper Dimmel and apprentice Daz waiting.

"You are finished with mid-sun meal already?" asked Raef.

"We did not require much after your party," said Dimmel. "Come, it is time to prepare you."

"Prepare me?"

"You have never seen a Keeper's wedding, have you?" asked Dimmel, "There are few of us, and you are the first of your generation to marry. There are special robes for such occasions and sacred clothing to wear under that."

"Wait till you see all of it!" said Daz, "Father showed me while we were waiting for you."

"Why have I not seen these sacred wedding clothes?" asked Raef.

"We have to keep a few surprises from our youngest Keeper," said Dimmel.

Prime Keeper Bremen arrived at the Keep and led them to a back room, one Raef had seen many times, and withdrew a large key from his robe. Raef watched

Bremen slide the key into a metal slot that he had always thought was part of the ornate decorations on the walls. Bremen turned the key and pulled open a plank wooden door, revealing a tiny room where ornate clothing hung as well as rolled parchments, a golden metal headpiece, and other ornaments that Raef could not even guess their purpose. Bremen began handing clothing to Daz.

"You can remove your clothing, all but your undergarments, and we shall prepare you," said Prime Keeper Bremen.

First were crimson hose that went over Raef's legs. Then trousers that only came half way down his legs, sort of billowy things that tied at the knee. The result were half-trousers that poofed out in what Raef considered ridiculous fashion. Then a linen shirt of pure white over which was placed a crimson tunic of stiff wool. On top of that Bremen placed a vest covered in blue beads that sparkled like a flowing river.

"I can scarcely bend over in all this," said Raef.

"You will not be required to," said Bremen, "Daz?"

Bremen handed Daz a pair of deer hide shoes with pointed toes and covered in flowery patterns of beads. Daz got to his knees and put them on Raef's feet, lacing up long leather straps halfway up his calves. The distinct scent of dragon wafted up from Daz and Raef looked around the room nervously. He hoped he was the only one who noticed, but he realized the other Keepers probably had never smelled the dragon before and did not know its scent.

Bremen and Dimmel took a very thick robe out of

the hidden room, and Raef held his arms out as they put it on him. It was blood red with vertical rows of darker beads running down it and a fluffy, cream-colored collar, its edges lined in gold. Raef felt twice his normal weight.

"I look like a jester," said Raef.

"You look like a king," said Dimmel.

Daz stifled a laugh.

They returned to the main meeting room of the Keep where Folor and Chaummer were waiting. An incense candle was burning and apprentices were present with fresh-cut fir branches held high. The Keepers circled Raef as the apprentices formed an outer circle and Bremen led an ancient chant Raef had never heard.

At three-quarter sun a messenger came to the Keep. The messenger whispered something to Daz who whispered something to Prime Bremen.

"It is time," said Keeper Bremen.

They took Raef, dressed in his finery, outside where it seemed every Intercessor in the village was waiting, all dressed in the finest clothing they owned. Prime Keeper Bremen took the lead, walking very slowly, followed by Raef, then Keepers Folor, Chaummer and Dimmel. The apprentices, including Daz, flanked the Keepers and all the other Intercessors followed behind, men first, then greenlings, women, greenlias and finally the younglings. In a normal wedding, Raef knew, the Intercessors would enter the Ceremonial Lodge where the wedding would be held. Only Intercessors would attend. Instead, Bremen led the Intercessors to the village square.

When they reached the village square Raef saw three of its four sides were lined with villagers. On the east boundary were the Merchants, to the west the Laborers and on the south the Warriors, wearing ceremonial feathered headdresses, leather chest pieces, beaded belts and animal fur kilts. Standing in the center of the line of Laborers was Naan, dressed in an emerald dress and a headpiece of tiny white flowers. In the center of the square was a circle made up of the village Nobles, the Prime Noble standing in the front. The Intercessors lined up along the northern boundary of the square as Prime Bremen led the Keepers and Raef to the middle of the square. In the very center of the square, on a tall circular pedestal, stood Master Matik, dressed in a smoky gown that flowed down past the pedestal and onto the ground.

Matik raised her thin arms and held them up dramatically. Six Warriors in full dress and painted faces marched from their ranks to six large clay pots stationed at the four corners of the square and at the midpoint of the longer, east and west sides. The Warriors carried torches of fire. The Warriors dipped their torches in the pots and fire erupted from each, only the fire burned green like tongues of grass. Raef heard murmurs from all around him. Matik lowered her arms and looked to the Keepers. Prime Keeper Bremen and Raef's father led Raef to the center pedestal. The Nobles parted, and Raef climbed a set of stairs to stand next to Matik on the pedestal. Then Matik turned east to where Naan stood beside her mother. Yamrah and another woman Raef did not know led Naan to the pedestal, where she ascended the stairs to stand next to Raef. Her eyes were dazzling, Raef thought.

The lilting tune of flutes and harps began to play the lines of a traditional wedding melody, and Raef turned to see the same minstrels Matik had hired for their meal in the inn. The familiar strain filled the air. Then from nowhere came a resonating blast that sounded almost like the dragon's growl. Raef glanced around, but saw no one playing an instrument capable of making such a sound. The stringed instruments began to play slower, more dissonant notes. A rumble came from the direction of the black smith shop on the west edge of the square. It sounded to Raef like a very large drum, though he had never heard anything so deep or loud from a drum. More rumbling came and more growling horns blew, hidden somewhere behind the Common Lodge, it sounded like. Then the six Warriors each tossed a small sack into the firepots sending dazzling sparks into the sky. Raef and Naan turned wide-eyed to Matik.

"Flash powder," whispered Matik.

Four drummers emerged from the smithery, each with a barrel-sized drum strapped to their chest, playing a slow beat as they walked to the center of the square. From behind the Common Lodge six trumpeters emerged playing long brass horns while behind them came four men carrying the longest wooden horn Raef had ever seen. When they all reached the center of the square one of the four men carrying the long horn stepped back to the mouth piece and blew a resonating blast that seemed to rattle the air. Then the Warriors threw another bag into each pot and another shower of sparks shot into the air with a bang. Then there was silence. The entire village looked around at one another, as if to determine what had just happened. Raef and Naan smiled at each other and then at Matik. Raef knew this was unlike any wedding ceremony ever witnessed in the Great Province.

"Villagers of Fir Hollow!" said Matik, pausing dramatically before continuing, "I give you, The Wedding."

One of the Warriors in ceremonial garb approached the platform and Raef finally recognized him as Chaz. Raef smiled; he had not recognized his friend under all the face paint. Prime Rodon also approached from the line of Warriors. The Nobles around the platform walked off to the side, leaving only the Prime Noble and his wife. The Guild Prime of the labor sector and his wife approached, as did the Prime Reever and Second Reever of the labor sector. Prime Keeper Bremen and Folor were already at the center to represent the Intercessors, but Raef's mother, Malta, approached now, standing next to Raef's father. Raef was astonished to see all five Primes of Fir Hollow taking part in the ceremony.

The five Primes walked up the stairs onto the platform and faced the village. Matik stepped down and stood by Yamrah.

"One Intercessor who journeyed alone," said Prime Bremen.

"One Artisan who will leave her home," said the

Prime Reever.

"One man who will lead us all," said Prime Rodon.

"One woman will herald the call," said the Guild Prime.

"One marriage unites us as one," said the Prime Noble.

Keeper Bremen stepped behind Raef and Naan, took each one's hand and held them up. Raef closed his fingers over Naan's smaller hand as Bremen chanted ancient words over them. Bremen then wrapped a silver cord around their joined hands and stepped away. Then Prime Rodon stepped behind them, held his hand high over their heads and began to chant in a language Raef had never heard, in a near shouting voice. When he stopped, the Warriors let out a cheer. Rodon stepped back.

The Prime Noble stepped in front of the pair and held their clasped hands high.

"Village of Fir Hollow," called the Prime Noble, "As Prime Noble of this village, with the authority granted me by the Council of Overseers, I declare Raef, Keeper of the Intercessors, and Naan, Artisan to the Province, man and wife, eternally wed in the customs and traditions of the Great Province."

Many of the villagers startled as the six brass horn players let out a blast, then six women in grass-colored dresses emerged from the crowd and began dancing in the middle of the square. Raef tried to discern who they were, but they moved too fast. The six Warriors in ceremonial garb joined the women in festive dance. It was not a wedding dance, as far as Raef could tell. Matik re-emerged, taking Raef and

Naan by there joined hands, and pulled them down the steps and out to the very center of the square.

"Well," said Naan, "I see we are going to dance now!"

"I do not know how to dance," said Raef.

"There is nothing to know," said Naan, "just move with me."

Raef began to spin and dip in slow circles as the minstrels began to play. Soon it seemed the entire village had joined them, dancing around the square. Raef even saw Keeper Bremen dancing with his wife. As the sun grew low villagers left a few at a time, but returned with food prepared in their homes. Raef's mother beckoned them to sit with she and Folor and Yamrah, who had set a cloth on the ground with food. The minstrels never allowed the music to stop.

It was nearly dusk when the celebrating ended and most families had gone home. An unusually cold wind hit the village as Dimmel and Daz brought a cart from the Intercessor stable.

"This is for you to use," said Raef's old mentor, "A wedding gift from the Intercessor clan."

"That is so kind," said Naan.

Dimmel and Daz bowed and left. Dark clouds began to gather over the village.

"What an unusually strong wind," said Naan.

"A summer storm," said Raef, "Unusual for Fir Hollw."

They mounted the cart as the wind continued to grow. Raef turned the cart west, driving slowly through each street and passing each home. Families waved from the windows. As they crossed back over the stream to the east side, Raef steered the cart south.

"Where are you going?" asked Naan.

"The Warriors came to our wedding. I wanted to pass through their sector as well."

The wind began to howl, and Raef could see the trees that lined the village dipping low in the darkening sky. It began to rain.

"We are going to get wet!" said Naan.

Raef snapped the reigns, and the single horse moved a bit faster. The windows of the long Warrior homes were shuttered. Raef drove the horse on the southernmost road in Fir Hollow, one side of the road lined with homes, the other only with trees.

"At least the wedding celebration went well," she said.

Raef looked at her. She was smiling as drops of water hit her face. Suddenly a gale dropped down on them and the rain became a downpour.

"This is quite wild!" said Naan.

"You seem to like it," said Raef.

"Of course!"

A blinding light and ferocious boom shook their cart, frightening the horse almost past Raef's ability to control it.

"That sounded really close!" said Raef.

He flicked the reigns, and the horse began to trot. Then the sky exploded with light, blinding Raef, as thunder shook the air. The horse reared up and nearly upset the cart. The flash ended in an instant followed by the deep cracking sounds of splitting trees. Raef could see nothing in the dark after the flash. Naan let out a scream as the sound of colliding trunks surrounded them and the ground began to shake.

"Trees!" said Raef, "Trees are falling on us!"

He held the horse still as the air rushed around them and the ground shook. The cart bumped, and Raef heard wood splintering.

"We were hit!" he said.

Crashing continued all around as branches whistled past his face in the dark. Raef let go of the reigns and held on to Naan. The noise subsided and the rain mysteriously let up.

"Are you all right?" Raef asked Naan.

"Yes, nothing touched me."

The wind and rain slowly died down and all grew quiet. A yellow glow came from the forest, and Raef looked to see the shattered stump of a tree burning just a few spans away. Raef and Naan stood up in their cart, surveying the damage in the glow of the small fire. The horse snorted and pawed the ground, unharmed and surprisingly calm. They were surrounded by the shattered trunks and broken bows of ancient trees.

"Let me see how bad it is," said Raef, "We may have to walk."

He got out of the cart, his legs brushing thick fir branches. The scent of sap filled the air. Just ahead of the horse only shards remained of what had been an ancient fir. Above the back of the cart three trunks had collided and wedged themselves to a stop only a fraction above Naan's head. The entire cart was essentially circled in fallen trees, any of which would have smashed the cart to bits had it hit. Raef carefully inspected the cart itself, but there was no sign of damage or trace of a scratch from even a falling branch.

"The cart was not hit," said Raef.

"Are you certain? I felt the cart bump and heard wood splinter."

"I felt it too. But, Naan, there is nothing. No damage at all."

"Is the cart stuck here?" asked Naan.

"I think I can clear the tree in front of us. It was smashed to bits."

Raef tossed aside the splintered remains of the log in front of them and returned to his seat in the cart. He gently shook the reigns, and the horse carefully started off again.

"How in all the Province did we survive unharmed?" asked Raef.

"It does seem quite unreal."

"Those trees came down right on top of us."

"But they stopped just before they hit us," said Naan.

"Do you think it could mean anything?" asked Raef.

"I was wondering the same."

They rode in silence down the path, making their way back north to the Intercessor sector.

"Perhaps I am making too much of it," said Raef, "but it almost feels like a sign from the Great Spirit."

"What kind of sign?"

"Well, he did not allow us to be harmed," said Raef, trying to think what it could mean.

Then Raef felt a rare moment of clarity. Words

came to him that he was quite certain had not come from his own thoughts.

"Zul, the Great Spirit, approves of our union," said Raef.

He listened to the words that had come from his lips. They surprised him.

"Zul protected us from harm," Raef continued, "He will do so again in the future. He will not allow anything to come between us."

"You know this?" asked Naan.

"Yes, somehow I am quite certain of it."

Naan was quiet for several moments.

"It is a bit unsettling to think we will need protection again," said Naan.

"I was thinking the same."

"Still, it is a good sign, not a bad one. Overall, that is."

"Yes," said Raef, "it is good to know we are worth protecting."

Raef put his arm around his new wife as they rode slowly through the dark streets. He felt lightness in his chest he had not felt since he was very young.

# PART SIX

## UNRAVELING

# 37

"Was that really you who stopped the trees from hitting them?" Erif asked the spirit beside him.

"Yes."

Erif diverted his gaze from the water to his feet.

"Was that really a sign?" asked Erif, "Are you really protecting them?"

"Yes, Erif."

Zul moved closer and put a hand on Erif's shoulder.

"Is that so hard to believe?" asked the spirit.

"But, why? He has betrayed you since he was a youngling."

"He does not yet see as clearly as you."

"How is that an excuse? This is not just some villager who has lost his way. He claims to be a Keeper, yet he befriended your enemy, the enemy of us all. He has caused who knows how many people to become ensnared by the dragon. Those devoted to you are following him to ruin! And now he has married this wonderful woman. She does not deserve what will happen to her. She is now married to this, this Dragon Child."

Erif walked a few steps away and began pacing in the sand.

"What is harder for you to accept, Erif, that Raef has done so much evil, or that I continue to pursue him?"

Erif turned shadowed eyes toward Zul, "Why do you pursue him?"

"It is because I love him."

A tear formed in Erif's eye, "Why?"

"Because, as a youngling he asked me to take him. To take him as a father takes a son. And down inside, under all he has done, he still wants to be my son. I will not abandon him."

"You should have abandoned him, Zul, seasons ago."

"He is my son, Erif. I will not."

Erif slowly sank to his knees and began to weep.

Naan was expecting. Raef grinned to himself as he kissed her goodbye so he could get to the sunrise homage before the chanting began. When the few deciduous trees in the forest had begun to glow the colors of the sunset, Naan had told him they would be having a child. It was a strange thought for Raef, being a father, but he was happy. He had reached his twentieth season over the summer and now his second season as a Keeper. He knew he had entered the seasons of a man back in Black Rock, but it was only now that he finally began to feel a little as if he actually were a man. Raef walked to the Ceremonial Lodge through the hard streets dusted in snow.

Raef smiled at Daz as he and the other apprentices held fir branches high for him to walk under. The other Keepers nodded as Raef made his way to the front. He glanced at them and smiled, walking to the front to stand with them. Sunrise homage was the same as always with the male villagers, all those who were greenlings and older, passing in front as Bremen blessed them. As always the Keepers left after the villagers had gone, the apprentices entered to store the fir branches and put out fires and incense. Daz locked the door and followed Raef to the Keep, where Raef hung the key on its hook.

Raef then led his apprentice toward the Healing Lodge to check on one of the villagers of their sector.

"Will we be finished by one-quarter sun?" asked Daz.

Raef looked around to be sure no one was in hearing distance.

"You are spending an awful lot of time with our old friend," said Raef.

"So do you!"

"Not since I was married, Daz."

"It makes no difference; you did all the time before."

Raef remained silent as they continued on to the Healing Lodge.

"Well?" asked Daz.

"We shall see," said Raef.

They visited the sick woman in the Healing Lodge and then did their rounds in the West End. Raef released Daz at one-quarter sun as the greenling was nearly coming out of his skin wanting to go to the forest. Raef watched the greenling dart into the trees and he recalled his own earlier seasons doing the same. Raef shook his head and returned to the Keep.

In the Keep he went to the back rooms where ancient scrolls were kept. He had become sloppy in his mentoring and decided he needed to search the scrolls for things he had yet to teach his apprentice. He came across a very dusty scroll he was sure he had never read. He opened it and in it found drawings of the dragon along with old stories of it. At first he rolled it shut, fearing he would be caught looking at something forbidden. Then he remembered these were scrolls for the Keepers, and he was a Keeper. He cautiously opened it again, still feeling a bit guilty.

The scroll said very little about the dragon and even less that was accurate. He read mostly warnings and tales of it attacking villages and killing villagers, none of which Raef believed ever happened. He found himself remembering his seasons at Black Rock, lying out care free on the basin floor, exploring endless caves full of gems, and feeling water beat down on his head as he swam under the waterfall at the north rim. He closed the scroll and sat back on one of the benches in the room, closing his eyes and remembering what it felt like to ride the dragon's back as it did loops over the Great Basin. There was nothing in Fir Hollow like that.

"Where in all the Province have you been?" asked

Naan as he entered his hut.

"I was studying in the Keep."

"It is long past mid-sun, and your meal is now cold."

"I am sorry; I was preoccupied."

"With studies? That can wait. I was beginning to worry that something had happened to you."

"I am sorry, Naan. A Keeper's duties can be very taxing."

She eyed him, and he could not tell if she was angry or being playful. He sat and ate, deciding not to try to find out.

# 38

As winter closed over Fir Hollow it became obvious Naan was expecting. Village women began to dote on her whenever Raef and she went anywhere. Raef mused at the unusual amount of attention Naan and the unborn baby drew. It was as if the village expected the baby to be something unusual or special.

Reaf's duties were not going so well, however. He began having difficulty concentrating and frequently forgot things he was supposed to do, which was very unlike him. It was a struggle to remember chants. He forgot who was sick and needed visiting in the West End. He would find himself entering one of the Intercessor lodges and forget why he had come. He was embarrassed when he was asked what he had come for and he had no response.

On one such occurence he found himself entering the Intercessor kitchen then immediatetly wondering why he had come. He noticed Nilo carving a deer carcass and decided to strike up a conversation, as if that had been his purpose all along.

"Nilo," said Raef, "good to see you again. You

must be nearing greenling's end."

Nilo looked up at him and paused, wiping his knife on his trouser leg and putting it aside. He did not smile.

"Greetings, Keeper."

"Nilo, it's me, your old friend. You have no need to address me so formally."

"As you wish," he said, "Yes, you are correct, I will reach my sixteenth seasons come spring."

"I will be sure to attend your ceremony."

Nilo shrugged as he picked up his knife and carved a strip of venison. Raef watched and waited, but when Nilo did not continue the conversation he left to visit the Healing Lodge.

Raef was careful to keep an eye on the sun and return home before sunset for last meal. He did not want Naan to be upset at him for arriving home late. He found her sitting on a stool in the center of the single roomed hut, painting on a large canvas set upon an easel.

"Oh, Raef, you are home already."

"It is nearly sunset."

"Oh, my, and I have not begun last meal."

Naan stood up and began to collect her supplies.

"Here," said Raef, "I will move your things to the wall for you."

"Thank you, Raef. It is so hard trying to paint and keep the hut clean and the cooking going. I get lost in my work and lose track of time."

"See, you as well as I do that."

Naan hastily hung a pot of water over the central fire. She pulled some potatoes from a sack and began to dice them on the table. Raef tried to fold up the easel so it would take less room against the wall. Even when folded it left very little room to walk between it and the table.

"This hut is so small, Raef," said Naan. "I wish we could have someplace larger. And we will have a youngling running around soon."

"Naan, I am the youngest Keeper. The others have larger families. There is no money for us to have a larger home built, and I don't have the skills to cut timbers to build a proper home myself."

"Your father no longer has a family at home. Neither does Bremen. Why can't some money be spared from your precious coffers so we do not have raise a youngling in this barn?"

"Naan, listen to you. Since when were you concerned about wealth? We are doing fine as we are."

Naan threw the diced potatoes into the stew, pulled dried meat from another sack, and began chopping it.

"I scarcely have room to paint in here. That is how I earn for our family, Raef. I have a commission from Pine Creek, but it will never be finished the painting on time if I have no room to work."

"Then work in the square or something."

Naan stopped cutting, put her palms down on the table and hung her head.

"Raef, I am sorry. I am only frustrated. I am worried I will not finish in time, or that the Pine Creek Nobles will not like it."

Raef came to her and put his arms around her.

"Naan, it is okay. We will be fine. You are an Artisan, trained by the greatest of masters. You have nothing to fear."

She leaned her head to his chest, but then stood up again, wiping a tear from her eye.

"Thank you, husband. I will have this ready in moments. Have some ale and rest."

Raef tried to help her, but she would not allow it. He sighed, hung his robe on the wall, poured a mug of malt, and sat on the bench nearest the window. The sun was setting earlier. Winter was here. Raef did not like winter. Out over the meadow he could imagine the image of Rail, flying away to Black Rock, just as he had seen it thirteen seasons past. He felt his eyes drooping shut and his mind filled with memories.

"Raef!"

Raef's eyes popped open. It was nearly dark outside.

"Raef, I have been calling your name over and over. Come eat, the meal is ready."

"Oh, sorry, I was just…thinking, that's all."

"Well, come think over hear so you can eat as well."

Raef moved the bench over to the table as Naan spooned potage on two trenchers. He dipped his knife in the pot to wet it, then dipped it into the salt cellar and wiped it over the pottage in front of him.

"I was trying to talk to you as I was cooking," said Naan, "but you never answered."

"I apologize, my love."

"I just wanted to tell you what happened when I ran into your sister at the square this sunrise."

"Certainly," said Raef.

He tried to listen, but found his mind drifting off

to other things. He smiled to at least appear more interested. When Naan was done with her story, Raef found he could not remember what she had said. He quickly changed the subject so she would not know.

It was difficult getting to sleep that night even though he was tired. When Naan fell asleep he got up and sat by the window, looking out over the meadow. It did not help him sleep but comforted him somehow.

# 39

Next sunrise Raef woke feeling groggy and unfocused. During homage he found himself not chanting, but staring vacantly ahead as visions of the dragon danced before him. After homage Keeper Chaummer and Daz accompanied him to assist with carrying blankets to three families on the West End. Upon returning Raef paced back and forth in the Keep, not wanting to complete his rounds. He could delay them, he decided, but he was uncertain what to do with himself until then. He paced frantically back and forth, his mind a clutter of images. A distant memory flashed of a small youngling flying through the air, end over end, as high as the treetops, then caught gracefully on Rail's soft head. The dragon lowered its head, and the youngling rolled to the ground, ending on his back in the grass.

"That was amazing!" said the youngling in Raef's memory.

Raef paused, then darted out the door and to the kitchen. Nilo was there, pulling things from a shelf to prepare something. No one else was in the building.

"Nilo," said Raef, "how are you this sunrise."

"I am well."

"Do you think the kitchen could spare you for a bit this sunrise? I thought you might accompany me on a short trip."

"A trip? Where are you going?"

"I was just recalling a place we used to visit, seasons ago. A place you used to think was amazing."

Nilo diverted his gaze from Raef to the opposite wall.

"I do not want to go back there."

Raef took a step closer, standing over the greenling.

"Nilo, I can smell it on you. I know you have been not long ago."

Nilo's face tightened, and he looked at the floor.

"Not with you. You are a Keeper. I can't."

"Who do you go with? Do you go alone? Is it still at the same meadow we used to visit?"

Nilo was silent a long time, looking at the floor.

"I go with Nomo, a young scribe," he finally replied.

"I know of him."

Then Nilo sighed and moved to sit on a tall stool. His stance relaxed as he sighed and looked up at Raef.

"I do not want to go anymore, but I cannot stop myself, Raef. I tell myself each sunrise I am done with it, with…that thing. We are released from the dormery after mid-sun meal, but I am not required to report to the kitchen for some time. That's when I go. Almost every sun, I go almost every sun."

Nilo looked at the ground, looking deflated and

ashamed.

"I know, Nilo. I know how it is to try to stay away but find we cannot."

"It is not only Nomo. A lot of the apprentices, not all, but many have gone with me. And Sena, a greenlia, she comes with me sometimes."

"Does it possess your thoughts?"

"Yes, some suns it is difficult to think of anything else."

"It is the same with me."

"Raef," said Nilo, "There is something else, something I feel even greater shame over. I took a youngling. He was with only nine seasons. He was playing at the forest edge after mid-sun when I was on my way to see Rail. I cannot believe I did such a thing."

"You had only eight seasons when I first took you to meet Rail."

"I remember."

"I had only six,"

Another kitchener entered the room. Nilo stood and resumed his work.

"I will not bother you with this again, Nilo," said Raef.

"Who is it?" asked Nilo as Raef was leaving.

"Who is who?"

"It is your apprentice, is it not? That is who you go with now."

The other kitchener gave them a puzzled look, then turned away to work.

"Blessings on your final greenling season," said Raef.

"And to you, Keeper," said Nilo.

Raef hurried through his rounds in the West End and then returned to the Keep. His conversation with Nilo replayed in his mind. He felt a saddness over what he planned to do next but it was if something had over taken him that he could not control.

Daz returned from assisting Keeper Chaummer just before one-quarter sun. Raef was waiting outside the Keep, his red robe already folded and stored inside. Daz stopped, smiled, and pulled his robe off before following Raef into the forest.

They stayed with the dragon until past mid-sun causing both to miss mid-sun meal. Raef had difficulty convincing Naan he had been unexpectedly called away. Daz told Raef that sunset he had received a beating from the dormeress for missing a meal.

Raef realized the eloborate deceptions he used to keep his two worlds separate were unraveling. It frightened him terribly to think what would happen if his two worlds met. It was too painful to consider the consequences so he vowed to himself to try harder to prevent his time with Rail from being discovered. The next sun he and Daz were careful to return to the village before mid-sun meal.

# 40

The snow formed a blanket over the village as winter solstice approached. Raef and the other Keepers became busy with preparations for the ceremony of Season's End. Much seasoned wood was needed for the ceremonial bonfire. The Laborers finished storing the last of the crops and salting meat to dry, so the Prime Reever sent them to assist the Intercessors collecting wood. Raef was tasked with overseeing wood collection while the other Keepers oversaw other details, such as the making of evergreen and cinnamon scented candles. The entire Intercessor sector was busy making preparations, and Raef found no time to sneak away.

On sunrise after homage Raef led Daz to the Keep, took the key from his apprentice, hung the key on the wall and dismissed Daz. Raef watched the greenling run to follow Keeper Chaummer then began to walk out himself to attend to the Laborers he was charged with overseeing during wood collection.

"Keeper Raef," said Bremen, just as Raef started to

step out the door.

Raef stopped walking and tilted his head back, "What now?"

Keeper Bremen paused and cocked his head.

"That is a disrespectful manner in which to greet one's Prime."

Raef lowered his head and pinched the bridge of his nose between a thumb and finger.

"My apologies, Prime Bremen. I have been feeling a bit overwhelmed."

"As are we all," said Bremen, "but we lead the Intercessors, even the entire village, during these ceremonies. We must be vigilant to do so with proper dignity."

"You are correct, as always, Prime Bremen."

"You need not call me 'Prime' here inside the Keep, young Raef. We are friends, after all. Let us simply remember to speak kindly to one another."

"Your forgiveness, Bremen. I am feeling sapped, and it is still early."

"I was wondering, my friend, if you might be so gracious as to lead the final chant of Season's End bonfire."

"Me? But the final chant is the most important chant of the ceremony. Should you not lead it?"

"There are no strict traditions as to which Keeper leads the chants of Season's End. The bonfire is but one event, albeit the final one, in the ceremony. I have plenty to lead. You should continue to take your place as a leader in Fir Hollow."

"Of course, Keeper Bremen. I am honored."

Raef smiled to himself. This was an unexpected

honor. He bowed gently and left to tell Naan the news. It would surprise her to visit so early.

"Naan!" said Raef as he entered the hut, "you will be surprised to hear what I have been asked to do."

Naan was nearly finished with her painting for Pine Creek. Her palates of pigment were spread all over the floor. She made a long stroke with her brush and did not look up as she responded.

"Yes?"

"Keeper Bremen has asked me to lead the final chant of Season's End!"

"That is nice, Raef. I am sure you will do marvelously."

She did not look up but made another long, slow stroke, then leaned back and peered at her work.

"What do you think?" she asked.

"But, what about my chant?"

"I said it was nice. How do you like it? I think it is nearly finished."

"Naan, I am trying to tell you...never mind."

Raef paused, waiting for Naan to look up at him, but she took another brush, this one with an earthy color, and ran it across the canvas. Raef stepped back outside. The sun was still just above the treetops. He sighed and began walking toward the square. Once there he found a seat on a stone bench, one that had a back rest, and rested. He leaned back and closed his eyes, letting the pale sun warm his face.

He remembered lying flat on his back in the Great Basin. He could sleep until nearly mid-sun, right out on the basin floor if he wanted. No one would bother him. Then Rail would come with food. The food was perhaps not as good there, he had to admit, but sometimes he could catch a quick ride on the dragon before it left again.

Flying through the air was something he truly missed. Flying made him remember a trick he learned at Black Rock. He would crawl into the dragon's mouth, it would coil its neck back, then thrust forward and spit Raef high into the sky, farther than anyone else ever flew. Only a few Dragon Children were ever able to repeat that trick. The recollection caused him to smile, recalling his fear of getting into Rail's mouth as a youngling. The dragaon's mouth had seemed so foul to Raef when he was younger. He wondered why it no longer did. Daz had surprised him a few suns past when he stepped into Rail's mouth to show Raef he was not afraid. The greenling was truly surprising.

A chill brought him out of his daze. He sat up as a second cold breeze brushed his face. Raef looked up, seeing the sun, now at mid-sky, pass behind a cloud. He leapt off the bench and hurried back to his hut.

"Where have you been?" asked Naan as he entered.

Raef saw that mid-sun meal had already been set on the table.

"Just resting out in the square," he said.

"You are late," she said, slapping him playfully.

After the meal Raef rested by the window, drinking hot tea and looking out over the meadow. A fog had settled down over the meadow, and Raef watched the vapors glide above the dead grass.

He knew he could rest a bit. The other Keepers would take a longer meal as well, to rest. They always did in winter. His life was good now, he decided. He inhaled the fragrant tea vapors as he watched the fog flow over the meadow. Naan was saying something, but he had not quite heard. He wondered what it would be like to ride Rail through fog. It would be thrilling, Raef decided.

"Raef!" called Naan.

"Oh, sorry, what was it?"

"Raef, I am right here talking to you and you are not listening."

"I said I was sorry. What is it?"

"I was asking when the ceremony will be."

"What do you mean? The end of the moon cycle, as always."

"Sorry, I was not sure if solstice was exactly that sunset or not. I am an Artisan, remember, and am not accustomed to paying attention to all the details of the ceremonies."

He tried to imagine again flying through low fog on the dragon's back. Naan was saying something again, interrupting his thoughts.

"What!" he said.

"I am just asking questions, Raef, you do not need to be angry."

He sighed, "I am not angry."

"I was just asking who else knows you are leading the final chant."

"Oh, I didn't know you had listened when I told you that."

"Of course I listened to you. I am your wife, after all."

"You are the only one I have told."

"But Keeper Bremen knows, right?"

"Of course Keeper Bremen knows. He is the Prime. He is the one who asked me to do the chant."

Naan became quiet and walked back to the table and removed the cloth from it. Raef drank some tea and sat back, closing his eyes. Yes, it would be fun to ride the great dragon in a fog. Especially a dense fog. He had never done that before. He could imagine the mist swirling around Rail's wings as they gracefully stroked the air. It might be a bit wet, however. Dense fog could make a man wet, and flying through it might get him more so.

"Well, I think it is a fine idea," said Naan.

Raef sat up with a jolt. Naan was now sitting next to him, looking out the window. She held a cup of tea. Raef groaned internally.

"Can I tell my women friends?"

"About what?" said Raef.

"About you leading the final chant. Raef, are you even listening to me at all?"

Raef let out a long sigh.

"Sorry, I guess I am just tired. We have been quite overwhelmed."

"You seem really distracted. Are you sure everything is okay?"

"Yes, I am sure. I am only tired."

"Well, all right, but I am a little worried about you."

"I am fine, I promise."

Raef tried to act patient and wait for Naan to finish her tea, talking to her now and then. When he saw that she was finished, he took their mugs to the table and rinsed them out in the basin of wash water. He was relieved that Naan began getting out her brushes again and sat before her canvas. Raef looked out the window at the sun. He had a bit more time. He closed his eyes and rejoined his flight with the dragon.

# 41

Winter arrived and with it the Season's End Ceremony. This was one of few ceremonies that entire families attended. Each family brought something that had come from the fields, but was now dry and useless. A crackly corn husk, a trencher so old it was as rock, a few old stalks of wheat, a bit of cowhide, or a vegetable turning to dust.

Families had put them aside to save for the celebration at least a moon cycle past, so they would appear sufficiently old. Prime Keeper Bremen chanted Crops End as families brought their aged fare to the front of the Ceremonial Lodge and deposited them on a large soiled cloth on the floor. Often the smallest youngling of a family was allowed to drop the family token onto the small heap.

Apprentices lit the winter candles once all the tokens had been deposited. The lodge filled with an aroma of fir. Fir trees were one of the only plants still alive to scent candles with this time of the season. Bremen led more chanting until the sun finally set. The villagers then moved to the square, where select

Laborers had already started a bonfire. Intercessor apprentices carried the four corners of the old cloth, full of decaying offerings, in front of the procession.

Once the village had circled the fire, the corners of the cloth were closed and tied. It was given to the Prime Reever who tossed it onto the bonfire. The village sang an ancient song of endings, then Bremen lead a chant for the end of crops and then another chant for the end of labor.

Finally, as the bonfire licked the inky sky, Raef walked proudly to his place in front and called out the ancient chant of winter sleep and rest. The village joined him in the final stanza.

Naan came to Raef's side afterwards and they watched the fire together. Families slowly drifted away to return to their beds. Thus marked the end of labor in the fields for another season. Raef was happy it had gone flawlessly. Many Laborers would be allowed to rest for half a moon cycle starting the following sunrise. Raef decided that this part of winter was perhaps not so bad.

Winter deepened, slowly spreading its frosty carpet across the village. Even the green bows of the fir trees were covered in white and hung low with the weight. As the air chillded the muddy roads of fall froze and became solid to walk on. Puddles became like glass and window shutters on the huts were seldom open. Villagers walked about covered in layers of clothing, their faces so obscured by scarves that it was difficult to tell who was who.

Raef found that sleeping was easier this winter, as Naan was always next to him to warm him. She had completed her painting for Pine Creek it had been well received. The Nobles of Pine Creek had paid her more than the commissioned wage. She had begun to work on additional, smaller paintings, which took up less room in the hut. Naan told Raef she hoped to sell them in the markets in spring.

Spring arrived, thawing the remains of winter's death and the Laborers began to plow the fields as rain muddied the streets. Daz reached his fourteenth season, despite the fact he still had the appearance and stature of a youngling. Raef and Naan were among those who commemorated the arrival of Daz's fourteenth season at one of the taverns.

Naan became large with child and the village midwife began stopping by their hut each sunset to check on her. Irah, who had rarely visited since Raef's return to Fir Hollow, began to visit Naan frequently, as did Malta and Yamra, shooing Raef out of his own hut on sunsets they wished to visit. Raef found himself visiting taverns to share a mug of ale with the scribes and apothecaries of the Intercessor sector, something he had never done prior. They seemed to appreciate a Keeper choosing to pass a sunset with them.

# 42

As the moon cycle of expected birth arrived, Raef began to stop by his hut numerous times each sunrise and sunset to check on Naan. Her feet began to swell when she stood long periods, and Raef massaged them for her. He began preparing meals when she was tired. He brought her daisies from the field and helped her stand when she got up from a bench or stool.

Early in the final moon cycle of spring, Raef lay next to Naan on their bed, staring upward in the dark. He could scarcely make out the ceiling as Naan had asked him to shutter the window because she felt cold. It was spring and he did not think it was too cold. He preferred to see the moonlight filtering but he did not tell this to his wife. Naan rolled toward him, her protruding stomach nudging his side.

"Oh, sorry," said Naan.

"You are still awake?"

"Yes, it is so hard to sleep with a round stomach like this. No matter which way I lay I soon become uncomfortable."

"Is there anything I can do?"

"Oh, no, no. You have been so good to me these moon cycles I have been with our baby."

Raef placed a hand on her stomach. He felt something push back against his palm quite strongly.

"I cannot sleep either," said Raef. "Excited about the baby, I suppose."

"What shall we name it?" she asked.

"I do not know. Names are such tricky things."

"I do not like my name at all."

"You dislike 'Naan?' I think it is a lovely name."

"My parents were certain I was to be a male. They had no names for females selected. The midwife named me."

"You never told me."

"A trivial detail. She was apparently an old woman. Naan is such an old name, not one used any longer."

"I cannot think of any name I really like either," said Raef. "And it is hard to have two names, one for a male and one for a female. What do we do with that? Do we save the unused name for a future child?"

"Then let us break with tradition and call our child something completely different. Something not used for naming. Something we could use if it is male or female."

"Do you want to curse the poor thing?" asked Raef, "Our little one would be mocked starting the sun it was born."

"First, stop referring to our child as 'it' and second, you should welcome breaking tradition. Come, Raef. I am an Artisan and you are a very unusual Keeper. Fir Hollow will be disappointed if we do not follow our most uncommon wedding with a uniquely named child."

"Well, how about rather than a name, we call our child by a number."

"A number? That would certainly be different. What number?"

"We will give it a number when we see it. A number fit for it."

Raef felt her hug him. He hugged her back best he could with her stomach in the way. She stopped talking and soon began to snore quietly. He closed his eyes to sleep but rest did not come.

Summer solstice celebration was next moon cycle, and he was hoping he could lead part of it. He wondered what he could do to show Bremen he was capable. He needed to name his baby. Numbers began to run through his head as he tested them in his mind to see which had the potential for naming a child. He had no experience with infants at all and wondered if he would have patience with it. And he had to remember not to call his baby 'it.'

An uncomfortable feeling began to grow in his chest. There were so many things to worry about. The feeling grew until Raef felt as if he might panic.

A shadow crossed his mind as a memory returned. He recalled standing somewhere, some place calm. His body instantly relaxed and the anxiety left his chest. In his memory Raef looked up and saw a shadow passing over him. It was a dragon with wings the span of a fir tree and a tail longer still. Under his feet he remembered feeling smooth, damp rock. In his mind he looked down and saw he wore no shirt and his chest and stomach were covered with inky grime. He inspected his palms and found hem soiled as well. He felt himself smile. It didn't matter here. Nothing mattered here.

# 43

The following sunrise Raef and Daz were in the West End bringing a remedy from the Healing Lodge to an ill woman. The Healers could have brought it, but Raef wanted a more personal touch and Daz was interested in the healing arts and herbal remedies. Daz had even mixed the remedy, under close supervision of the Apothecary. They entered the small home, and Daz held a folded linen toward Raef.

"Why are you handing it to me?" asked Raef, "You know how to administer it."

Daz smiled and began unwrapping the linen as a greenlia of the family brought a mug of hot tea.

"Keeper Raef!" someone called from the street.

"I will see who it is," said the greenlia, after handing Daz the mug of tea.

Raef watched Daz sprinkle three pinches of the dried herbs into the tea.

"Keeper Raef," said the greenlia, "it is almoness Irah, your sister, here to fetch you. She says it is urgent."

Raef stepped away as Daz held the mug to the ill

woman's lips. His sister, Irah, was in the street, bouncing up and down.

"Raef, Raef!" said Irah, "the baby is being born right now!"

Raef felt his practiced expression of calm leave his face.

"Now?"

"Yes, our mother, Yamra and the midwife are with her now. They asked for you to come."

"Yes, yes, I am coming!"

Raef turned toward Daz and the ill woman.

"Daz, my baby is being born. Remember your learning and finish up here. I am leaving for my hut."

"Can I come after?"

"Focus on what you are doing, apprentice. This woman is your first responsibility."

Raef did not wait for a response but dashed out to the street and hurried with his sister to his hut. When they finally neared his hut on the far-east side of the village, his father, Folor, was outside waiting. Folor grinned wide.

"Well, son, you are about to be a father," said Folor.

"Yes, yes," said Raef, "it is hard to believe."

"How does it feel?"

"I...I am not sure. I was not expecting it to happen quite yet."

One of the benches from inside had been brought outside and was up against the outer wall of the hut.

"This is where the men get to sit," said Folor, "this is one time we have little say in what happens."

Raef smiled and sat next to his father. Irah went

inside. Raef could hear Naan gasping and crying inside. He began to feel slightly dizzy. Keeper Dimmel came down the road, and Raef took the opportunity to step away from the cries coming from the hut to greet him. Keepers Bremen and Chaummer were not far behind and soon several other Intercessors were gathering outside the hut. A loud gutteral sound, almost like a scream but deeper, came from inside, then the tiny cry of a baby was heard. A few moments later Raef's mother opened the door.

"A female!" said his mother, "It is a female."

He smiled at his mother. A female. He had imagined it would be a male. He had never even imagined himself with a daughter.

"Can I see her?" he asked.

"Not yet," said his mother, "but you will be the first called in."

She disappeared inside again, and Raef sat on the bench. He felt men slapping his back, but he did not look up to see who they were. It was odd not to be allowed to enter his own hut.

"Do not feel badly," said his father, "it is this way for all men. Babys are women's territory, and we are only allowed in when they are good and ready."

"Even Keepers?"

Raef heard the other Keepers laugh.

"Yes, young Raef," said Keeper Bremen, "even Keepers. Birth is the time Keepers lose our status to the midwife."

Raef tried to laugh. More people were coming down the road. He saw Daz sprinting through the crowd toward him. Keeper Bremen caught the greenling and bent over and whispered in the greenling's ear. Daz smiled at Raef but stayed behind the other Keepers.

"I am a father," Raef thought to himself.

Things had happened so fast since returning to Fir Hollow. It seemed not so long ago Raef was a lonely greenling in Black Rock and now he was married and a father. At the moment, none of it seamed real.

A soft hand on his shoulder brought him back to his senses. He looked up to see his mother standing over him.

"Raef, your daughter is waiting to meet you."

Raef stood up and walked to the door. He knew everyone was looking at him and felt an awkward grin on his face. He entered his hut, and walked to the bed where Naan reclined against rolls of blankets, holding something wrapped in cloth. Yamrah sat on the floor leaning over Naan. The midwife was wrapping up crimson stained linens in a far corner. The musk of sweat and sharp tinge of blood hung in the warm air. Raef hurried to Naan's side as Yamrah stepped away. Naan's hair had been combed, but her face was flush. Raef stroked her hair, and she beamed up at him.

"Who is this?" Naan said to the bundle, "Who came to see you?"

Raef looked down as Naan pulled back the cloth to see a tiny face, eyes tightly closed and face scrunched as if in pain. The infant's eyes opened for a moment and looked in his direction.

"She is so small," said Raef.

"You can hold her," said Naan, holding the bundle to him.

Raef stared dumbly at the bundle, only its face uncovered, closed tightly again, ruddy and sprinkled with waxy bits.

"This is your daughter," said Naan.

Raef gently took the bundle, noticing how light it was. He could feel her wriggle a little as he held her. The infant opened her eyes and looked upward. Her pupils opened wider, then shrunk as she became very still.

"I cannot tell if she can see me," said Raef.

The midwife came to Raef's side, putting a hand to the tiny infant's head.

"Give her some time to learn to use her eyes well," said the midwife, "it is the same with all infants."

Raef pulled back the cloth a little to see more of this infant. She was so rosy looking and her mouth so delicate.

"Is she not perfect," said Naan.

"No one is truly perfect," said Raef, "but this one is nearly so."

"What is her name to be?" asked the midwife. "Naan would not tell me. She said to wait for you."

"Raef, I know," said Naan, "she should be 'Nine.'"

"Nine?" asked Raef.

"Almost perfect," said Naan.

"Yes," said Raef, holding his daughter up so her nibbin of a nose brushed his, "she is indeed a Nine."

"What are you two talking about?" asked Yamrah.

"Our daughter's name is Nine," said Raef.

"What kind of name is that?" asked Yamrah.

"An almost perfect name," said Raef.

"First the wedding, then this," said Yamrah, "I

don't know what to think of you two."

"I think it is quite wonderful," said Raef's mother.

"What is the village coming to?" asked the midwife, standing up.

Raef looked up at the midwife and raised his eyebrows.

"Your pardon, Keeper Raef," said the midwife, "I will be going now, but will return at sunset to check on the mother and daughter."

"Blessings on you, midwife," said Raef.

The older woman left, huffing quietly. Raef smiled, knowing she had wished to say more about the name.

"Do I look presentable?" asked Naan.

"You look wonderful," said Yamrah.

"Then let the others in," said Naan.

Raef handed little Nine to Naan and opened the door to the hut. People began to come in, one at a time, to see the infant. The Keepers came first, then the others. Raef sat on a bench along the wall. He could not stop himself from smiling. Daz sat next to him as villagers came and went.

Raef's mother went to her home and returned later with mid-sun meal for Raef, Naan and Yamrah. The visitors save Daz left to their homes. Folor stayed as well to share the meal with them. Afterwards Raef sent Daz to finish the rounds and stayed with Naan and little Nine. Folor and Malta left but Yamrah stayed and would not allow Raef or Naan to lift a finger as she brought them anything they needed.

When sunset came Raef's mother returned to cook again and the midwife visited again to check on Naan and Nine. The midwife reported all was well and left again. When she departed Yamra, Folor and Malta left as well, leaving the new family alone for the first time.

"She is so amazing," said Raef, holding his daughter.

"She is," said Naan.

That night they put little Nine in a bassinet Folor had made. Nine was placed by Raef's side of the bed. Naan was still sore after the birth so Raef wanted to be the one to lift the baby for feedings. Raef had prepared himself for little or no sleep, expecting Nine to wake often to eat. Nine slept half the night before waking. Naan, on the other hand, woke at the smallest sound, waking Raef to check on Nine. When the sun began to shimmer Raef was indeed groggy from little sleep, but more because of his wife than his daughter.

# 44

Yamra and Malta were at the hut early to help with first meal. Keeper Bremen, Keeper Chaummer and Daz came after sunrise homage was over to bless Raef, Naan and little Nine. Raef was told to stay home and help Naan as long as he was needed. Chaummer and Daz would see to Raef's duties. Later that sunrise Keeper Dimmel visited to see the baby and wish them well. Raef sat on a bench, holding Nine while looking out over the meadow. He was content.

Raef was enjoying being home with Naan, and having all the work done by Yamra and his mother, but by the eighth sun he was getting restless sitting around so much. Naan finally told him to leave.

"Go back to work or something," she said, "I appreciate your concern, but you are making me nervous the way you pace around our little hut."

Raef did his New Leaf washing at sunrise, had first meal with Naan, then went off to homage. The apprentices smiled for him as he walked beneath the fir branches they held. It appeared there were a couple of new apprentices now, young faces smiling timidly as he passed by. Homage passed uneventfully and Raef followed the other Keepers out where he collected his apprentice and headed for the West End.

"What shall we do this fine sun's journey, Master?" asked Daz.

"Whatever we like, I suppose," said Raef, "most of the villagers are out working in the fields, and Chaummer said no one is sick in our sector."

"And after mid-sun?"

"You have completed your work in all the Intercessor fields of study," said Raef, "I suppose we will have to do some exploring or something. I really do not feel like working especially hard."

"This is the best apprenticeship ever," said Daz.

They crossed the stream to the West End and began walking through the streets on the northern half. Raef noticed that the roofs which had been repaired over winter still looked strong. He was pleased. They made their way to the last row of houses on the far west side of the village. Raef paused and looked over the huts and houses. A pair of young men walked quickly past them, headed for the fields. As they passed an aroma wafted off of them Raef was familiar with.

"It is late to be starting work," said Daz.

"Indeed," said Raef knowingly.

He watched them as they hurried up the street then passed through a gate into the fields. Then he turned, walked between two houses and into the forest. Daz scampered after him.

"Where are we going?" asked Daz.

Raef did not answer, but pushed through a grove of maple saplings. Shortly they came upon a small clearing of matted grass. The strong must of dragon filled the air.

"Where are we?" asked Daz.

"One of the secret places."

"Secret places?"

"The dragon's secret places."

"Oh."

"I came here as a youngling at times. I had an older friend who lived nearby."

"You had a friend living in the West End?"

"Friends of my father, I believe. But I had to stay with them once and the son took me out here to see Rail. This is where he came to see the dragon."

"Are there many of these places?"

"Probably two or three outside each village."

"The dragon visits other villages?"

"Oh, yes. All the villages, even outside the Great Province."

"Outside the Province? I did not think there was anything beyond the Great Province."

"There is, young Daz."

Daz walked out into the center of the clearing, held his arms out and spun slowly, looking skyward.

"How did you come to know so much about the dragon?"

"It has taught me."

Daz bent over and pulled a dragon hair from the grass. He held it high in the air and watched it as the breeze made it sparkle and flutter. He released it, and it danced in the breeze before disappearing into the trees.

"I went back to see it again," said Daz.

"The dragon?"

"Of course the dragon. When you were away with the baby."

"Just once?"

"Well, no. I kind of went every sunrise. You know, before mid-sun like we used to do."

"We probably have time to go this sunrise," said Raef.

Daz fell back into the grass and moved his arms through the blades at his side.

"This is the best apprenticeship ever."

That sunset Yamrah did not come to the hut to help with last meal. Naan was nearly back to full strength and no longer needed help.

"It smells wonderful," said Raef, removing his robe and hanging it on a wall.

"Just put your tunic in that pile of clothes over there," said Naan, "I will do some wash next sunrise."

Raef removed his tunic and tossed it into a small pile of cloth in the corner. His shirt was all he needed anyway during summer. Raef held Nine as Naan placed a pot on the table and sliced the trenchers. Raef continued to hold Nine, looking at her little face as he ate.

"She can see me now," said Raef, "I can tell she sees me now."

"Of course she can," said Naan, "the midwife says they learn very quickly in the early moon cycles."

Raef held a finger to her palm and Nine grasped it in her tiny hand.

"She seems to learn more every sun," said Raef.

They had last meal and relaxed outside, watching the sunset in the cooling air. Naan still slept little, waking at every gurgle Nine made at night, but Raef only smiled when Naan woke him to check on the baby. He amazed even himself at his patience with Nine and his wife.

"We should just let her sleep between us," said Raef when the moon was mid-sky, "Then I wouldn't need to sit up to get her from her basinet."

"Raef no," Naan replied, "you would roll over on her and crush her."

Raef felt himself smile in the dark.

"I would do no such thing. It would just be easier, that is all I am saying."

He felt a playful slap on his arm.

"Do not even consider it," said Naan, "she stays in the bassinet."

# PART SEVEN

## UNMASKING

# 45

Raef rose and looked out the window. The sky was clear but somehow not very blue. He liked that it was silent in the streets this early. He had sunrise to himself.

He did his New Leaf washing and put on his red Keeper's robe. Naan gave him bread and cheese for first meal, he kissee Nine, and he left to perform sunrise homage. After the ceremony he and Daz toured the West End, finding nothing out of place and no one ill. They went to their secret place early, laying out in the grass until a shadow cast over them, blocking the sun. Raef sat up and watched the great beast land next to them. Daz had already removed his shoes and instantly began scrambling up the dragon's neck. Rail turned its great head to Raef and spoke softly.

"Raef, it is time."

"Time?"

The dragon moved its eyes in the direction of the greenling climbing its snaky neck.

"Now? But what will the Keepers say? The

dormeress? It will not go unnoticed. Daz is well known, no one will believe he simply ran off."

"They will accept it. It has always been the same."

Raef stood and walked to the dragon's side. He placed a hand on one of Rail's glassy scales. It was several times the size of his hand. Daz crawled onto the dragon's head and lay down. The dragon flicked him high into the sky, then caught him on the way down. Then Rail lowered its head and Daz rolled off onto the ground. The greenling stood and looked at Rail.

"Don't put me down, I want to go again."

"I will miss you, Daz," said Raef.

"Miss me?"

The dragon slowly extended a claw and circled Daz with two talons. Daz lifted his arms as one talon closed across his chest and another his back.

"What are you doing, Rail?" asked Daz.

"It is taking you to learn the last of its secrets," said Raef

"I don't understand."

"Do not be afraid; Rail will not let harm come to you."

Daz looked up at the dragon. Rail appeared to grin, although Raef was never sure about the dragon's expressions. The beast spread its wings across the clearing, then flung them down and shot into the sky. Raef watched them disappear in the eastern sky. He could hear Daz shouting something at Rail, but could not make out his words. When they were out of sight, Raef turned and began to walk back to Fir Hollow. He tried to imagine Daz's reaction when he saw the

Great Basin.

Raef entered the village in a daze. How was he going to explain Daz's disappearance? Daz was his apprentice, and Raef was charged with knowing where he was at all times. He looked up to see the sun mid-sky so he walked to his hut. He hung his robe and started to walk to the table when he caught Naan's glare.

Naan looked angry. Nine was asleep in the bassinet, but something was out of place. The meal. There was no food on the table and no scent of food cooking.

"Naan, what is wrong?"

Naan glared at him and held up her hand. From her fingers dangled a long sparkling strand.

"I found this on your tunic when I washed it."

Raef felt the color wash out of his face.

"Raef, I know what this is. It's a dragon hair."

# 46

"The time has arrived," said Zul.

"The time for what?" asked Erif as he stared into the flowing water.

"The time of great pain."

Erif found himself wanting to look away from the image of Naan and Raef. He began to pace quickly back and forth in front of the vision.

"What is wrong, my Warrior friend?" asked Zul.

"I don't know. I don't want to see this part, that's all."

"You know what is happening?"

"Yes, I know."

Erif turned away from the water and took four paces in the opposite direction. He looked out over the colorless sand and boulders. He felt his heart racing in his chest.

"Do not look away, Warrior. Look into his eyes. See what he is feeling."

"I do not want to see."

"It is the most important event in all his seasons, Erif."

Erif lowered his head and slowly turned back to the water. He looked into Raef's eyes.

Raef stared at the strand in his wife's hand. He had forgotten to have Daz check his back before returning home mid-sun past.

"Naan, I would never…"

"Stop it. Stop lying. I grew up on the West End where parents do not watch their younglings so closely. I remember greenlings who ran off to play rather than work in the fields. They would come back with these after playing in the forest. They told stories of playing with the dragon and pulling these from its head."

Raef's mind went fuzzy, and his vision blurred. He reached for the door to hold himself up from falling. He searched his mind for something to say. There was nothing.

"I also remember they disappeared after that," continued Naan, "They never came back. You and I both know why."

"Wait, no, Naan, I don't know anything about that…that whatever it is in your hand."

"Do not lie to me, Raef. You were gone five seasons when the dragon took you. You know all about it. And I know more than you think."

Naan dropped the hair on the table and stood, folding her arms and looking out the window.

"When I was a young greenlia, a greenling took me

to the forest. He took me to a place, and I saw it. I saw the dragon. I think the greenling was trying to impress me, but he only terrified me. One thing I do remember, though, that thing was covered with these hairs. All up and down its hideous spine."

"Naan, but, I…I don't know how that got on my tunic. I would never…"

"Raef, I will not be lied to, not even by you. Your mind has been somewhere else for moon cycles. You are gone longer than any Keeper needs to be. You come home late with no good excuse. Especially just before mid-sun meal, which you are almost always late for."

She turned to him, and her eyes flamed.

"That is when you see it. It is, I know I am right."

Raef felt himself tremble. He looked at Naan, then at Nine sleeping, then turned and bolted back outside. He started walking, as fast as he could. He realized he did not know where he was going. He went to the square. It was empty as everyone was at home having mid-sun meal. He walked north past the Council Hall and then through the streets of the Noble sector with its huge multi-level homes. He walked south and through the Warrior sector passing rows of long, dome-roofed homes. Then he headed west and went through all the streets of the West End between rows and rows of dilapidated huts. Then he stopped. He was tired. There was no place to go. He had just walked out on his wife and infant daughter. He could not do that. He began to tremble as he realized he would have to return. It was either that or leave Fir Hollow and his family. He did not want to do that.

Very slowly, he plodded back to his hut to face his wife. He found her crying and holding baby Nine.

"I do not know what I am going to do," said Naan when he walked in. "I do know I cannot live with someone who befriends the dragon. You put us all, even Nine, at risk. This house will not be another Moss Rock."

Raef stood in silence. The memories of his life played across his mind like actors on a stage. Rail was in almost every scene. He could not remember when Rail was not there, always present but always hidden. He looked at his wife, a pure being in spite of her troubled past, and his daughter, the very image of spotlessness. The stark difference between he and his family sliced the room in two.

"I do love you, Raef, but I need time to think."

"What will you do?"

"Do not ask that now. I fear the answer I would give."

"I do not know what to do now," said Raef.

"Go eat somewhere else," said Naan, "and eat somewhere else for last-meal as well. You can sleep here but do not expect me to speak to you. I will tell you when I know what I am going to do."

Raef left his hut in a daze. The rest of the sun was a fog. When he returned Naan and Nine were asleep. He dared to lay down next to his wife but found it nearly impossible to sleep.

# 47

Raef was woken before dawn by someone calling his name from the street. He rose groggily and pulled his trousers over his legs, tied them, then put on only his Keeper robe before opening the door. Keeper Dimmel stood in the street looking rather anxious.

"Have you seen Daz?" asked Dimmel.

"No, not since before mid-sun last."

"The dormeress woke me just past mid-moon saying he did not return to the domery. Not for mid-sun meal, then not for last meal, and not even at sunset to sleep."

Raef felt his stomach grow cold. Dimmel began to pace back and forth in the street. Raef came outside, shut his door, and walked closer to his old mentor.

"He is gone, I know it," said Dimmel, "He has run off, perhaps to another village."

"Why would he do that?" asked Raef, "he was doing so well as an apprentice."

Dimmel stopped pacing and glared at Raef.

"Doing well? In what sense was Daz doing well?"

Raef felt himself take a step backward.

"Daz has not been himself for some time," continued Dimmel, "I see him far less, of course, but even I can see how lethargic he has become. He does not show proper respect for his elders or even for the Keepers. The dormeress says he goes missing frequently. She sends other apprentices to find him, but he seems to be missing from the village. When he returns, he has no good answer to where he had been."

"I…I am sorry to hear that," said Raef.

"You are sorry? Raef, Daz started acting this way only after he became your apprentice."

Keeper Dimmel stepped closer and peered into Raef's eyes. Raef looked at the ground.

"After homage I will send the apprentices, all of them, to search for Daz. He is no longer a youngling, but he is still my son."

"I will look as well," said Raef.

Dimmel turned and looked out into the meadow. Then he began his way back down the road toward the Ceremonial Lodge. Raef went back into this hut. Naan was awake, feeding Nine.

"It was you, was it not?" asked Naan.

"What was me?"

Naan looked down at Nine, stroking her head as she spoke.

"The dragon took Daz, didn't it? You took your apprentice to see the dragon and now he is gone. You son of evil. You son of a dragon. Who else is dead because of you?"

"Daz is not dead! No one is dead. You don't understand."

Naan's head jerked up, and she glared at Raef.

"Oh, I understand all right. It is everyone else in this damned village who does not understand."

Tears began to run down her cheeks. Raef's heart raced. He wanted to run, but he wanted to comfort his wife. The province seemed to spin around him.

"Go," said Naan, "go bless the village at your sacred homage. Go walk the streets of the village in your robe and smile so everyone thinks it is okay. I will not be here for mid-sun meal, eat were ever you like. I will see you at last meal. I will tell you then what I decide to do."

Raef started to leave when he realized he was not properly dressed. He took his robe off and put on his shirt and tunic, then laced up his shoes. He did not do a New Leaf washing or eat first meal. He simply left for the Ceremonial Lodge, though it was far too early.

Sunrise homage was tense and unpleasant. None of the Keepers or even the apprentices would look anyone in the eye, not even each other. Those who came for blessing were especially quiet. The village already knew about the disappearance, Raef realized.

After homage Raef went to the West End to do his rounds. Villagers nodded to him, but no one smiled. When anyone spoke to him it was strictly about village business. No one mentioned Daz, no one offered words of solace. This is how the village always acted when someone vanished. It was as if the village had a collective determination to pretend nothing had happened at all.

Raef ate in a tavern at mid-sun meal. The tavern was empty save for himself and the innkeeper. After mid-sun he did his best to keep busy, checking on the Healing Lodge and inventorying the candles in the Ceremonial Lodge. When the sun fell low in the sky one of the older apprentices reported to Raef that Daz had not been found, and it had been determined he had run away to another village. Further searching had been called off by Prime Bremen.

Raef left the Ceremonial Lodge and began the walk home. He came across Nilo on the way, who was heading home from his work in the kitchen. Nilo gave him a knowing look.

"It took him?" asked Nilo.

Raef nodded as imperceptibly as he could.

"To where it took you?"

"To where it takes everyone."

"I do not wish to be taken," said Nilo, "but I fear I will be."

"Then stay away from it. You know that is the only way."

"I try. It is just...it is so hard. I always go back."

"As do I."

"Why has it not taken me? I have fifteen seasons and celebrate greenling's end in two moon cycles."

"I cannot say. Perhaps because you do not wish to be taken."

"Did you want to be taken?"

"I had no idea such a thing happened at all. I was very frightened when it took me away."

"But you came back."

"Yes, but it took me five seasons to have the courage to do so."

"Then the stories of you being lost all those

seasons in the forest are not true."

"None of the stories are true, about me or about…it."

Nilo paused at the dormery door.

"I must go now," said Nilo.

"I shall see you next sunset."

"Perhaps."

When Raef returned to his hut, Naan was home. There was a pot cooking over the fire, but the table was piled high with folded clothing and blankets.

"What is all this?" asked Raef.

"I am leaving Fir Hollow," said Naan.

"What?"

"I spoke with your sister and your mother. I told them everything."

"Everything? About the dragon…Daz…Naan have you lost your senses?"

"No, I have only just come to my senses. Do you know what I learned? I learned that they already knew you visited the dragon. They have always known."

"What!"

"They have always known, your father as well, apparently, yet said nothing. Not to anyone."

Raef stood stunned. His mind grasped futilely at what Naan had said. Naan came to his side and took his hand. Her face was kind.

"Raef, I do not know what happened to you when the dragon took you. You were scarcely more than a youngling. I do not know what happened to you all those seasons you were missing. I do not believe the story you were wandering the forests. You never said such a thing; that was Keeper Bremen's story. I can tell you struggle with dark spirits. The dragon did something to you. Perhaps it has you under some kind of spell. I look at you and see you do not know what it did to you either."

"Then why are you leaving?"

"I am not leaving you. I am not really leaving anything. I am going to something."

Raef sat on a bench, pushing the blankets on the table in front of him to one side. Naan sat next to him.

"Your sister told me she had heard one of Healers speak of someone who healed dragon wounds. We went together to the Healing Lodge, and they sent us to and old man who was once a Healer but is now too old to practice the healing arts. We did not tell anyone about you, we said we knew someone who had been put under a spell by the dragon. The old man seemed to believe us. He said it is rumored that there is a Soul Healer who lives somewhere in the Three Sisters Mountains."

"A Soul Healer? I have never heard of such a thing."

"It is only a rumor. The old man said there is a tiny community living somewhere near the Three Sisters Mountains in the south. And up on one of the mountains, he did not know which, lives a Soul Healer. The Soul Healer, it is believed, can help people ensnared by dark spirits. He is not a Keeper, but knows deep truths about the spirit world."

"Do you believe these rumors?"

"I have to. I am going myself to find this Soul Healer. I am taking Nine with me. I need answers for myself about what has happened to you."

Naan closed her eyes and took a slow breath. When she opened her eyes she took Raef's hand again.

"Raef, you have to make a choice. I cannot live with this kind of evil in my house. You may either come with us to see the Soul Healer, or you must leave us."

# 48

Erif took a deep breath and let out a ragged sigh.

"She is a woman of great courage," said Zul, "She looks for truth, even when it is painful."

"She still loves him," said Erif, "even after such betrayal."

Erif looked at the wise old spirit.

"But, Zul, is that not weakness?"

"No, Erif, it is her greatest strength."

"Raef could betray her again. How can she stand even the thought?"

"It is a risk, but to love is to risk. To love completely, as Naan does, is to risk completely."

Erif looked again into the water. Raef's head lay in Naan's lap and she stroked his long hair.

"It is ironic," Erif said, "men are supposed to be the strong ones. Sometimes I think we have it all wrong. Women are more courageous to give their hearts like that. I think they are the stronger of us."

Zul smiled. "The greatest courage often goes

unnoticed."

"I do not want to continue missing such things," said Erif.

"Oh, my son. If only you could see how much you have grown. You already see far more than most."

Erif reached down and touched the water where the image of Naan's cheek was. The water rippled and the image faded.

"Be strong," he whispered.

Raef sat in his parents' home, head hung low. Around the table, seated on benches and stools, sat his mother, father, sister and brother-in-law, and Naan. Nine was sleeping in Naan's arms. Naan was repeating everything she had discovered. The dragon hair, all the times Raef had been late returning home, and the disappearance of Daz. Raef's father hung his head. His mother cried softly. Irah's face burned red, her eyes squinted and piercing in Raef's direction. Wren sat stoically, facing the wall behind Raef, his face stern.

"We should have helped him," said Malta, quietly, "Folor and I knew something was wrong, even when Raef was a youngling."

Naan shook her head slowly.

"He came home one sunset, smelling very odd. There was a dragon hair stuck to his shirt," said Malta, tears in her eyes.

"Malta, you did not tell me that sunrise past," said Naan, "You found a dragon hair on your son and did nothing?"

Irah turned to her mother, "Mother! I cannot believe you and Father let this go on. You are Intercessors and Father is a Keeper."

"Do not act self-righteous, Irah," said Naan. "I have spoken with Raef and gotten more of the story. You knew Raef called the dragon by name as a youngling. You knew of all his trips into the forest. Surely you noticed the odd smells when he came home as well as your parents. You knew Raef was timid, but oddly unalarmed when the dragon attacked Rodon. You knew Raef had no good explanation for where he was the five seasons before he returned from wherever the dragon took him. You have no excuse either."

Irah sat in silence, her face locked in defiance.

"Your mother and I tried," said Folor quietly.

Raef noticed how meek Folor looked. He had never seen his father look this way before.

"I talked to Prime Keeper Bremen about Raef stealing away to the woods and coming home smelling … inhuman. I told him about the dragon hair as well."

"You did?" said Raef.

"Yes," said Folor, "but Keeper Bremen seemed flustered and embarrassed. He said for us not to worry about it. He said younglings are often curious about the dragon, but grow beyond it in time."

Naan slapped the table, "I cannot believe it! Even the Keepers knew? It is as if the entire village has been allowing this to go on in front of their eyes, and no one was willing to stop it."

Raef's parents hung their heads. Wren looked at

the far wall. Irah glared at Raef.

"Well, if none of you will, I will put an end to this," said Naan calmly, "Irah and I discovered rumors that an old man, a Soul Healer, who lives somewhere down south, in the Three Sisters Mountains. This Soul Healer may be able to help Raef. It is only a rumor, but I am going. Raef has agreed to come as well."

"Father, Mother," Raef said, "I am so ashamed and sorry. I tried to stay away from it, but I could not. Even after I returned to the village I kept going back to see it."

"No, no," said Malta, "we should have paid more attention. It is we who have failed you."

"You did not fail me, mother."

"We did, your father and I. We knew about DeAlsím taking you to see the dragon. It was not hard to figure out. We knew also about Rocecé. He became so jaded he could no longer cover his tracks."

Raef sat stunned, "You…you knew about DeAlsím and Rocecé?"

"We were very suspicious," said Folor.

"But you let Raef spend time with them!" Naan shouted.

"As I said," said Malta, "we failed Raef."

"Mother, it is not just me," said Raef, "up on Black Rock Mountain, that is where the dragon takes everyone it captures, there are hundreds of villagers up there. From all over the Great Province."

Raef's mother looked at his father. Folor sighed and looked away.

"We may have failed you in the past," said Folor, "but we will not this time. We will do everything we can to help you."

Raef looked at his father. Folor looked old and tired. Broken. Raef realized he felt compassion for his father, not anger. He was a little surprised that he did.

# 49

The next sunrise after homage Raef followed Bremen to the Keep. Raef removed his Keeper's robe and handed it to the Prime Keeper.

"I can no longer serve as Keeper. I have broken the vows of the Keepers. I do not wish to say more, but I must resign my position."

Bremen accepted the robe and looked sorrowfully at Raef. "I may have some notion of what you speak, Raef. My best wishes, even my blessing, are with you."

"I am leaving with my family to go search for someone who can help me escape the snare I have found myself in."

"Your memory remains close to mind. You will not be forgotten."

Raef stepped out of the Keep and looked around. Assistants were cultivating herbs in the garden for the apothecary. Kitcheners were arriving for work to prepare food for the poor. Apprentices ran here and there, off to one mentor or another for a sun's labor. This had been his life. He had known the smiles of Intercessors all around, the respect of the village, the sense of purpose in his calling. It was all gone now, all of it. He plodded toward his hut, meandering between houses rather than taking the road. Three younglings scampered past on their way to lessons. A man bowed as he passed. All this will be gone.

When he arrived at his hut a small two-wheeled cart pulled by a single horse was out front. The wedding gift from the Keepers. They had sold all else they had for food for the journey and a tent. Naan was already sitting in front, holding Nine. Raef got into the cart and took the reins. He was not good with horses, but it was easier when the horse was strapped to a cart. He looked down at his infant daughter. He wondered if Nine would ever know her grandparents. He snapped the reins, and the horse pulled the cart down the road.

They traveled to the center of Fir Hollow and then took the road leading out of the south end of the village. Raef had never been anywhere south of Fir Hollow. Three small mountains, all in a row, stood in the distance. The mountains got shorter going from right to left: Older, Middle and Younger Sister. The two tallest mountains each came to a point, still topped with white. The smaller one had a distinctly flat top, not tall enough for snow this time of the season.

"Naan, I have no idea how to find this Soul Healer."

"Zul will guide us."

"Zul never helped me with the dragon before. Why do you think the spirit will help us now?"

"I just do. I have to."

They passed the last house in Fir Hollow and the forest closed around them on either side as they left the village.

———.◇.———

When the ink had dried from recording his last vision, Erif took the parchment it was on and began to sew it to the others. It had taken many parchments to record all the visions he had seen, and as he sewed this last one to the others he realized it made a very long scroll. He finished the seam and tested it to be sure it would hold, then began rolling the entire scroll into a tight cylinder. He bound it with three leather straps; one at each end and one in the middle. He held the scroll in his lap, gazing down on it.

Erif realized the villagers would not like what this scroll said. The Provincial Overseers would likely forbid its reading outright. Erif put the scroll into a leather bag and tied the mouth tight. Then he placed it in his wooden storage box to keep it dry. He picked up his long sword and admired it's polished blade. Forbidden or not, the Great Province would hear the words on this scroll.

# HOW TO HELP THE AUTHOR

If you enjoyed reading Raef's adventure in *The Other Side of Black Rock*, your rating would be highly appreciated. Just go to your favorite bookseller and leave a review—even a single sentence or two will help!

Thank you!

John W Fort

## ABOUT THE AUTHOR

John W Fort was born in Texas, moved to the Pacific Northwest as a child, and lived for two years in Brazil in his twenties. He has a love for the outdoors, music, and old cars which he pursues when not writing.

Diagnosed as hyperactive and attention deficit as a child he chooses to embrace the oddity and mental frenzy it provides rather than seek a cure. John loves deep spirited conversation, but only in person, having a general disdain for social media.

He lives with his wife and two children in Oregon.

## ABOUT THE FORBIDDEN SCROLLS

*The Forbidden Scrolls* is a chronicle of secrets a society does not want to admit to and topics they would rather ignore. As we see secrets and taboo subjects only harm those enforcing them.

Set in the medieval tim e period of the fictional world, The Great Province, a banished warrior, Erif, records his visions of a young boy, Raef, growing up and trying to make sense of the secrets and lies his village keeps. Everything Erif writes is forbidden but he is determined to complete his record of the visions and return the scrolls to The Great Province to confront them with their lies.

*The Forbidden Scrolls* include:

Book 1: The Shadow of Black Rock
Book 2: The Other Side of Black Rock
Book 3: Under the Burning Sun

The series will continue...

Made in the USA
Lexington, KY
09 December 2019